BREATHE

SARA FUJIMURA

BREATHE

Tanabata Wishes
Enterprises, LLC

Tanabata Wishes Enterprises, LLC
Gilbert, Arizona
United States of America

ISBN-13: 978-0-692-12590-8

For my sister and my "sisters"

ONE

HAPPY BIRTHDAY, AMERICA. Goodbye, childhood.

I pull the water-heavy air deep into my corset-less chest. The scent of tree bark, firecrackers, and pending rain come with it.

"Well, it's been nice knowing you." I pat the old apple tree's fissured bark right above our carved initials. "But I really must go. I have an important ball to attend tonight. A hundred of Mama's closest friends and all of my classmates wait with bated breath for my official introduction to society."

As I prepare to leave my favorite hiding spot since I was seven, Daddy's bottle-green Cadillac Phaeton turns into our courtyard. I freeze, hoping the apple tree's lush foliage is adequate cover. My breath catches as Daddy's chauffeur slides out of the driver's seat and rushes to open the passenger door.

"It's going to be a long night, Marco. Go have Angelina fix you something to eat." Daddy hands Marco his black leather bag—which goes everywhere with him—before climbing out of the Cadillac with a groan.

"Thank you, sir." Marco's voice echoes around the

courtyard. "First, I want to check the Phaeton's engine. Tonight of all nights wouldn't be a good one for a breakdown."

"You're a good man, Marco." Daddy claps Marco on the back. "Your father would be proud."

"My father would know how to fix that odd clicking noise."

"Yes, Mr. D'Orio could always diagnose a car's ailments with miraculous ease. That was his gift. Maybe it's your gift, too?"

"About that, sir. Could I possibly —"

Daddy fumbles for his gold pocket watch. "Look at the time. My wife will have my head. I'll let you get back to your tinkering, Marco."

"Yes, sir."

I cling to the tree's weather-beaten trunk as Daddy limps at a snail's pace beneath me and then up the shallow steps to the kitchen. Meanwhile, Marco gathers Daddy's medical accoutrements while whistling. His playful tune bounces around our tiny, brick-lined courtyard. Just as he passes under the apple tree, the wind picks up. A letter flutters off the top of the crate of medicines, and Marco mumbles what is probably an oath in Italian. He puts the crate down on the steps and chases after the letter which now rests at the base of my tree. I tuck my feet up and pull a branch in front of myself. Marco slides off his chauffeur's cap and wipes the sweat from his brow. He must have visited the barber this morning. Marco's sometimes unruly dark curls are trimmed and oiled flat into a wave. Not that I've been studying his countenance over the past month since he took this position.

"A lot on your mind today, Miss?" Marco snatches the letter from the base of the tree but doesn't look up. He leans against the tree trunk and surveys our surroundings. "The courtyard is clear. Do you require assistance getting down?"

My face burns.

"No." I clear my throat and repeat with confidence. "No, I do not."

Marco looks up and finds my hiding spot immediately. "It's an important night for you, no? New dress. Official escort. I'm sure it's a lot for a young girl like you to handle."

An indignant fire lights in my belly. "I seem to recall that *you* are also seventeen."

"Eighteen. My birthday was in April."

"Barely eighteen then. I'm sure driving us to the Bellevue-Stratford Hotel is a lot for a young boy like you to handle, no?" I mock.

"Believe me. I have been a man for a while now."

"Don't be vulgar."

"Who's being vulgar? My father—God rest his soul—is gone and Dom is overseas with the doughboys. As I said, I've been a man for a while now, at least in my home." Marco looks up at me and smiles. "Do I need to climb up there and help you down? 'Cause, I could do that for a damsel in distress."

I wish Marco could see his expression when I stand up on the branch and scoot out on the limb toward the side of our house.

"I was teasing." Marco jerks up straight. "Don't go any further, Miss. You'll fall."

I pretend to lose my balance even though my bare feet grip the limb with ease. Marco swears and rushes underneath me. His arms spread wide to break my fall. I laugh. I let go of the branch above my head and slide into the open window of my bedroom with all the ease of someone who's been doing that trick for a decade now. I peek my head back out the window and stare down at Marco.

"I'm not a damsel. And I don't need your help. I'm a modern woman." And to retain the last word, I tug the window sash sharply closed.

I do, however, need Angelina's help to be a modern woman. Especially with this blessed corset.

Angelina peeks her head around my door. "You are ready to dress for your party now, Miss Virginia?"

Unlike her little brother's, Angelina's voice still carries a melodic Italian accent.

"I would like a glass of lemonade first. I am over-heated." I dab at a trickle of sweat rolling down behind my ear with my sleeve. I thank Providence that at least I had enough foresight to throw my old work dress over my shift before ducking out my window earlier.

"Yes, Miss."

After Angelina closes the door, I wander back to the window. I know Marco won't still be there, especially with a rain shower threatening to come, but I look anyway. Part of me is disappointed that he isn't there. Now I know I must be getting ill. But not tonight. Tonight is my time to shine. My dance card is already full. I grab my old friend Teddy from his place of honor on top of my bookshelf and brush the dust from his nearly threadbare head.

"Oh Romeo, Romeo, wherefore art thou Romeo?" I repeat the lines I once delivered during our class discussion of *Romeo and Juliet* to class clown Anna, which completely dampened the romantic element of the piece. Such is the hazard of attending an all-girls school.

I run my finger over the coarse stitches I put in Teddy's ear when I was about seven. Mama insisted that she didn't

4

have time to fix Teddy before bedtime and I couldn't sleep without him, so I performed the surgery myself. I chuckle at my clumsy knot. I've come a long way with my needle skills since then.

Angelina raps on my door and enters with a glass of lemonade, thankfully with many ice chips floating on the top. I open up my hope chest and place Teddy on top of one of the skillfully stitched linens I've done this past year to prepare for my future home. The room turns fuzzy and gray when I stand back up. I grab the bedpost to fortify my uncooperative knees. Angelina's dark brows furrow.

"I'm fine. I didn't eat enough at luncheon today." I sip my lemonade, letting the cool liquid slide down my irritated throat.

Angelina pauses but then goes dutifully to my wardrobe to pull out my white silk gown. She drapes it on my bed before putting out my freshly-polished high-heeled shoes.

I pray no one will recognize this dress from Kit's eighteenth birthday extravaganza from nearly three years ago. At least the seamstress was able to rework the dress into something more modern. With the war raging on in France, I heard that Margaret Vaughn had to buy her debut gown off the rack at Wanamaker's. She vehemently denies it, of course.

Angelina gushes in Italian as her calloused fingers slip over the luxurious fabric. She mostly talks to herself as she pours the silk over my head and down my now tightly-corseted torso. Mama hired Angelina to also dress my hair. She pulls Granny Jackson's silver-handled brush through the knotted strands of my hair with her deft but gentle hands. Angelina makes a surprised noise and pulls out an errant apple tree leaf. I don't offer up an explanation, and she doesn't dare ask.

I watch in my vanity mirror as Angelina brings my dark hair up to a high gloss. She tucks and pins and rolls my hair into a dramatic coif. Thank heaven, I was able to talk Mama into letting Angelina do my hair instead of going to Mrs. Davenport, Mama's crotchety hairdresser. The two of them would have insisted on some old-fashioned Gibson Girl atrocity that a family of squirrels could make into a comfortable nest. No, this will be much more stylish and modern. Angelina truly has a gift. It's a wonder she doesn't dress ladies' hair for a living instead of working in our kitchen. I'm sure my classmates would be lined up around the block to have Angelina dress their hair for their debuts, Christmas parties, and such. The pain in my temples spreads down into my neck, but I hold my head still so that Angelina can add baby's breath, navy ribbon, and three red roses—barely out of their bud stage—into my hair. Angelina tuts and talks to herself as she makes adjustments.

"Beautiful," Angelina proclaims after she tucks the tiny apple tree leaf back into the decorations in my hair.

I suppress the urge to embrace Angelina. Somehow, she has taken this tree-climbing, ugly duckling and transformed her into an elegant, swan-like debutant.

"Virginia!" Mama pokes her head around my door. "You are going to be late to your own party. Come down immediately. Your father and I will be waiting in the Cadillac."

"I'm almost finished, Mama."

Angelina buckles my shoes and then hands me my gloves and fan. I snatch my diamond-studded, silk evening bag—honestly, they are paste jewels, but they look authentic—off my bed. At the door, I remember myself because it is past the time for Angelina to return to Little Italy and her own family.

"Thank you, Angelina. You did an excellent job."

"It is my pleasure." Angelina does a very unnecessary curtsy. "Miss Virginia, your head is very hot. I feel it as I work. Would you like some medicine before you go?"

"No. I'm fine, Angelina. And do not mention this to my father. You know how he worries at the tiniest things."

"Yes, Miss."

I rush down the staircase, but skid to a stop at the front door to—as my mother would say—comport myself like a lady. When I open the front door, the Cadillac waits on the street with my parents and Marco tucked inside.

"A lot for a young girl like you to handle. Hmpf," I mumble.

I can feel Marco's gaze as I descend the stairs to the sidewalk. Between my headache and these heels, I wobble to the Cadillac like a new born colt. Marco remembers his job and meets me at the passenger side door.

"Are you certain that you are well?" Marco's overpowering spicy hair tonic makes my vision swim. "Your cheeks are flushed. And I'm certain your mother doesn't allow you to wear rouge."

"I am perfectly well. No need for concern." I don't mind a little extra coloring tonight. Now I won't have to pinch my cheeks like Kit does because indeed my mother prohibits us from wearing cosmetics.

Marco opens the door, and I slide into the Cadillac next to Mama. I lean over to smooth the wrinkles out of my dress. When I sit up again, my head throbs like someone is using it as an anvil.

Daddy peers over the top of his newspaper. "You look lovely, Ginny."

"Thank you, Daddy," I say, but he's already buried his

face back into today's gloom and doom.

"This heat is oppressive." Mama's fan snaps open with a whip-like crack." Did you remember your fan, Virginia? A lady always comes prepared. She does not perspire."

Mama and I fan away in silence all the way to the Bellevue-Stratford Hotel. It does not help. To distract myself from the vise-like pressure in my head and the rivulets of sweat rolling down the back of my neck, I study Marco instead. At least, the back of Marco's head. Also occasionally the side of his freshly-shaven face when he looks over his shoulder to pass around some delivery truck or the occasional country folk riding into Philadelphia in their old-fashioned, horse-drawn carriages. Marco pushes away a trickle of sweat that sneaks down the side of his face toward his formal coat. After all, men are allowed to perspire. The temperature in the car soars, and the town passing outside blurs. I close my eyes to make it all stop.

"Virginia." Mama taps my leg with her closed fan breaking me out of my daze. "I said, we're here."

Mama ignores Marco as he assists her from the Cadillac. She flicks her deep sapphire silk dress impatiently as Daddy and I collect ourselves.

"Miss Jackson." Marco offers his hand when it is my turn.

My vision grays when I step out onto the Cadillac's running board. I grab Marco's hand to steady myself. Marco's dark eyes telegraph his concern, but he thankfully stays quiet.

"Come along, Virginia. Our guests are waiting." Mama clings to Daddy's arm for the benefit of the public. Events like this are the only time I ever see my parents pretend like their marriage is happy and contented.

As we enter the foyer of the hotel, the pain radiating up

from my hips is so intense that I nearly collide with Everett Winthrop the Third, my appointed escort for the evening. I shiver. Not that Everett isn't accomplished, attractive, and descended from one of Philadelphia's founding fathers, but—as Anna likes to say—he doesn't ring my bell. Everett is, however, currently at the top of my mother's list of potential husbands. My parents allow me a moment with Everett as they drift toward the dramatic plush staircase leading to the ballroom on the second floor.

"Happy Birthday, Virginia." Everett leans in to kiss my cheek.

I turn my head so he kisses the hair above my ear, and probably a rosebud or two. Everett attaches my now gloved hand to his arm and gives my hand a squeeze.

"Miss Virginia, wait," Marco's voice calls from behind.

We turn to see Marco standing just inside the gold and gilt lobby, holding my purse out. Everett walks stiffly towards him.

"You will refer to her as 'Miss Jackson.'" Everett snatches the purse out of Marco's hand and returns to me. "The nerve of those people. To think they can refer to us by our Christian names. I'll have a word with your father about it."

I look back over my shoulder as we walk away. Marco continues to stand there. His hands clench into fists at his sides.

"No, don't. Everyone makes mistakes." I wrap my arms lightly back around Everett's right arm and look up at him. "Let's not spoil the evening."

Everett's scowl melts into a smile. He leans in. "Anything for the birthday girl."

As we follow behind the crush going up the staircase, I hear Marco muttering in annoyed Italian. Part of me doesn't blame him. Everett is insufferable. I concentrate on putting one foot in front of the other until we enter the hotel's magnificent two-tiered ballroom. I look at the sea of faces around me and sitting up in the balconies overlooking the area. Everett peacocks as he leads me around the perimeter of the room like a prized pony to receive well wishes and empty compliments from my classmates and their high society parents. All eyes are on me. All the people who have been a part of my life for years and yet know nothing about me. Except for one.

"May I cut in?" Anna doesn't wait for Everett's response. She grabs my arm and pulls me out of his grip.

"You made it!" I say. The cavernous room suddenly fills half full.

"Father and I made a deal. I allow Aunt Gertrude to chaperone and dress me for this evening without protestations, and Father allows the two of us to come to Philadelphia for this most miniscule of visits. And by allow, I mean that I badgered him for weeks about it until I broke him. Therefore…." Anna twirls around in her peach dress. "I am all yours tonight. Especially as your dear sister has missed the boat. I bet your mother was apoplectic."

"It was a train, not a boat, and Mama took to her bed for a full day." I wince remembering Mama's tirade after receiving Kit's telegraph from California. "Daddy had to give her laudanum to calm her nerves. Or maybe it was simply for *his* nerves. Either way, he's ordered me never to use the word suffragette—"

"*Suffragist.* Unless she is heaving bricks through windows while in California. Then again, maybe Kit is a suffragette."

"She most certainly is not. At least, I don't think so. Daddy says we are not to utter that word in our household again. Kit will be in the doghouse until the next century."

Anna laughs, but then her face hardens. "You look like hell."

"Anna!"

"My apologies. I forgot. I'm a lady tonight." Anna pulls her gloves off. One hand reaches for my pulse as the other rests on my forehead. "Correction, you feel like hell."

"An-na!"

"Ginny, you're sick, and you know it." Anna takes a step backward. "It's from going to Devil's Pocket, isn't it?"

"Don't be ridiculous."

"It is. You went down there two days ago on my behalf. The incubation time for influenza—this Spanish flu, the papers are calling it—is one to four days." Anna steps back in and takes my hand, even though she shouldn't. "This is all my fault. I only wanted to help Mrs. Flanagan. I should have never asked you to go down there."

"Just because I don't agree with what you are doing, doesn't mean I won't keep a promise."

Anna squeezes my hand. "You are a good friend, Ginny. The best."

"The best? The sick. I wish I would have taken Angelina up on her offer to fetch me some aspirin." I rub my throbbing temples. "But as Mama says, we are women. We endure. Tomorrow, I shall stay in bed all day."

"Speaking of enduring, here comes Everett." Anna slides her gloves back on. "With your mother. Good luck, my friend."

Anna ducks away and heads toward the crowd of people who don't accept her either. Anna, Kit, and I are quite the trio.

"They're waiting for you." Mama grabs the purse from my hands and herds us toward the dance floor.

The crowd parts as Everett and I walk to the middle of the ballroom. The leader of the palm court orchestra Mama hired introduces us and says a few words. The words sound like a muffled buzzing in my ears. I glance around the crowded room trying to find Anna. Instead, I catch Cecelia's eye. I don't recognize her at first. For as long as I can remember, Cecelia has always come wrapped in a white nursing apron and a gentle smile. Tonight, this handsome matronly woman wears a deep emerald gown and a frown of concern. She taps on Daddy's arm with her fan and whispers something to him.

The crowd claps at the end of the orchestra leader's speech, pulling me back to the task at hand. Everett positions us to dance a traditional waltz, just as Mama firmly instructed him to do. I argued for a jazz band but lost. Everett, of course, sided with my mother. Anything to keep our private dance lessons going for another week or two. Everett leans forward and whispers something in my ear. Probably sweet nothings. I nod, pretending like I can hear anything over the blood pounding in my ears.

Endure, Virginia. That's what women do.

Everett's face crowds my vision. I watch his lips count the downbeats, but I still miss the step off. Everett pushes me into motion anyway. I stumble backwards a few paces as the room starts to tilt. I hear a bell ringing in the distance. It has nothing to do with the countenance of my dance partner, and everything to do with my head striking the parquet floor in a most undignified manner.

"Get away from her, you insufferable idiot," Anna's voice echoes from somewhere deep in my mind. "I'm sorry, Ginny. I'm so, so sorry."

"Step back, everyone, please," Cecelia's voice is as soothing as her cool hands on my face. "Stay with us, sweet Ginny."

But I can't will my eyelids open. The weights on my limbs drag me under.

TWO

"MOTHER, PLEASE ALLOW me a moment." Kit's voice echoes up from downstairs. "I haven't even had a chance to remove my hat."

She's home. I am equally irritated and ecstatic. Though I appreciate Cecelia's countless games of 500 with me while my home was under quarantine, I look forward to putting my playing cards away for a bit and having someone else to talk to. Meanwhile, Cecelia is probably glad to sleep in her own bed tonight. The settee in the parlor is not comfortable for an hour, much less seven nights. My lungs feel like raw sausage, and my mind is quickly turning to porridge, but Daddy refuses to let me leave my bedroom. Granny Jackson's ancient chamber pot under my bed adds to the humiliation. I can't wait to hear all of Kit's adventurous tales from California. Though we may have to save the juiciest ones for after Mama has turned in for the night.

"Don't scrape the wallpaper!" Kit and Mama shout in unison.

A series of thuds, grunts, and mild oaths echo up the stairs. I hear one of the picture frames in the hallway collide with the floor.

"Could you open the door for me, Miss?" Marco's voice is tight. "Please."

The doorknob turns, and my stomach clenches. I pull the bed sheet up to my chin and contemplate ducking all the way under it. The door swings open, and Kit blows into our room like a hurricane. Marco staggers in two steps behind her under the weight of Kit's steamer trunk.

"Put it by the fireplace, Angelo." Kit places her hat box and traveling gloves on our vanity. "Angelina can unpack my trunk after luncheon today."

"It's Marco." My voice sounds unnaturally low and gravelly.

"Marco D'Orio." Marco executes an overly dramatic bow. "At your service, Miss Katherine."

"Ah, yes. Marco. Angelina's younger brother." Kit steps between Marco and me to block his view. "And our new chauffeur, I hear."

"I am." Marco peeks around the Wall of Kit to look at me. "You are looking better, Miss Virginia."

My empty stomach clenches. These stupid, little girl braids. I should have never agreed to them after Cecelia's humiliating sponge bath yesterday. My cheeks burn. Thankfully, I can blame them on my fever.

"You gave your family quite a scare." Marco pulls a small paper cone out of his vest pocket. "Angelina instructed me to give these to you. She says you have a notorious sweet tooth."

"I do not." My stomach contradicts me with an audible growl.

"I'll return the lemon drops then." Marco tucks the paper cone back into his vest pocket.

"Don't be ridiculous, Ginny. You love sweets." Kit steps to the side to block Marco's view again. "Thank you,

Marco. I will take them. Also, thank you for helping Father carry Ginny up the stairs after she collapsed at the party."

My cheeks flame again realizing that truth. Of course, my father wouldn't be able to carry me up a flight of stairs by himself. He hasn't been able to carry me up the stairs since I was a small child.

"Though he vehemently denies it, my father isn't the spry young man he seems to think he is. I'm happy to hear that you will be assisting him," Kit says. "At his age and with his bad leg, Father shouldn't be driving or lifting heavy things at all. I'm glad he has a boy to do the heavy work for him now."

The smile on Marco's tanned face quickly fades. "Yes, Miss. I hope to do more for Dr. Jackson than chauffeur and lift patients. I am eager to learn more from him. I hope to—"

"Excellent. I'm sure Father could use the help. Well then, that will be all."

"Yes, Miss." Marco doesn't even acknowledge me as he leaves the room.

Kit closes the door behind him. She unwraps the top of the paper cone and pours out three lemon drops into my outstretched hand.

"The cheek of that boy." Kit pops a lemon drop into her mouth, too. "Shall I put these in a safe place? At least until Mother leaves for her meeting tonight?"

I nod, though I would be happy to eat the whole bag promptly. Kit nudges the piece of molding under the window with the tip of her leather boot. It pops out with ease after a decade of use. She pulls out the pint-sized Mason jar I keep in the cavity and adds the lemon drops to my secret stash of sweets. Kit ducks down and slides the jar, along with a few scraps of paper, back into the hidey-hole.

"If you want some candy later, let me know. I am happy to fetch them for you." Kit pushes the piece of molding firmly back into place. "Mother says that you are *not* to leave our room. She will send Nurse Cecelia up after luncheon to empty your...." Kit affects a snooty English accent, "*chamber pot. Is this 1818 or 1918? Chamber pots. My word.*"

Yet another reason why Mama is not Daddy's nurse. She doesn't have the constitution to empty bedpans, or chamber pots in my case. At least Mama didn't ask Marco to do it.

"What a morning." Kit pulls the topaz hat pin out of her favorite blue, wide-brimmed, ostrich-plumed hat, an extravagant 20th birthday present last year from Cecelia. She sticks the pin into the silver-mounted hatpin stand on our vanity and nestles her beloved hat into its box. "I am so relieved to be rid of my chaperone. Widow Clark vexes me so."

"I am sure the feeling is mutual." My throat might feel like raw sausage, but the lemon drops have greatly improved my mood.

"Don't be a brat." Kit lifts Teddy—who has magically reappeared out of my hope chest and onto my bookshelf again—and hurls him at me. He misses my bed and hits the floor.

I push up on my elbows. "How was California? Did you go to any dances? Meet any handsome young men?"

"All in due time, Baby Sister. I promised Mama not to overly excite you during your convalescence."

I groan and flop back down. Kit scoops the book Mama left for me off my bedside table.

"*The Ladies' Book of Etiquette and Manual of Politeness.*

What drivel is this?" Kit thumbs through the dusty tome. "It was published in 1860. Times are changing, Ginny. We are a new breed of modern women. Surely, I have something better in my possession."

Kit looks down the over-stuffed bookcase next to her bed. She pulls out a few books and places them on my bedside table. I don't want to read those ones either.

"Now, Mrs. Eleanor Fitzgibbons says a modern woman is well-versed in what is going on both inside and outside of her home." Kit paces around our room like a schoolmarm lecturing me. "A modern woman is able to converse at length at dinner parties and salons about current affairs. She has an educated opinion and expresses it eloquently without raising her voice and sounding like a deranged harpy."

I chuckle. Kit stops her lecture to dip down and pick Teddy off the floor. "Perhaps, I need to spend some more time working on that last part."

Kit tucks Teddy into bed with me like I'm six and pats him on the head. "I concur, Teddy. The *New York Times* would be the perfect light reading material before luncheon."

Kit slumps into our overstuffed chair and places her traveling bag on her lap. She digs around in it until she pulls out a newspaper and then a small block wrapped in wax paper. Kit sniffs the block and lets out a contended sigh.

"Angelina and her mother made more of their heavenly lavender soap. Cecelia procured some for us." Kit places the palm-sized block on the vanity before digging out a second one. "There's one for you also, so don't pilfer my soap. Now, where were we?"

Kit flicks open her newspaper and reads report after

report about the war machine in foreign lands. My mind soon wanders. I picture Anna up in Boston helping her widower father attend to sailors and other servicemen already back from their part in the war. Men missing limbs. Men missing their sanity. The thought is so depressing that I go back to playing my favorite childhood game of finding pictures in the heavy lines and exaggerated patterns of the gaudy wallpaper in our room. Why Mama chose such a horrific pattern for our nursery is beyond me. Kit drones on. I find the stuffed bear with a missing ear in the jumble of swirls above Kit's head. On a good day, if I stare long enough, the patterns begin to move. With the laudanum still fogging my brain, the green and yellow designs don't only move, they swirl around like a tornado.

"Let's redecorate our room." I close my eyes to make the tornado stop.

"Excuse me?" Kit chastises me for interrupting her gloom-and-doom report.

"We're not little girls anymore. Let's make our bedroom something more fitting for two modern women."

Kit snaps the wrinkles out of her newspaper and folds it. "I don't plan on living here much longer."

I bolt straight up in bed and am rewarded with a fit of coughing. After I catch my breath again, I say, "You've accepted Mr. Jeffries marriage proposal?"

Kit's face pinches. "Don't be ridiculous. I am not that desperate. Just because I'm almost twenty-one doesn't make me an old maid. Plus, I have no intention of leaving Radcliffe without a degree in my hand. Despite what our parents say."

"*Bon chance*, dear sister, especially after you missed my debut."

"From what I hear, so did you, *dear sister*." Kit's words

hit their mark.

I wince. I'm sure my dramatic exit has been discussed at length by Rittenhouse Square's residents by now. The tinkling of a bell downstairs signals luncheon.

"Oh, good. I'm famished." Kit tucks her newspaper back into her traveling bag. "Plus, I hear that Angelina is making Peach Melba for dessert since we have an overabundance of peaches presently." Kit claps her hands together like she's five. "You know how I love a good raspberry sauce. I will make sure they send some up to you. The ice cream would help soothe your throat."

Kit bounces out the door and down the stairs. I wait, and I wait. Visions of peaches and ice cream and raspberry sauce fill my addled brain causing me to drool. Finally, Angelina comes upstairs with my luncheon. A peachy aroma clings to her clothes as she places the tray in front of me. My heart falls when she lifts the cover off my meal.

"Beef tea?" I slump down in my pillows.

"I make your grandmamma's recipe. Just as the doctor says." Angelina pours me another glass of water and places it on my tray.

I stare at the pathetic excuse for luncheon.

"Maybe I can bring up ice cream for you later?" Angelina must feel as sorry for me as I do for myself. "If the doctor says yes, of course."

"Oh, please. I mean, thank you, Angelina. And thank you for the lemon drops. They are my favorite."

"I know. Marco's, too." Angelina stops at my door and looks back. "He picked them for you."

A warmth settles in my stomach after Angelina leaves. It's not from the revolting beef tea either.

THREE

TIME MOVES AT a snail's pace as my lungs continue to heal. The summer will be over, and I will have nothing to show for it at this rate. With this oppressive heat, every little thing grates on my nerves, especially Kit.

"I don't know why we have to ride with the Sharps to the art exhibit." Kit bursts into our room, interrupting my reading. Again. She snatches her ostrich-plumed hat off its stand and pins it into her hair. "Isn't that why father hired what's-his-name?"

"Marco," I say.

"I shouldn't be going to this event at all, but I've run out of excuses," Kit says, confirming my suspicion that she isn't listening to me at all, as per usual. "Oh, for the love of all that is holy." Kit crams her gloves in her handbag and stomps out the door. "Yes, Mother, I am coming presently!"

As soon as I hear the front door close, I hook up my boots and grab my latest letter to Anna to post. Since I am dressed—thankfully without a corset on my still aching chest—I am determined to leave my house today even if it is to simply stand in the courtyard. Moving at the speed of an elderly woman with consumption, I descend the stairs. In the hallway rests today's mail. A silver dollar sits on top of Mama's overflowing correspondence to half the population of the United States. I add mine to the middle of her pile, hoping Mama won't notice the extra three-cent charge. The top letter of the in-coming stack catches my attention. It's addressed to Daddy, but the postmark is from here in Philadelphia. In her tell-tale, tight, perfect penmanship is Nurse Cecelia's name and address. I peek into Daddy's office, but he's still out. I place Cecelia's letter in the center of his desk on top of a few other pieces of correspondence.

The smell of peaches wafts down the hall on the heavy summer air. My mouth waters. I follow the scent down the hall and to the kitchen. Angelina and a number of her extended family members gossip in Italian in our kitchen as they work. I know it is gossip because as soon as I walk into the kitchen, everyone stops talking.

"Good afternoon, Miss Virginia." Angelina tops off a glass jar of peaches in sugar syrup and wipes her hands on her white apron. "Would you care for some peaches? We have plenty, as you see."

"Yes. That would be delightful."

Angelina digs through the basket on the kitchen table until she finds a prime specimen. She washes it off in the kitchen sink and dries it for me.

"Please, I am not an invalid." I take the peach from Angelina and a knife off the table. The perfectly ripe peach releases rivulets of juice as I cut it into bite-sized morsels. I cram a chunk into my mouth and lick the excess juice off my fingers. The taste explodes across my tongue. "Oh, this is delightful."

Just as I cram another sticky piece into my mouth, Marco bursts into the room, a bushel of peaches perched on his shoulder. The room erupts in boisterous Italian. Marco gently places the basket on the floor before making the rounds. Each of the middle-aged aunts kisses him on both cheeks and make clucking comments about how strong or handsome or something he is based on the amount of peacocking Marco does around the room. Marco continues to laugh and strut, picking Angelina off the floor and spinning her around until she smacks him in the head with her dishtowel.

"Miss Virginia!" Marco launches himself toward me, his dark eyes twinkling.

I back into the kitchen counter, wiping the juice dribbling out the corner of my mouth on my sleeve. The aunts erupt in laughter.

"You are looking better," Marco says, pushing the point of the knife away from him. "Back to climbing trees yet?"

"Soon. Tomorrow probably." I place the knife down on the counter. "You are in good spirits today."

Angelina wraps an arm around her brother's waist. "Your father has agreed to make Marco his assistant."

I blink. "But Daddy made you his assistant in the spring."

Marco's blinding smile dampens.

Angelina gives him a squeeze. "No, Dr. Jackson has agreed to teach Marco how to doctor. At least until Marco can go to doctor school himself."

"Medical school, Angelina. Medical." Marco turns his piercing gaze to me. "Did you think I wanted to be a chauffeur for the rest of my life?"

Angelina snaps at him in Italian.

Marco removes his protective arm from around his sister's shoulders. "Call me when you have the last of the peach pits cleaned. Mrs. Jackson wants them delivered to the Red Cross this afternoon."

"What could the Red Cross possibly want with peach pits?" I say.

"The peach pits are burnt down into charcoal for the doughboys' gas masks. Helps keep the mustard gas—and God knows what else—out of my brother's lungs." Marco grabs a peach out of the new bushel and rubs it on his shirt. "If you aren't too busy, feel free to grab a knife and do your patriotic duty."

A fire lights in my belly, and I can't contain the words that rush out. "My patriotic duty? What about your patriotic duty? Aren't you eighteen now? You don't have to wait to be drafted."

Angelina squeaks. The aunts don't need a translation. All four of them cross themselves. I wince as Marco's mouth opens and closes like a fish stranded on dry land. He smacks his peach back on the table, scoops up the basket of cleaned peach pits at his aunts' feet, and crashes out the kitchen door. The aunts tut among themselves, never making eye contact with me.

"I've lost my appetite." I wipe my sticky hands on the dishtowel and head toward the door.

"Miss Virginia," Angelina calls after me. "I'm sorry. Marco, he forgets his station. Please don't say to Dr. Jackson."

Though it is indeed within my right to relay this conversation to my father, I won't. "My father has enough on his mind right now. I don't need to add to his worries."

"Thank you, Miss." Angelina does a very unnecessary curtsey.

Marco is in the hallway when I exit the kitchen. When I try to pass him, Marco puts out his arm to block my way.

"Let me by," I say.

"Wait."

"I beg your pardon."

"Wait. *Please*."

"I wasn't going to tattle to my father, but now—"

"Would you stop thinking about yourself for two seconds?" Marco's eyes flash with anger, but he drops his voice. "Dr. Jackson received some distressing news. Give the man a moment to comport himself."

I stop and listen. Daddy's voice echoes from behind the cracked door of his office.

"Oh no. Oh no no no. Why, Cecelia, why?" he says.

I push Marco's arm out of the way and race up the hallway. I burst through Daddy's door to see him slumped over his desk with Nurse Cecelia's opened letter in his hands. I rush to him and kneel down beside his chair.

"Daddy, what's happened?"

Daddy looks at me, his eyes glassy. "Cecelia has joined the Army Nurse Corps. She accepted a training position at Camp Wadsworth in South Carolina. She left this morning." Daddy shakes the letter. "Why, Cecelia, why?"

The truth suddenly strikes me in the stomach. "Because Dr. Porter said she was too old. That soldiers want to be comforted by fresh-faced angels, not someone who could be their mother. Remember? It was around Christmas time. Dr. Porter was here and you three were discussing the war effort and doing your patriotic duty. Should you enlist again? Should you stay behind and serve Philadelphia? Cecelia mentioned that she had considered enlisting and you two had a jolly laugh about it."

Daddy winces. "I didn't want to lose her to the Red Cross, too...or the Army, for that matter. And now...."

"Cecelia is doing her patriotic duty," I say. Cecelia has been more of an aunt to me than any of Mama's younger sisters. No one will ever be able to fill her shoes. "I admire her adventurous choice, but I will miss her so."

"I will, too." Daddy pinches the bridge of his nose. "Why didn't she tell me, Virginia? I would have talked her out of this foolhardy idea."

"That is *exactly* why she didn't tell you. She didn't want you to talk her out of what she felt called to do." I wrap my hands around Daddy's large, callused ones. Tears well up in my eyes. "I never got to tell her goodbye. Or even a proper thank you."

"I didn't either." Always pragmatic, Daddy adds, "I don't know how I will ever replace her, especially now with so many nurses overseas."

"Would you like to place an advertisement in the *Philadelphia Inquirer*? I'm certain Kit could write a good one."

"No, I will ask my colleagues at the hospital."

"Daddy, what if something—"

"Don't. My old heart couldn't bear it." Daddy pulls his hand from mine and clears his throat. "Please, leave me be, Ginny. And tell Marco to go home. Or fiddle with the automobile. Or something of use. I want to be left alone this afternoon."

Marco. I bite my tongue. Now is not the time to bring up that arrogant boy's new position. I kiss the top of Daddy's rapidly graying head before backing into the hallway and closing the door. I rest my forehead against the heavy door. My heart breaks, for him, but for me, too. I've lost my ally. My champion. The one who insisted that I should be allowed to go to medical school if I wanted to.

Someone clears their throat from the hallway. I wipe my eyes on my sleeve and turn around.

"Pardon me. Is there something I can assist your father with?" Marco's eyes telegraph his genuine concern.

"No. In fact, my father has given you leave for the rest of the day."

"It's that bad then?"

"It's none of your concern." I turn on my heel and walk briskly toward the stairs.

"If Nurse Cecelia isn't returning, then it *is* my concern," Marco says from the base of the stairs, confirming my suspicion that he's been eavesdropping the entire time. He comes up to the step below me and lowers his voice. "I can do wound care and help set bones, but I don't know anything about—" Marco gestures at me as he struggles to come up with the words.

"Obstetrics and gynecology," I say with false confidence.

A redness creeps up Marco's neck to his ears. "Yes. That."

"Well, becoming a doctor requires *that*, so maybe you should rethink your aspirations."

"I know I haven't worked here long, but are you always so sharp-tongued? The gossip is that you are the pleasant sister. Are they wrong or do you save your ire specifically for me? If we were in grade school, I would presume that you actually fancied me."

"Don't flatter yourself. If we were in grade school, you would be the boy pulling my pigtails and leaving snails inside my desk."

Marco laughs. "I wish I could deny that, but unfortunately, it is probably true. Ask Angelina. My knuckles were rapped on a daily basis sometimes."

At her name, Angelina comes down the hallway from the kitchen. Finding us halfway up the stairs together, Angelina tells Marco something sharply in Italian. Whatever it was causes him to back slowly down the stairs.

"Always lovely to chat with you, Miss Jackson. Alas, the Red Cross requires their peach pits per instructions of the missus of the house, and I do not wish her ire."

Marco pantomimes a formal bow before heading toward the kitchen with Angelina. What a peacock. An idea pops into my head. I scurry down the stairs, grab my letter to Anna off the sideboard, and race back upstairs again. My chest is tight and my breathing raspy, but I feel better than I have in ages. Better than even before I came down with the influenza.

⸎

"WHAT THE DEVIL?" Marco says when he slides into the chauffeur's seat and finds me sitting in the back seat.

"Manners, Mr. D'Orio." I adjust my hat and pull on the emergency pair of gloves Mama keeps in the Cadillac. The gloves don't complement my outfit, but today is not the day to be a fashion plate. I have a new course to chart. "To the Red Cross first, please. And then a stop at the post office and Miss Nan's Confectionery. I'm sure my father needs some peppermint buttons to help settle his stomach after today's distressing news."

Marco turns around in his seat to face me. "I can't drive you through Philadelphia like this."

"Then put your cap and gloves on and play your part, Mr. D'Orio. We have a chauffeur for a reason."

For the second time today, Marco is speechless. I flick open Mama's emergency fan and attempt to move the stifling heat around the automobile. Marco runs an exasperated hand through his hair and mumbles to himself in Italian. He pulls the chauffeur's cap over his untamed waves and tugs on his gloves.

"The Red Cross, Miss," Marco announces after our silent ride across town. "Please allow me to deliver the peach pits. If word gets back to the Missus about this, she will have both of our heads."

Though I had no intention of walking into the Red Cross toting a bushel of peach pits like a farmhand, I enjoy vexing Marco. I wave a dismissive hand at Marco granting him leave. He pulls on his chauffeur's coat even though the mercury is above 85 degrees for certain. Marco opens the trunk and heaves two bushels of peach pits onto his broad shoulders. I may have watched him a little too intently enter the building. He does strike a cutting figure.

Several minutes later, Marco returns. He opens up the driver's side door and hurls his coat across the bench seat. It hits something that tinkles. I slide up to peer into the front seat.

"What are those?" I say, looking at the two small paper boxes in a cherry crate sitting on the front seat.

Marco slides behind the wheel. "Medicine."

"I can see that."

"I didn't steal it. It was to be delivered today. It's for Mr. O'Connor. The son. The one who's the undertaker." Marco nonchalantly turns the boxes so that I can't read their labels, but I already recognize the packaging.

If I question why we are delivering Salvarsan to the son of one of Daddy's first patients, then I will have to explain how I know what the medicine is used for. Darn Anna for complicating my life again with her unconventional choices.

"Well then, what are we waiting for?" I sit back in my seat and play dumb. "To Devil's Pocket, Mr. D'Orio."

"Do you want me fired? Don't answer that. I absolutely cannot bring an unchaperoned debutante into Devil's Pocket."

"Do you want Mr. O'Connor to have his medicine today

or not?"

Marco takes off his cap and runs his hand through his hair. His cheeks puff in and out as he weighs his options. Finally, Marco fires up the Cadillac.

"I will deliver them in record time, Miss. I promise it will be only a slight inconvenience for you."

I take my gloves off. "As long as we are home before five, we shall be fine. You completed your tasks, and I had a spot of adventure. No one else needs to know."

As we leave the finer section of Philadelphia, Marco looks in the rear mirror at me. "The gossips were wrong about that, too. *You* are the unconventional sister, not Miss Katherine."

That makes me smile. We drive in silence until we pass a church. A woman Kit's age dressed in black shuffles out the front door dabbing at her cheeks with her handkerchief. She shifts a baby on her hip and takes the hand of the smaller of two children trailing behind her like baby ducks.

"It must be difficult for your family with your brother being overseas," I say.

"It is."

"I will pray for his safety."

Marco dips his head. "Thank you, Miss."

Marco doesn't expand on that thought. And though I know it would be inappropriate—not to mention impolite—to inquire about your chauffeur's personal life, I suddenly want to know. I have a burning desire to know him better.

"Is that why you want to be a doctor? To make more money for your family?" I say. Mama would be horrified by my uncouth behavior.

Marco covers up his shock with a small laugh. "No, I

genuinely want to be a doctor. The higher salary would be helpful though for my family. As I mentioned on your birthday, I am the man of the house. Angelina and I work full time. Mamma does piecemeal work for the factory when she can get it. Isabella and Giorgio need to stay in school for as long as they can. But if the war drags on and I get drafted—" Marco looks back over his shoulder at me. He's said too much. "I apologize, Miss Virginia."

"No apology necessary. If we are going to embark on this adventure together, we should at least be acquainted," I say, and a cocky smile returns to Marco's face. "In the most polite and appropriate way, of course."

"Of course." Marco swerves the Cadillac over to the side and parks. "The post office, Miss Jackson."

Mama likes to remind me whenever I complain about being stifled that when she was a girl, ladies weren't allowed to travel outside their home without either their father, brother, uncle or husband. But I am here. Alone. And the feeling is euphoric. However, I'm not stupid. I attend to my errands at the post office and Miss Nan's Confectionary while Marco waits in the Cadillac.

When we arrive at Devil's Pocket shortly after, Marco deposits his chauffeur's cap and gloves on the seat. He slides the two packages of Salvarsan into his pockets. "I promise not to be gone long."

I nod and leave him to his business. The last time I was here, Devil's Pocket almost killed me with Spanish influenza. I have no desire to let someone finish the job today. Instead, I sit in the Cadillac sweating like a goose simmering in its own juices. If this is what being a modern woman entails, it is highly overrated.

A sudden tapping on the glass interrupts my cat nap. I grab my fan like a dagger. Marco laughs from the other side of the window before sliding into the Cadillac. He fires up the engine and looks back over his shoulder at me. A satisfied smile cuts across his face.

"Thank you. We made a difference today. I promise."

"Happy to be of assistance, Mr. D'Orio." I feel quite smug as we head home. I mailed a letter by myself, and I haven't coughed in hours. I even resisted temptation—in the form of Mr. Hershey's delightful chocolate "kisses"— and only bought peppermint buttons for Daddy and a few lemon drops for me. Patriotic Americans ration their candy intake for the sake of our boys overseas, of course.

"Jesus, Mary, and Joseph." Marco suddenly swerves to the side when we enter Rittenhouse Square and find the Sharps' automobile parked in front of my house. "They're back early. What do we do? Should I put you out here and keep going?"

"No! I'm not even supposed to be out of my room."

Someone behind us honks.

"Keep going." I duck down in the seat, praying that Mama won't see me. "Park in our courtyard like you always do. Hurry. Before they finish with the hundred required niceties with The Sharps."

Marco turns into our courtyard and jerks to a stop. I'm out the door before he has a chance to open it for me.

"Where are you going?" Marco hisses from behind me when I don't head for the kitchen door.

"Give me a boost."

"Pardon?"

I turn when I get to the apple tree. "A boost. Do you want to keep your job or not?"

Marco bends down and laces his fingers together. I step into them. With a grunt, he pushes me up until I can hook my toe in the crook of the tree. I'm up the tree in record time. Marco stands under the tree limb both trying not to be improper and yet ready to catch me if I slip. If I fall and break my neck, he will lose his job for certain. I stifle my coughs as my lungs spasm in retaliation for this foolhardy endeavor. I stumble through my open window seconds before I hear the front door close downstairs.

"Virginia." Marco's hushed voice rises up from the courtyard.

I lean back out the window. Marco stands below with my paper cone of sweets. The top rolled down tightly. Marco tosses the package up to me, and I nod in thanks.

Footsteps are coming up the stairs. My heart pounds as I tear the hat out of my hair, toss it onto my hat stand, collapse into bed and pull up the bedclothes though my boots are still on. I hide the cone of sweets under my pillow.

"Mama," I say between coughs when she enters my room a moment later.

"Gracious, Virginia." Mama sits down on the edge of my bed. "Is your fever back?"

"No. It's…hot…today."

"I imagine, especially under all these bedclothes." Mama reaches down to pull them away, but I stop her. "You are acting queer. Shall I fetch your father?"

I shake my head as I continue to cough. Mama reaches for my carafe and tumbler and pours me the last of the water. I gulp it down, hoping to settle my lungs. She pats my hand until my cough finally subsides.

"Well then. Enough lollygagging. I must attend to business." Mama stands up and shakes the wrinkles out of her somber-colored skirts. "I'll send Angelina up with a dinner tray shortly. You obviously need several more days of confinement. I don't care if your father is a doctor. A mother knows these things."

My mother knows nothing, and I'd like to keep it that way.

I wait until I hear Mama's footsteps descending the stairs before throwing the stifling bedclothes off me. I unhook my boots and sneak over to my wardrobe to put them away. As I cross back toward my bed to retrieve my cone of sweets, I hear whistling in the courtyard. I peek out the window. Marco is down below with the hood of the Cadillac up and his backside hanging out of it. I jump back out of sight when he ceases his tune and stands up straight. A moment later, I dare another look. Marco stands with his back to me clad only in his undershirt, with his suspenders drooping down around his hips. His jacket and work shirt hang over the car door. He holds up a piece of machinery to the sky examining it. I watch in fascination as all the muscles in his arms and upper back contract as he replaces the piece and tightens it back into place. I know what the human body looks like. All of it. At least on paper. My father has a whole library of books on how the human body works. Anna and I have borrowed a few specific books over the years. Yet, this example is completely fascinating. Scientifically-speaking, of course.

The whistling turns into humming and then into a soft Italian tune. Maybe it's a love song. Or maybe it's an original composition about the vexing family he chauffeurs around Philadelphia. Who knows? All I know is that everything sounds better in Italian.

I lean out the window. "Psst. Psst."

Marco stops whistling and turns around. He smears a streak of engine grease across his brow while wiping away the perspiration. Finally, he looks up. I put my index finger to my lips and gesture for him to come underneath the window. When he does, I hold the parcel of sweets out of the window and let it fall directly into his dirty hands. He smiles up at me. I nod. My first adventure has ended quite satisfactorily.

FOUR

TO HIS CREDIT, Daddy does entertain my somewhat self-serving suggestion that he hire Anna to replace Cecelia for the rest of the summer. That is how desperate he is for a nurse. Marco is not pleased. Yes, Marco can lift patients and drive Daddy around. But, Daddy has also lost a few Rittenhouse Square patients because of Marco.

"It's not proper," Mama says at luncheon a week later. "Mrs. Sharp said her youngest daughter—the one in the family way presently—is going to Dr. Lakes for her care."

"Why?" Daddy stabs at his potato salad as if it has personally wronged him.

"She didn't say." Mama ducks her head, making me doubt the truth of that statement.

"Well, Lydia did." Kit leans to the side a bit so that Angelina can remove her luncheon plate and replace it with a dainty dish of peach sorbet. "She said she didn't feel comfortable having a man in the room while being examined. I pointed out that the person who delivered her older sister's last three babies was also a man. And that my father did a fine job of it."

"Thank you, Katherine," Daddy says.

"It's really Marco she objects to," Kit plows on. "When I

pressed her further, she finally told the truth. She doesn't want an immigrant in the room assisting. Male or female."

Angelina clatters some plates on the tray. Mama gives Kit a withering look, and my sister has the good sense to hold her tongue until Angelina leaves the room.

"I am simply reporting the facts." Kit digs into her sorbet with gusto. "The Sharps are such snobs."

Daddy sighs. "It's not only the Sharps. I've had two more Rittenhouse Square patients say they want to be attended by a real nurse. Not a chauffeur who thinks he's a nurse. I need a woman for the job. I even telegraphed Henry yesterday."

My heart leaps. "Dr. Carter is going to send us Anna?"

Daddy pulls a piece of paper out of his pocket and smooths it out. "Henry telegraphed me back this morning. He said: Don't be a jackass. I need Anna here. Hire Virginia. Regards."

"No," Mama says.

"Then Katherine." Daddy smacks the telegram on the dining room table.

"Absolutely not," Mama and Kit say at the same time.

"You know the sight of blood gives Kit the vapors, Daddy," I say. "And then there are her opinions about politics, especially women's suffrage. Those give high society ladies the vapors."

A deep crease forms between Daddy's eyebrows. "We are losing our livelihood because of this. These are your friends, Eleanor. Come attend to them. Just for a few weeks until I can find someone to replace Cecelia."

Mama blusters at the ridiculous idea.

Daddy's face softens, and a chuckle slips out. "So what you are trying to say is that I should stop being a jackass and hire Ginny?"

"Yes. I want to go to medical school," I say, and Mama blusters some more about how unseemly the job is for a young lady. "Anna and I already have plans to attend the Woman's Medical College of Pennsylvania. I might as well test the waters now."

"She does have a point, Eleanor. I need a nurse starting this afternoon. Which of you three will be accompanying me? You choose, dear wife."

Mama pushes away from the table, her face flushed. "You may take Virginia, but only until you find a new nurse. Katherine, you and I will write another advertisement presently."

For once, Kit wisely chooses to be agreeable. "Of course, Mother. I can deliver it on my way to the library this afternoon."

"Well then," Daddy says, pushing away from the table. "Now that the matter is settled, please be ready to depart in thirty minutes, Ginny. We are going out today. I have a standing date with two of your grandfather's favorite patients."

I'M ALREADY WAITING in the Cadillac when Daddy arrives with his black bag. He groans and rubs his bad leg.

"You must stop sleeping in the parlor, Daddy." I pull a peppermint out of my—Cecelia's old—nursing apron. "It's not good for your leg nor your back."

"Thank you for your concern, Nurse Jackson." Daddy takes the peppermint from my palm and pops it in his mouth.

"Undoubtedly after today's luncheon, you will be sleeping there again tonight."

Daddy sighs. "Undoubtedly."

Marco slides into the front and startles. "Miss Virginia, I didn't realize you would be accompanying us today."

Daddy beams and pats my knee. "Yes. I have finally found an answer to my problem. At least until the end of the summer. Then I guess I'll have to release Virginia back to her mother for Red Cross events and tea parties and other such womanly things after school."

"What if I am not interested in Red Cross events and tea parties and other such womanly things after school?" I say.

Daddy laughs though I am deadly serious. "To Devil's Pocket, Marco."

Devil's Pocket. Home to many of Philadelphia's Irish families. Why Anna concentrated her efforts here is unfathomable to me. Maybe because it's the only place in Philadelphia where a red-haired girl like herself could easily blend in? We pass the Naval Hospital and enter the group of small courts that overlook the Schuylkill River. Marco turns down a narrow street. A pair of young children squats near the stoop of a weather-beaten brick building, digging at something in the dirt. A young mother who doesn't look much older than Kit sits above them peeling carrots. It's Mrs. Flanagan, the woman I delivered Salvarsan to on Anna's behalf. The one with syphilis caught from her lecherous husband and spread to the eyes of her now blind, youngest child. The one who may have given me the Spanish flu. I finger my nursing mask. I won't make that mistake twice. We pull to a stop at a similar building a little further down the street.

"I will need you to stand by the car today, Marco." Daddy leans forward and puts his hand on Marco's shoulder. "Otherwise, I'm afraid that our tires will be missing when we return. Today's paper had an article about immigrant hoodlums absconding with a gentleman's tires. Can you fathom it? Who knew that rubber was such a hot commodity on the black market?"

The vein in Marco's temple throbs, but he nods his head anyway. "Yes, sir."

"The Lemon Squeezer is under the driver's seat. Brandish it, if you need to. I require my tires."

"Lemon squeezer?" I say. "Are we making lemonade in Devil's Pocket today?"

Marco and Daddy share a knowing laugh. My face burns. Marco reaches under the seat.

Marco holds the small handgun across his palm for me to see. "A Smith & Wesson .38 Caliber Lemon Squeezer Double action revolver."

"Which I hope never to need. But it never hurts to be careful," Daddy says. "Speaking of which, mask on, Nurse Jackson, at least until we arrive upstairs. Your lungs are still weak."

I follow Daddy up the tenement's stairs. The half-rotted planks groan under our weight. Bile rises up in the back of my throat as the stench of sewage, rotten vegetables, and smoke assault my nose. I pull my handkerchief—the one with the yellow roses decorating the corner—out of my pocket and hold it up to my mask-covered nose. I breathe in deep. Though I doused the handkerchief with the last of my rose water before I rushed out the door, it does nothing to improve the odor. Now everything smells like sewage-garbage-smoke with flower petals sprinkled on the top.

"Mr. O'Connor was your grandfather's closest boyhood friend." Daddy and I both breathe heavily after three flights of stairs, and we still have another to go. "Unfortunately, time has not been kind to him. Time and Diabetes Mellitus.

I fear I will have to take another toe today."

"Toe?" I pull up short.

"Yes, I will probably need to amputate it. If this is going to be too much for you, I should walk you back to the car now."

"No, of course not." I steel myself. "I was only surprised. That's all."

I wanted another adventure. Next time, I should be a little more specific.

"Good afternoon, Mr. O'Connor!" Daddy yells across the room after Mrs. O'Connor lets us in.

"Aye. Afternoon. Is that you, Charles, come for a visit?" Mr. O'Connor squints at us from the threadbare chair he's lounging on.

I take a sharp breath. Daddy failed to mention that Mr. O'Connor is already missing several toes. In fact, the lower half of Mr. O'Connor's right leg is gone, his trouser leg tied in a knot like the end of a sausage.

"Aye, sir." Daddy shakes what's left of Mr. O'Connor's right hand, two of the digits missing.

Mr. O'Connor squints at me. "And who might you be? Is this your darling Eleanor?"

Daddy chuckles and gestures at me to remove my mask. "Oh, heavens, no. This is my daughter, Virginia."

"Ah, the obedient daughter." Mr. O'Connor laughs, and Daddy along with him.

My stomach clenches, but I keep my mouth closed. I cram the nursing mask in my pocket.

"Well then, let's have a look, shall we?" Daddy unwraps the stained, filthy bandage from around Mr. O'Connor's left foot.

I put the rose-scented handkerchief up to my nose to counteract the smell of sweet, rotting flesh wafting up from the bandage.

"Virginia, can you assist me, please?"

Daddy hands me the trail of bandages to hold. His nimble fingers work to free the section of the fabric adhered to Mr. O'Connor's oozing wound. Bile rises up in my throat as a strip of skin clings to the bandage. I take a deep breath to push the bile back down. I will not fail on my first day. As Daddy pulls the bandage across the fourth toe, the skin at the base of it begins to rip. *Until the whole fourth toe completely falls off!*

"Oh, dear God." I drop the bandages, with the toe still stuck to it, and rush to the window.

The garbage heap down below doesn't quell the rolling in my stomach. I try to push the toe out of my mind. I think of my apple tree. Anna's fluffy white cat, Snowflake. Marco laughing at my incompetence. Anything to make that toe go away.

"I'm sorry, Mr. O'Connor," Daddy's voice is smooth like caramel as he delivers the bad news. "All of them have severe diabetic gangrene. The third toe is going to have to go and probably the one beside it soon after. Should I take both of them today and be done with it?"

"Take the whole damn foot, Charles," Mr. O'Connor grumbles.

I continue to stare out the window as Daddy prepares for the task. I hear the clank of metal instruments and the clink of medicine bottles being set out on the table.

"Nurse Jackson, will you be assisting during the amputation?" Daddy says.

I take a deep breath to steel myself and turn around. The self-amputating toe still lies on the heap of bandages on the floor. Suddenly, the room begins to melt like wax dripping down a candle. I hold on to the window sill to keep upright.

Mr. O'Connor laughs. "Obedient, but maybe not cut out for nursing."

Daddy makes it across the room in three, limping strides. His strong hands grab me by the waist to keep me upright. His gentle, weathered face fills the space in front of me.

"Deep breaths, sweetheart," Daddy uses the caramel voice on me, too. "Go wait outside with Marco. I'll be out soon."

With the rose-scented handkerchief over my nose and mouth, I rush out the O'Connors' door without a farewell. I barrel down four flights of stairs and burst out the front door of the tenement building, just in time to empty the entire contents of my stomach into the gutter next to the Cadillac. I look up, expecting to see Marco having a jolly laugh at my weakness, but he's not there. I never want to eat potato salad or peach sorbet again.

Finally, Marco comes strolling down the alleyway. He glances up from his thoughts and catches my eye. He startles and jogs back to the car.

"Have you finished already?" Marco looks around for Daddy. "I only stepped away for a moment. I needed to take care of some...um...personal business. Where's Dr. Jackson?"

"He's doing an amputation." My stomach rolls at the mention of the word.

"That might be a bit much for your first day. It would probably turn you off from nursing all together." Marco notices my mess in the gutter.

My face burns.

"Did Dr. Jackson ask for me to assist him instead?"

"No."

"Oh." Marco, remembering his job, opens the door of the

Cadillac and offers his hand so I can jump over the soiled gutter. As I settle into the backseat, Marco climbs into the driver's seat and stares up at Mr. O'Connor's building. He drums his fingers on the window frame of the car. Sweat pours down his temples and drips onto his collar.

"Would you care for a lemon drop?" I use my left hand—the one that didn't touch Mr. O'Connor's soiled bandages—to hold out the paper cone of sweets toward Marco.

Marco looks over his shoulder, and a small smile spreads across his face. He takes one. "Thank you."

It takes a few moments, but I am able to successfully get one yellow sphere out of the paper cone and into my mouth, too.

"Would you care for another?" I say several minutes later to be polite, but it's mostly for my benefit. Anything to get the smell of potato salad and gangrene out of my nose.

"Thank you," Marco says as he takes another and a third one as we wait for Daddy to finish his onerous task.

Finally, Daddy reappears. Marco rushes to the front door of the building and collects my father's black bag.

Daddy slides in beside me and pats my hand. "The next one won't be so hard, I promise. Most days, it's more of a social call than a medical one."

"Dr. Jackson, do you have time to see another patient today after Mrs. Maguire?" Marco says as we pull away from the curb.

"I don't know. It's getting late. I promised to have Virginia home in time for an early dinner." Daddy turns to me. "Your mother is hosting some sort of salon this evening. For the Red Cross? Or maybe it was the Flower Market ladies? Who knows? I can't keep up with all of your mother's doings. Be a good girl and assist her tonight. Your dear father can't bear another night on the settee. His old bones aren't up to it anymore."

A good girl. An obedient daughter. The words grind my soul.

Marco looks over his shoulder. "Sir, it's a little girl. A baby who isn't growing."

"How can I neglect a child?" Daddy squeezes my hand. "Of course, we will see her. Is this a family friend of yours, Marco?"

Marco pauses for so long that I wonder if Daddy will repeat himself.

"She's a special little girl to me. You'll see," Marco says.

"Alright then," Daddy says. "But first, Mrs. Maguire."

"I WAS A washerwoman for some of the finest families in Philadelphia in my day," Mrs. Maguire says, as Daddy and I settle in on her stained and faded parlor furniture. "I washed for your da's family for many years, I did. Your mam's, too."

"And a fine job you did, Mrs. Maguire. My mother—God rest her soul—wouldn't allow anyone else to even touch her grandmother's antique table cloths." Daddy pats the woman's gnarled and spotted hand before taking her pulse.

"Aye, so she did. Och, where're my manners? I haven't offered ye tea. I even have a bit o' shortbread today." Mrs. Maguire rocks back and forth attempting to get to her feet.

"Please, Mrs. Maguire, rest. My daughter would be happy to make us tea."

Daddy gives me a reassuring nod despite my flustered

look. I've never made tea before. In fact, I've never made anything more complicated than a cheese sandwich.

After scrubbing my hands thoroughly, I dig through the kitchen to find all the pieces for an acceptable tea tray, including the shortbread. I almost set my apron on fire while boiling the water, but otherwise, I would call my first attempt at tea a success. My confidence dips when I pour Mrs. Maguire's tea, and something resembling dirty dishwater comes out of the chipped china teapot. The splash of milk makes it look even less appealing.

"Oh dear, it barely has the strength to get out the pot." Mrs. Maguire chuckles and pats my hand. "That'll be fine dear. Waste not, want not. We're in a war after all."

"One lump or two, Mrs. Maguire?" I continue my charade as a refined hostess.

"One, please."

"Would you care for a piece of shortbread?"

"Yes, please. How delightful you are, Eleanor."

Before I can correct her, Daddy shakes his head at me. Adding to his peculiar mood, Daddy also declines a sugar cube and a piece of shortbread, though everyone knows I inherited my sweet tooth from him. I add a second sugar cube to my pathetic example of tea to make it potable.

Mrs. Maguire nibbles on a piece of shortbread with the few teeth she has left. "My, isn't this shortbread lovely? Such a blessing to have a little fresh butter again."

Mrs. Maguire prattles on to Daddy about the good ole days and people long dead. Honestly, administering to Mrs. Maguire isn't that much different from the teas I suffer through with Widow Clark. She talks about her gout and the pain in her back and her tooth and her elbow and her pinky. Mrs. Maguire seems to suffer from an acute case of loneliness. Loneliness mixed with a large dose of old age.

"Are you still doing your facts and figures, Eleanor?" Mrs. Maguire says to me.

"Pardon me?"

"Do you still keep your da's books? You were always busy with your facts and figures. And me, I can barely compute the egg money without using my fingers and toes."

I don't know how to answer. Though I suddenly understand why Mama spends hours rectifying the household account down to the penny.

"Eleanor's uncle sold the family business a long, long time ago, Mrs. Maguire." Daddy comes to my rescue. "A year or so after we were married."

"Well now, that's a shame." Mrs. Maguire looks at me. "Do you remember that blue dress? The one the color of cornflowers with lace on the collar. Oh, how cross yer mam was about that dress. I tried every laundry trick I knew, but nothing would get that ink out. I bet you couldn't sit down for a week after that."

"I had forgotten all about that," I play act.

"I'm so glad ye picked Charles." Mrs. Maguire pats Daddy's hand. "A good man he is. A handsome man. When are you going to have some wee ones?"

"I have two girls, Mrs. Maguire," Daddy says.

"Girls? Well, you're gonna have to get to work, young man." Mrs. Maguire lets out a hearty laugh. "Ye need a son. Someone to follow in his da's footsteps and carry on the Jackson name."

"I'm afraid that's not meant to be." Daddy's voice has a regretful tone.

"Maybe one of his daughters can follow in his footsteps?" I say.

Mrs. Maguire laughs. "Aye, maybe, Eleanor. The times have changed since I was a lass. Begorrah, I wouldn't have even learnt to write my name if it wasn't for ye, Eleanor. I'll never forget that."

"Ah, time is passing quickly by us, isn't it?" Daddy puts his empty teacup down and nods at me. "Now, Mrs. Maguire, before we go, do you have any other health complaints?"

"My hands have been aching me something awful lately, and my knees and…." Mrs. Maguire's repeated list of complaints continues long after I gather the tea things and bring them back to the kitchen.

I wash and dry all the dishes. Another first for me today. As I put away all the tea things in the worn, but clean, kitchen, I realize what was missing before. Food. I peek into the pantry and the icebox. I tally up exactly one-half of a loaf of bread on the counter, less than a quart of milk in the icebox, and three turnips in the pantry. The shortbread in my stomach suddenly feels like a brick, especially after I ate Daddy's piece while retreating to the kitchen. I also took the last of Mrs. Maguire's sugar cubes. With the combination of poverty and rationing, it's unlikely that she'll be able to obtain any more, at least this month. When I sweep back into the other room to wipe the table off, I bring my handbag back into the kitchen with me, the coins of my weekly pocket money jingling in the bottom. I stack the coins next to the teapot and tuck the last of my lemon drops inside the antique sugar bowl as penance for my gluttony.

Daddy stands at the front door when I return from the kitchen, Mrs. Maguire attached to his arm like a grand lady.

"We really must go. Please take care of yourself, Mrs.

Maguire." Daddy pats the top of her hand. "I'll come check on you again soon."

Mrs. Maguire reaches out her gnarled hand and places it gently on the side of my face. "Be good to yer mam, Eleanor. I know she can be tryin', but she just wants what's best for ye."

"Yes, ma'am."

Mrs. Maguire leans in like she is going to kiss my cheek, but instead whispers in my ear, "Don't you worry none. Your secret's still safe with me."

Now I definitely want to stay, but Daddy rushes me out the door after a few last pleasantries. We find Marco pacing beside the car, sweat circles marking his shirt.

Daddy pops open his gold pocket watch after we are settled in the car. "Is it that late? We need to head home."

"But, sir," Marco says.

"We promised to see a baby," I say.

Daddy melts into the corner and closes his eyes. "All right. One more for today. I'm not as young as I used to be."

It only takes a few minutes to arrive at another tenement slum. Daddy allows Marco to carry his black bag up another four flights of stairs. Marco lightly raps on the last door at the end of a long hallway. A child howls in the background. Marco knocks harder. The door cracks open, and a disheveled young woman about Kit's age opens the door, a red-faced baby attached to her hip.

"The baby's lungs are clear. That's a good sign," Daddy says as the young mother lets us in. "Marco here tells me that your child is doing poorly, Missus…."

The woman's peaches-and-cream complexion turns to strawberries-and-cream.

"It's Miss," Marco answers for her. "Miss Siobhan

49

Shannon. And this is Doctor Jackson and his daughter, Miss Virginia Jackson."

"It's a pleasure to make your acquaintance," *Miss* Siobhan Shannon says with a dip. "And this howling monkey is Colleen. M'daughter...*my* daughter, sir."

I am not so sheltered as to not know that children are occasionally born outside of wedlock. However, I have never met a woman so brazen as to admit to it, especially on first introductions. I can't help but wonder if Anna has counseled—or should have counseled—Miss Shannon in the past, but I don't dare ask it. Daddy and Dr. Carter have been friends since medical school. I'm afraid Anna's secret doings wouldn't remain secret for long.

"C'm here, Colleen." Marco takes the baby from Miss Shannon and bounces her about a bit. "Give your poor mamma a few moment's peace."

The baby's wails cease though there are still pools of tears in her big hazel eyes. She grabs at Marco's face until she hooks his lip in her tiny fingers like he's a prized trout. I cover my laugh with a cough.

"How old is the child?" Daddy sets his black bag on the roughhewn kitchen table and opens it up.

"Six months," Marco says, Colleen still attached to his lip.

Colleen doesn't fuss when Daddy places the stethoscope on her back to check her lungs. She's too busy attaching her other hand to Marco's ear.

"Was Colleen a Blue Baby?" Daddy moves the stethoscope to the baby's chest.

"No, sir." Miss Shannon wrings her hands.

"Does she suffer from vomiting or diarrhea?"

"No, sir."

"Are you nursing her regularly?"

"I try. I just don't know if it is enough." Tears well up in Miss Shannon's slate blue eyes.

Pasty skin. Thin hair. Brittle fingernails. You don't need a degree in medicine to see that both this child and her mother are suffering from malnutrition. Probably for a long time now.

Daddy places his stethoscope back in his bag. "I'm afraid, Miss Shannon, that your daughter is suffering from marasmus."

"Severe malnutrition," Marco and I say at the same time.

"She needs more food." Daddy smooths down the tuft of brown hair sticking up from the little girl's head. "If your milk is drying up, then procure some Mellin's Food and mix it with cow's milk."

Miss Shannon bursts into tears. "I wish I could. I swear, Dr. Jackson, every penny that comes in this house I use for my daughter. I am nary a drunk nor gambler. But every month I find it more difficult to stretch my money and ration books."

"And the baby's father? Can he take some responsibility?"

Miss Shannon and Marco share a knowing glance.

"No." Miss Shannon drops her head. "Not right now. Maybe in the future. When his family will accept me."

Daddy tugs Colleen from Marco and inspects her a bit more. "Otherwise, other than malnutrition, your daughter is healthy. No infections or other maladies that I can see."

"Thank you, sir. I swear, I will try harder." Miss Shannon accepts Colleen back from Daddy. The baby resumes her fussing.

"I'll come again the next time I'm in Devil's Pocket," Daddy says. "Marco, remind me to bring the Mellin's Food with me. I have some extra in our supply closet."

"Yes, sir." Marco nods though he knows as well as I do

that we don't keep Mellin's Food in our supply closet. Daddy can be gruff sometimes, but it's well known that he has a soft spot for children. Maybe because he had hoped for a larger brood of his own? Maybe a son, like Mrs. Maguire insists he should have.

"I should pay you something for your trouble," Miss Shannon says.

"That's not necessary, Miss Shannon. We were visiting an old friend in the neighborhood. But now, we really must go." Daddy herds me toward the door.

Marco lingers behind as Daddy and I head for the car. I try to eavesdrop, but the sound of Daddy's boots on the rickety stairs drowns out most of the conversation. I do catch a few words though.

"I'll try," Marco says. "I promised I would, didn't I? Mamma is so stubborn."

Daddy ushers me directly into the car before closing the door. He doubles back to the front door of the tenement building and stops Marco. Oh, how I wish I could read lips or had extraordinary hearing. Whatever Daddy says to Marco results in a shamed, wounded dog look. It's a far cry from the peacock who strutted around my kitchen only a week ago.

Daddy slides into the back of the Cadillac with an irritated sigh. "We will *not* mention this last patient to your mother. I've tried to shelter you from such improprieties, but alas they do exist." There are a lot of improprieties I cannot mention to my mother, mostly thanks to Anna's doings. "I'm afraid that you've had to grow up rather fast today. I'm sorry about that. Maybe your mother is right. Maybe this isn't an appropriate job for a young lady. Perhaps Marco is better suited for the job."

Marco sits up straighter behind the wheel. Meanwhile, I

feel like a child who's had her favorite toy snatched away.

"Please, Daddy. I promise not to vomit anymore," I plead, but Daddy shakes his head. "And I *do* know of these worldly things. In fact, I know very well why Agnes Griffith left school in the middle of the term for a sudden trip to her distant relatives' home in Idaho. And it most certainly was not for the potatoes!"

Daddy's mouth drops open, and Marco looks over his shoulder at me in disbelief. The Griffiths are Main Line royalty, but that didn't protect them from the salacious gossip.

"You will *not* repeat such things," Daddy snaps. It confirms my suspicion that the day Agnes's mother brought her in to see Daddy had nothing to do with the food poisoning mysteriously happening every morning for two months, as reported.

"But I do know these things, Daddy. And as Kit always says, we shouldn't be afraid of knowledge. Knowledge is power."

"The nonsense they fill the girls' heads with at Radcliffe." Daddy shakes his head in disappointment. "All they are doing is preparing those girls for a life alone. Books are wonderful, but they won't take care of you in your old age."

"Well, my books and I shall take care of *you* in your old age, Daddy."

"Ah, my darling one, I'm afraid you will be the only one. Especially if your mother finds out about our adventures today."

"Perhaps we shouldn't elaborate."

"Agreed. My leg cannot take another night on the settee."

"Does that mean I may retain my position?" I press.

Marco perks up to hear the answer. Daddy is quiet for a bit before finally answering.

"Yes, Ginny, you may stay on." Daddy winces when I throw my arms around his neck. "But only until school starts. Then I need to give you back to your mother for training."

I sit back smugly like I've snatched my toy back. Marco wisely keeps his mouth closed. But he doesn't know that I have no intention of stopping after school starts. In fact, I don't plan on stopping until I leave for college.

FIVE

"MAN ALIVE, MOTHER was in such a foul humor this evening." Kit sits down at our vanity and unpins her hair. "Why must I always be the one who endures her wrath? Can't you play the role of Disappointing Daughter for an evening or two?"

Now that we're safely ensconced in our room, I can shed my robe. I open the bedroom window a little wider in an attempt to catch any breeze.

"I would take the role, but you are so splendid at it." I pick up Granny Jackson's silver-handled boar's hair brush and pull it through Kit's deep brown hair. "If only you would keep your mouth firmly closed, you would save yourself from much of Mama's wrath."

"I am a journalist, Ginny. I will not censor my words on paper nor at the dinner table."

"I'm not asking you to censor yourself. I'm asking you to stop inflicting every piece of gloom and doom you read in the newspaper on our family at meals."

The brush hits a particularly snarled section of Kit's hair.

"Ow!" Kit grabs my wrist. "You did that on purpose."

"I did not. Stop being such a baby. If you can't weather a simple hair brushing, then maybe you should be like those cinema ladies and bob your hair."

A sparkle lights in Kit's eyes. She tucks her long hair up into a bob-like length and admires herself. "I've been thinking about it. I even have the neck to pull the look off." Kit sighs and drops her hair back down. "Mother would disown me."

"Then do it after you arrive back at Radcliffe and send Mama a photograph. By the time you come home for Christmas, she may have come around to the idea."

"No, she would still disown me. Then you would inherit Granny's coveted silver vanity set." Kit picks up the silver hand mirror off the vanity. "That's why you are so keen on this idea. You want Granny's silver all to yourself."

"As I am more likely to get married and have a daughter to pass the silver down to, I think that it is only fair," I tease, but I hit a nerve.

Kit pops to her feet, puffed up like an agitated hen. "Do not write me off as a spinster quite yet, Virginia."

Kit walks to the window and kicks out the molding underneath. But instead of bringing back my jar of candy, she has a series of newspaper clippings in her hands.

"Do you know what the NWP is?" Kit says, keeping the clippings pressed to her chest.

"A group of scandalous women in bloomers? At least according to Mrs. Clark, that is."

"That was Eighteen-blessed-fifty-one, and wearing bloomers is now a perfectly acceptable fashion while cycling."

"Try telling Mama that."

"I have. Repeatedly. Her stubbornness puts a mule to shame."

"Pot, meet kettle."

"Don't be nasty, Virginia. It's not becoming of a lady."

"Neither is being arrested for being a suffragette."

"*Suffragist*. And I was released with a warning because it was my first arrest." Kit slumps down on the vanity chair. "But that day. That horrible day in November, I should have stayed by my sisters' sides when they were taken away. But I was afraid. I didn't want to be sent to Occoquan. I ran instead of standing my ground."

I wrap my arms around Kit's hunched shoulders and look at her in the vanity mirror. "You're a journalist, not a soldier. Words are your weapon. You can't do your part for the National Woman's Party chained up in the Occoquan Workhouse with a feeding tube crammed down your gullet like Miss Paul and Miss Burns and the others. Don't look so surprised. I do read the newspaper, occasionally."

"You sound like Grayson."

"Who?"

"Grayson Reynolds. Of the New York City Reynoldses. Star reporter for *The Harvard Crimson* and mentor to *The Radcliffe News.*" Kit shows me the top newspaper clipping.

I read the headline. *20,000 March in Suffrage Line. 500 Men in the Ranks. Women of All Ages Join in the Demonstration, Many Carrying Service Flags.*

Kit points to the middle part. "Grayson Reynolds, unapologetic supporter of the suffrage movement."

A fleeting smile crosses Kit's face. My sister is in love! I squeeze Kit's shoulders.

"You and Mama will be at peace again soon. You will be allowed to return to Radcliffe College this fall. You and your dear Grayson—star reporter for *The Harvard Crimson* and unapologetic supporter of the suffrage movement—shall be reunited again soon."

Tears well up in Kit's eyes. She pulls a second newspaper clipping on top. It's an engagement announcement from the *New York Times*. I vaguely recognize the family name of the debutante from one of New York's so-called "Four Hundred." I glance at the announcement. She's someone from a moneyed family. Someone who will be marrying Grayson Reynolds this winter. Someone who isn't my sister.

I tip my head against Kit's. "Now what?"

"I don't know. I need some time to rethink things. Maybe I don't want to return to Radcliffe College after all. Maybe I should move to Washington, D.C."

"Are you running *to* something or simply *away* from something?"

"Perhaps both." Kit wipes her eyes on the sleeve of her robe. "All I know is that things must change. I can't stay here, but the idea of returning to Radcliffe—and having to see Grayson and his soon-to-be wife around town—is more than I can bear right now. You're the one out and about, and I'm the one stuck at home with Mother rolling bandages. Most days I want to poke myself in the eye with my seafood fork."

"Please don't be envious. Mr. O'Connor's toe fell off today. Completely. Fell off." My stomach lurches at the memory.

Kit recoils. "But at least you are moving forward. I know you dream of medical school, Ginny. I want to help you go. I don't know how though."

"You can pay for my medical school with your inheritance money from Granddaddy Jackson," I jest. "Because Mama is never going to agree to my medical school matriculation much less the high fees that will undoubtedly come with it."

Kit folds her hands over mine. "I will give you part of it. All of it even, if I marry well."

"Promise?" I tease.

"I promise," Kit says in all seriousness.

"And Granny's silver vanity set?"

Kit pokes me in the side until I release her. "No, you greedy imp. You aren't getting the silver until I am soundly dead. Now go to bed."

I think about Kit's secret life as I climb into bed. Kit sheds her robe, turns off the lamp, and falls into bed with a weary sigh.

"So, what is this Grayson Reynolds like?" I say into the hush of our darkened room. "Is he handsome?"

"Very."

"Did he court you?"

Kit is quiet for so long that I think she's asleep, but she finally answers. "No. Not officially."

"Did you fall in love with him?"

"Madly."

"What does it feel like?"

"All of the ridiculous and trite expressions that you're forced to read about during English lessons. Heart flutters and butterfly wings and all that ridiculous rot."

"Did you kiss him? On the mouth, I mean."

Kit's pillow hits me in the face. "Yes. Multiple times in fact. Now enough. I'm not discussing the intimacies of my romantic life—or lack thereof—with my baby sister. Good night."

"Younger, not baby." I throw her pillow back.

"True. Now hush. I need my beauty rest."

As I snuggle down in my bed, I try to picture what this Grayson person might look like. As my thoughts slip into dreams, Grayson's undoubtedly pale features turn deeper. To olive skin and dark curls oiled down in a wave. To deep brown eyes that have little flecks of green in them. And when I step in and place my lips against his, heart flutters and butterfly wings and all the ridiculous rot takes over my body. And it is delightful.

SIX

MY NEXT TWO weeks of nursing aren't half as exciting as the first. No one loses a toe or, thankfully, any other appendage. Jimmy Barber probably lost some skin off his backside though on Tuesday after he, his newly-set broken arm, and his irate mama got home. It took immense restraint not to tell the little peeping Tom that he got what he deserved when he fell out of his neighbor's tree. And he most certainly did not receive a piece of candy from me at the end like the boy with the bean up his nose before him did.

Friday afternoon we have no patients at all. Instead, I spend the sweltering August afternoon dusting and reorganizing all of the bookshelves in Daddy's office. Meanwhile, he pretends to read his medical journal, at least until he snores so loudly that he wakes himself up.

"Everyone who has an ounce of sense has left the city for the summer." Daddy uses his medical journal as a fan. "This heat is oppressive."

"We should pack a picnic and go to Willow Grove Park tomorrow." I flop down into the leather chair across from Daddy's desk and wave the bottom of my skirts around attempting to move the humid air around the room or at least up underneath my skirt. "Even better, we should go to Atlantic City for the weekend and take a dip in the ocean."

"But you can't swim, my darling."

"True. And there are man-eating sharks."

"That was two summers ago. There probably isn't a shark left anywhere near New Jersey by now."

"We could still go and walk along the boardwalk. And purchase ice cream from the hokey pokey man. Wouldn't that be delightful?"

"Ah, I wish, Virginia," Daddy says wistfully.

Daddy and I are lost in our fantasies about ice cream and cool, ocean breezes when Marco comes through the doorway. I jerk my skirts back down.

"I fixed the tire, sir." Marco pulls a plain white cotton handkerchief with frayed edges out of his vest pocket and wipes at his sweaty brow. "The Phaeton is ready for its next adventure."

"You're a good man, Marco," Daddy says.

"Now we have no more excuses," I press Daddy again. "If we can't travel to the shore, or ride the rollercoaster at Willow Grove Park, can we at least go to a soda fountain for an egg cream or a lime rickey to escape this heat?"

To my utter surprise, Daddy agrees. "Yes. In fact, I believe I owe my old friend, Mr. Borrelli, a visit."

"If you are coming to Little Italy, Dr. Jackson, could you pay my mother a visit, too? The wheezing in her chest sounds worse to me, but she refuses to go to the doctor." Marco digs in his vest pocket for some coins. "I could pay you for your time, of course."

"Put your money away, Marco. It's not necessary." Daddy pushes up from his desk. "Now then, children, let's go have some ice cream. Virginia, go fetch a half dozen jars of the peaches. We should share our bounty with our Italian neighbors."

I suspect Daddy's generosity has much to do with how tired we both are of eating peaches, but I keep that comment to myself.

Marco digs in his vest pocket again. "Sir, may I buy some digitalis for Mr. Borrelli? He fixed Mamma's sewing machine recently, but he wouldn't accept payment from me."

Before Marco can count out his money, Daddy pulls a bottle of digitalis off the shelf and hands it to Marco. "Now both of us are settled up with Mr. Borrelli."

"Thank you, sir." Marco slides the bottle into his pocket. "I'll go prepare the Cadillac."

"WHAT IS THAT?" Daddy's head whips to the side as we enter Little Italy. "Pull over, Marco. I'll only be a moment."

Daddy bounces out of the Cadillac like a spry young man. I crane my neck to see what prompted the stop.

"Ah, I see. It's an automobile. A fancy one." I slump back in my seat and fan myself some more. "I'm surprised you aren't over there acting giddy with my father."

Marco slides off his cap and gloves. He knows we are going to be here more than a 'moment' too. "Everyone in Little Italy has heard of Salvatore's new Packard Twin Six. I'm sure he enjoys having a new audience."

"So, you are saying that you don't covet thy neighbor's fancy automobile?"

"No, I do not." Marco wipes something off the bottom of his chin with the back of his fingers. "As Papà used to say, 'We D'Orios might not have much, but what we do have comes from good, honest, hard work."

"This Salvatore must be doing something right to be able to afford such an impressive automobile." I peer out the open window again. Daddy runs a gloved hand over the cardinal red door of the Packard. "Daddy looks absolutely smitten."

"What is right and what is wrong sometimes depends on the viewpoint of the man."

Before I can engage Marco in a philosophical debate, Daddy hastens back to our automobile with an enormous smile on his face. Marco jumps out and opens the door. Instead of climbing into our automobile though, Daddy grabs a jar of peaches.

"Virginia, darling, the gentleman who owns the Packard has offered me a short ride in his automobile. Could you wait a moment longer?"

"I'm parched. I wish I would have brought some water for us." I feel guilty when the rare smile slides off Daddy's face. "Of course, Daddy. Please enjoy yourself. I am happy to wait."

Daddy looks over his shoulder at the exquisite automobile and then back at my sweaty, red face. His forehead creases as he weighs his choices.

"May I take Miss Virginia to Mr. Borrelli's shop to wait? I'm afraid she will get the vapors if she waits much longer in this heat." Marco's collar is wet with perspiration, making me doubt his sudden concern for my welfare even more.

"Yes." Daddy digs in his pocket and pulls out a silver dollar. He hands it to me. "Enjoy some ice cream, Virginia. Then I will meet you both at the D'Orios' home. It's the one at the end of the street, isn't it, Marco?"

"Yes, sir. The row house on the right with the yellow

roses underneath the window."

"If your mother is not there, you are to bring Virginia back to the car to wait. Understood?" Daddy gives Marco a pointed look, and Marco nods. "I will meet you there shortly."

"Here, take the gentleman some more peaches." I push the apple crate toward Daddy.

He takes a second jar out and cradles it in his arm. "Take the rest to your family, Marco. The D'Orio ladies worked hard. They deserve some of the spoils of their labor."

"Thank you, sir." Marco hands Daddy the Cadillac's ignition key. "We will walk. It's only a short stroll."

Of course, Marco isn't the one wearing a corset and multiple layers of fabric. As we start down the crowded street together, people openly stare at us. Marco lifts the apple crate up onto one shoulder.

"Shall I give you a tour of Little Italy as we stroll, Miss Jackson?" Marco says, unabashed at the stares. "I'm sure you haven't spent much time here."

Not outside of the Cadillac, no. "Lead on, Mr. D'Orio."

"Presenting, the Ninth Street Italian Market." Marco opens his hand like a showman. "This is *di macelleria*, where the best *prosciutto* and sausages in all of Philadelphia come from. Over there, *negozio del formaggio*, where you can buy the best *mozzarella* in all of Philadelphia."

"Moss and what?"

"*Mozzarella*," Marco over-pronounces the word. "It's a type of cheese."

"I see." The scent of butter and sugar wafts out of the next building. "This must be the bakery."

"*La paticceria*," Marco corrects me. "Here you can buy the lightest, sweetest *baba* in—"

"All of Philadelphia, I am certain. Is there anything in

Little Italy that isn't the best in Philadelphia?"

Marco pretends to be deep in thought. "No. We Italians are the best, especially when it comes to food."

We pass a shop with a bounty of fish and seafood displayed outside on blocks of rapidly melting ice. I am envious. Of the fish. If the smell weren't so horrid, I would love to stand next to the cool steam coming off of the blocks of ice.

"Will this heat ever abate?" I dig my ivy-patterned, Irish linen handkerchief out of my drawstring bag and dab at the sweat rolling down the side of my neck.

"Next we have Little Italy's best *gelateria*." Marco gestures to the sign stenciled on the front window. *Borrelli's*.

"I thought Mr. Borrelli sold ice cream."

Marco laughs. "*Gelato* is like ice cream. Only better because we Italians invented it."

"Of course."

When Marco opens the door, a sweet, fruity smell wafts out. I breathe in deep. A small contented sigh slips out of my mouth.

"Marco D'Orio!" A middle-aged man with a thick mustache booms from behind the counter. Undoubtedly, Mr. Borrelli.

Marco returns a hearty greeting and maybe a little bit of good-natured teasing, both of them talking as much with their hands as their mouths. I glance around the room. There are a few groups of girls, some mixed groups, and even a few couples tucked away in the corner. A group of girls about my age stops talking and stares at us. One whispers behind her hand to another, and they all giggle. I snap my head back to the front. Marco and the man haggle in Italian. In the end, Marco hands over two of the four jars of peaches that were intended for his mother.

I open up my purse to retrieve the silver dollar. "I have—"

"I have it." Marco pushes my purse away. Before I can protest, he whispers, "Please, Miss Jackson."

I close my purse and allow Marco his moment of pride.

"What you want, *bella*?" Mr. Borrelli says, his deep brown eyes crinkling at the corners.

I glance over the chalkboard written in looping Italian. Before I have to ask, Marco begins reading down the list for me. His words sound like melted chocolate in my ears: *fragolina, nocciola, panna cotta,* and *zabajone.* Those same words sound like fingernails down a chalkboard when he repeats the list, this time in English. Though my tongue wants chocolate, I point to *nocciola*, hazelnut, so that I can hear Marco say it again.

"Are you sure?" Marco says. "*Nocciola* is good, but *limone* is even better, especially on hot days. That's what I always have."

"In that case, I shall have the same."

"For you, *bella*." The man serves up a heaping scoop of white *gelato* in a cheap glass bowl and places a straw-like cookie in the side of it. He adds a dainty spoon to it. He hands the second one to Marco before opening up the cash register and pulling out a few coins.

"*Grazie*." Marco accepts the coins with a nod, their trade done. And then he promptly drops all of them into the coffee can next to the register.

I can't read most of the sign attached to the can, but some of the words don't require translation: *315th Infantry Regiment, 79th Division.*

"Is that the regiment your brother is in?" I nod at the coffee can. The newspaper reports on the 315th—"Philadelphia's Own"—often. Or at least, what the government censors will allow through.

"*Si*, our Domenico is," Mr. Borrelli answers before Marco can. "And many of our brave boys. Little Italy does her part. No one calls us slackers, right, Marco?"

"*Si*," Marco says, his voice suddenly quiet and tight.

"Thank you. This looks delicious," I say.

I follow Marco to the only table open. The one right next to the door. Now everyone can stare at us fully while coming and going. I put the last two jars of peaches in the middle of the tiny table like a chaperone. Meanwhile, Marco tucks the now empty crate under his chair.

"Ah, *gelato di limone*. Both sweet and sour at the same time. Sort of like life, no?" Marco digs into his bowl with gusto as I let the first bite melt on my tongue slowly. "Do you like it?"

"It is delicious," I say, and Marco raises an eyebrow. "I mean that genuinely."

"I told you. It is the best." Marco kisses his fingertips and then opens his hand like a flower.

"In all of Philadelphia," I finish for him. "On this, I concur."

I try not to gobble down my *gelato*, but it is quickly melting. After fighting the urge to lick my bowl clean, I dab at my lips with my handkerchief. Marco reaches over the table to examine the embroidered ivy leaves twining around the corners of my handkerchief.

"Did you do this?" he says.

"Yes. It took me two days to get the stitches uniform and even."

Marco takes the handkerchief from me and flips it over. He runs his index finger over the stitches and two knots. I decide not to mention how many times I had to pick out the stitches during the course of this project.

"These fingers." Marco holds up his right hand. "These fingers are good at changing tires and pulling out spark plugs. They are not so good at fine, detailed work like stitches."

"So don't be a surgeon. You can still be a good doctor."

"Was that a compliment, *bella*?" A smile splits Marco's face.

Before I can respond, the girl who was whispering about me appears at our table. The smile disappears from Marco's face.

"*Buon pomeriggio*, Marco," the girl, who looks like she stepped out of one of Kit's European fashion magazines, greets us.

Marco jumps to his feet, tucking my handkerchief into his vest pocket by mistake. "Oh, Sofia, *buon pomeriggio*."

This Sofia speaks to Marco in rapid Italian, while he shuffles from foot to foot. I hear *Sabato*, Saturday, one of maybe a half-dozen Italian words I know and something that sounds like *Tarzan*. Maybe she and Marco are planning to attend the cinema together tomorrow. Whatever they are discussing, Sofia makes me acutely aware that I am pressing in by repeatedly looking down her nose at me. I glance back at her group of friends. They are enjoying the show. I know these girls, even though I am not acquainted with them. We have a group just like them at the Miss Mildred Franklin School. They look down their noses and talk about me, too.

"I don't believe we've met." I stand up and offer her my hand. "I'm Virginia Jackson. It's a pleasure to meet you."

"Sofia Villani." The girl gives my hand a limp squeeze before releasing it.

Marco tugs at the collar of his shirt. I wait for Marco to continue the conversation, but he doesn't.

"My father and I came to visit…a friend, but then he saw your neighbor's new automobile. You know how men are. Easily distracted by the next new, shiny thing," I joke.

Miss Villani gives Marco a pointed look before bringing her attention back to me. "That they are."

"I heard that Mr. Borrelli's *gelato* is the best in all of Little Italy. And now that I've had it, I must concur. Well then…." I slide my handbag over my wrist and shake out the wrinkles in my gloves. "I'm feeling much better now, Mr. D'Orio. Thank you for your concern earlier. Now, I must get back to my father. It was a pleasure to meet you, Miss Villani."

Miss Villani gives me a nod of her head.

"A moment of your time, *Mr.* D'Orio." Miss Villani drags Marco by the elbow over to the table filled with her friends. The girls talk to Marco in Italian in loud, teasing tones.

"I hope you'll return to school this fall. I miss seeing your handsome face every day," Miss Villani says in English to make sure I overhear. She steps in closer to Marco and bats her eyelashes at him. "Who will walk me home each day if you don't return?"

Marco backs away with a strained laugh and hurried farewells to his classmates. He only stops long enough to take the apple crate with the remaining jars of peaches from me.

"Hey, Marco!" Mr. Borrelli hails us from behind the counter. He holds out one of my former peach jars which is now filled with *gelato* the same color as cherry blossoms. When Marco declines, the man insists. "For Angelina."

"*Grazie.*" Marco accepts the jar. "Oh, and Dr. Jackson asked me to deliver this to you."

When Marco holds out the bottle of medicine, the

haggling starts again. Finally, I take the bottle from Marco and put it into Mr. Borrelli's hand.

"My father insists."

"*Bella*, you come back soon, no?" The man's face softens.

I give him a nod but promise nothing. Marco adds the jar of *gelato* to the apple crate before perching it on his shoulder again. When we take our leave, the doorbell tinkles behind us like tiny wedding bells.

"I hope I wasn't keeping you from something?" I say as we walk down the crowded sidewalk.

"Ah, hmm. About that."

"No explanation needed. I am not interested in your social life." I point at my handkerchief poking out of his vest pocket. "I should probably take that back. I don't wish to make your lover angry at me."

Marco flushes but hands me back my handkerchief. "She's not my lover."

I look up at him and bat my eyes. "But who will walk her home each day if you don't return?"

Instead of stepping away, Marco links his arm through mine and pulls me in even closer. "Smile, *bella*, because Signora Brambilla is staring at us."

Sure enough, out in front of a general store with dozens of olive oil cans in the window, a graying, sour-looking woman stops her sweeping to glare at Marco and me.

"*Buon pomeriggo, Signora,*" Marco says.

Signora Brambilla returns Marco's jovial greeting with a curt nod of her head.

"The Brambillas come from Milano. We D'Orios come from Napoli. They think they are better than us. Hmpf. If Little Italy's biggest gossip is going to tell tales about me, I'm going to give her something especially juicy to gossip about." Marco leans in and gives me a peck on my cheek. I stumble over a crack in the sidewalk. "Careful there, *bella*."

Out in front of the brick row house with the yellow roses underneath the front window is the middle-aged version of Angelina. Marco releases my arm like it has suddenly caught fire. After strained introductions, Mamma D'Orio ushers me into their modest home. Behind my back, I hear what sounds like Mamma D'Orio's hand colliding with Marco's head.

"Please excuse our home." Marco's younger sister, Isabella, flutters around their parlor area removing books and laundry and other pieces of everyday life.

"I'm sorry to intrude." And I truly am. In fact, Mamma D'Orio's glare at Marco alone makes me want to bolt down the street and wait in the Cadillac.

"It is our pleasure." Isabella clears some of the piece work Mamma D'Orio does for a local factory off a worn, puffy chair and gestures at me to sit. "Please."

"We brought you something." I nod at Marco.

"Peaches." Isabella accepts her own family's handiwork with more grace than I would have. "Thank you."

"And *gelato*." I nod at Marco again.

"Yes, from Angelina's admirer, Mr. Borrelli." Marco hands over the rapidly melting jar of *gelato.*

"Gah. He is too old for Angelina." Isabella wrinkles up her nose at the suggestion. "Angelina wants a husband, not a papà."

I startle. Of course, Angelina would have a life and ambitions outside of the work she does at our home. It would be rude to inquire how old Angelina is, but surely she isn't much older than Kit.

As Isabella takes the jars to the kitchen, Mamma D'Orio sits down on the equally worn settee across from me. Marco squeezes in beside her, suddenly looking much younger than eighteen. We sit in a pained silence for a few moments, the dethroned queen staring at me.

"Mamma, where is Giorgio?" Marco says in English.

Mamma D'Orio tells a tale in Italian. Marco nods and says, "*Si. Si.*" a lot.

"Giorgio…is Giorgio," Marco shrugs at the end of the long tale. "He'll come home when he's hungry."

Isabella returns from the kitchen with a glass of lemonade for me.

"Please, Miss D'Orio. Don't go to any trouble for me," I say.

"You are our guest." Isabella serves me with a hundred times more poise than I possessed at her young age.

"Where is mine?" Marco says.

"God gave you two good hands." Isabella perches on the arm of the settee. "Make Mamma some, too. She's been washing your dirty clothes all day."

Marco grumbles but immediately heads toward the kitchen. I sip the lemonade, feeling like a pachyderm on display at the circus. A light rapping on the door interrupts Mamma D'Orio's staring. I have never been so glad to see my father in my life.

"Come. Come." Mamma D'Orio waves Daddy inside. She stares at me until I jump up from my chair. Though Daddy protests, Mamma D'Orio seats him on the throne. Daddy places his black bag down beside the chair. When Marco comes back from the kitchen with a glass of lemonade in each hand, Mamma D'Orio takes them both. She insists that Daddy accept one.

"Thank you." Daddy takes a long drink. "I was in the neighborhood and thought I would drop by. Marco mentioned that you have been feeling poorly, Mrs. D'Orio." While Marco interprets for his mother, Daddy looks around for a place to set his drink. I take it from him so he can dig his stethoscope out of his bag. "May I listen to your lungs while I'm here?"

Though Mrs. D'Orio fusses, Marco says, "Yes. Please do, Dr. Jackson."

Marco stands next to his mother as Daddy comes to sit down beside her on the settee. Do I reclaim my spot on the throne or continue to stand? I don't understand the rules of this odd game of musical chairs. I decide standing is the safest choice. The room silences as Daddy listens to Mrs. D'Orio's chest. You don't need a stethoscope to hear it. The wheeze that comes with each inhale.

"Is it consumption?" Marco says softly, worry etching his face.

Mrs. D'Orio fusses, her hands flapping around. She adds in English, "I am old woman."

"Nonsense." Daddy pats Mrs. D'Orio's hand. "But you have been through much this year. It would be taxing on anyone. Please rest more and allow your children to attend to you. Your heart is working too hard."

What Marco says in Italian to her sounds very much like, "I told you so."

Daddy tucks his stethoscope back into his bag. "Mrs. D'Orio, you are taking the digitalis every day, yes?"

"Yes, I make sure of it," Marco answers for her.

"As we discussed the other day in my office, Marco, all we can do right now is to continue to treat the symptoms." Daddy and Marco share a look, and Marco drops his head. There is no cure for heart disease. "But if things worsen, if her breathing gets harder or she has pain in her chest, then we will have to put her on bedrest."

"*Non.*" Mrs. D'Orio stands up. "I work. Every day, I work."

"Mamma." Marco reaches for his mother's arm, but she brushes him off. "Mamma!"

"Mrs. D'Orio, please. This isn't good for your heart." Daddy pats the seat beside him. "Your children don't want to lose you, too."

Mrs. D'Orio's English is better than she lets on because Daddy's words immediately extinguish her indignant fire. She settles on the settee. Her wheezing is even worse than before. Daddy digs a bottle of medicine from his bag and hands it to her. Mrs. D'Orio says something sharp to Marco. He rushes out of the room but returns a moment later with a black leather coin purse.

"Mrs. D'Orio, please. That's not necessary." Daddy refuses to take the few coins thrust at him. "Marco works very hard for me. It's the least I can do."

Mrs. D'Orio gives Isabella an order. A moment later, Isabella returns from the kitchen with a loaf of bread wrapped in a dishtowel. She holds it out to Daddy.

"Please accept it as our thanks," Isabella says, and Marco mouths his own plea from behind his mother's back for us to accept it.

"Thank you. It smells delicious." Daddy takes the loaf but immediately hands it off to me. "Now I know why Angelina is such a good cook. She obviously gets it from her mother."

Mrs. D'Orio beams with pride.

"Now then," Daddy says collecting his black bag. "My daughter and I really must go. My wife will be worried."

Mrs. D'Orio fusses and flutters some more before finally granting us leave.

"Thank you, Dr. Jackson." Isabella hands Daddy his hat and curtseys. "Mamma says, please visit our home again. Next time we will make dinner for you. Please bring your wife and daughters."

Daddy must have the same thought I do, based on the panicked look in his eyes. My mother would never agree to dinner with the hired help. And then there is Kit and her inability to control her tongue. I shudder.

"Thank you. That would be a delight," Daddy lies convincingly.

Mrs. D'Orio profusely thanks Daddy for employing Marco, invokes God's continued blessing on us, and—to our mortification—kisses us on both cheeks. A redness shoots up from Marco's collar to his ears, and he practically pushes us out the door. Marco follows us to the Cadillac which is now parked in front of his home.

"Forgive her. Mamma is very old fashioned. I keep telling her that Americans shake hands, but she never remembers."

"No apology needed. Things have been difficult for her—all of you—since your father passed. You are a doing a good job as the man of the house." Daddy pulls the ignition keys from his vest pocket. "It's late. I'll drive us home tonight, Marco."

"Thank you, sir."

As Daddy walks around the front of the automobile to get to the driver's side, Marco opens the passenger side for me.

"Thank you for the *gelato*," I say.

"My pleasure, *bella*...er, Miss Virginia."

I slide in next to Daddy.

"See you on Monday, sir." Marco gives me a shy smile before he closes the door. "Miss Virginia."

As we drive away, I have to ask what is on my mind. "Daddy, is Mrs. D'Orio going to die?"

"Everyone dies eventually, Virginia."

"You know what I mean."

Daddy looks over at me, a sadness in his eyes. "Yes. I give her five years, maybe less if she refuses bed rest."

"Does Marco know?" I remember the worry etched deeply into Marco's face.

"He hasn't asked me directly, but I suspect he already knows." Daddy reaches over and squeezes my hand. "Please be patient with Marco. I know he can be vexing, but try walking in his shoes for a bit."

"I'll try." I sniff the warm bread currently cradled in my arm like a newborn. "Oh, this smells delightful. If putting up with Marco includes more of his mamma's bread, I would even agree to court him."

I laugh at my own joke, but Daddy looks panicked.

"Don't say that. Especially not in front of your mother. She didn't even want Marco to be our chauffeur."

"Why?"

"Honestly, Virginia, I think you can surmise why she might object. But Mr. D'Orio was a good man. He died too soon. Helping his son was the least I could do after he passed."

"Daddy, I want to go to medical school. I am not about to give that up for some boy."

"Excellent answer." Daddy pats my head like I'm five. "Let's keep it that way. For a long, long, loooong time."

"Agreed," I say, but something tugs at me. Daddy didn't have to choose between being a doctor or a husband. Why do women have to choose one or the other?

As we head back out of Little Italy, we pass a new crowd huddled around Salvatore's Packard. Daddy takes one last longing glance and sighs.

"Let's pack a picnic and go to Willow Grove Park tomorrow," Daddy says like it is a completely new idea.

"Maybe John Phillip Sousa and his band will be in concert tomorrow night. I'm sure your mother would enjoy that."

"I would enjoy riding the roller coaster and purchasing ice cream from the hokey pokey man."

Daddy glances over at me, a new light in his deep blue eyes. "Me, too."

SEVEN

I AM BUSY enjoying the last few days of my summer holiday, when Kit bursts into our room, stomps over to our overstuffed reading chair, and drops Mama's household ledger book on my lap.

"I'm busy." I push the ledger off my book until it slides into the gully between my hip and the chair.

"You are not." Kit puts a hand on her hip.

I tip my book up so that she can see that it's L. M. Montgomery's *Anne of the Island*.

"Splendid choice," Kit says of one of her favorite writers. "However, this is more important right now. A modern woman needs to know—and preferably control—her own wealth."

"As my mathematic grades are higher than yours ever were, perhaps *you* should rectify the household accounts. You obviously need the practice." I hold out the tobacco-colored leather tome to Kit. When she doesn't take it, I toss it onto the vanity. "Besides, I heard Mama specifically ask you to do it."

Kit snatches the book off my lap and holds it tight against her chest. "You may have it back after you rectify the household accounts."

I leap up from my chair and grab for my book. Kit holds it over her head. Between her natural height and the heels on her pumps, I can't reach it.

"Give it to me." I jump for it. I don't reach the book, but my finger snags in the lace of Kit's sleeve and rips the hem.

"You little beast. This dress came from New York. You may have the book back after you rectify the ledger *and* fix my dress." Kit tucks my book under her arm and storms out of the room.

"Give it back!" I rush after her.

We sound like a herd of pachyderms going down the stairs, but I don't care. I'm not going to let my sister boss me around any longer.

"Mama asked *you* to do the ledger," I say when I hit the bottom of the stairs half a second after Kit. "I'm not doing your work."

I grab Kit's shoulder, turning her to face me. I latch onto the book still in her hand.

"Unhand me, Virginia." Kit pulls away, rotating us in an odd waltz down the hallway toward the kitchen.

"Not until you give me back my book." My hip bumps the sideboard sending today's mail fluttering around my bare feet.

Marco comes out the swinging door of the kitchen, a deep tray in his hands. He presses to the side, tray over his head, as Kit and I continue down the hallway toward him.

"Presenting the cultured and refined Jackson sisters," Marco mumbles after my elbow grazes his chest.

"Girls!" Daddy's voice echoes down the hallway, freezing us in our tracks. "You will comport yourselves like young ladies in my home. Katherine, I specifically heard your mother ask you to finish the ledger. Virginia, in my office. You will roll bandages. Both tasks will be completed by luncheon or neither of you will be eating it."

"Yes, Daddy." I take advantage of Kit's momentary distraction and snatch my book out of her hand.

"For heaven's sake, Virginia, go put on some stockings and shoes this instant. You are not a child anymore." Daddy runs a hand through his rapidly receding hairline. "Lord, grant me patience."

Marco attempts to cover his obvious amusement with a cough. My face burns, but at least I reclaimed my book.

When I return to Daddy's office a few minutes later—stockings and shoes firmly on—Daddy and Marco sit on opposite sides of his desk with the deep tray between them. Meanwhile, a pile of knotted tendrils of fabric waits for me on Daddy's exam table. I pull one out and begin the mind-numbing task of rolling it.

"Okay, Marco, now pull it through the other side," Daddy says.

I tilt my body until I can see the pig's foot resting on the bottom of the tray. Marco pulls a needle up until the catgut tightens and brings the gash slightly closer together.

"Not bad. Keep practicing." Daddy lifts his hand to pat Marco on the back but then remembers himself. "Sutures are a skill that takes a lot of practice."

Marco lets out an exasperated sigh when the catgut comes out of his needle. I stifle a laugh when Marco attempts to rethread it, his tongue sticking out the side of his mouth in deep concentration. I roll three more bandages while he struggles with this simple task. I could do it with one hand. Behind my back. Blindfolded.

"I'll never be a good doctor with these…these sausages for fingers." Marco waves his fingers in front of his face in disgust.

Daddy looks back over his shoulder at me. "Ginny, could

you rethread this needle for Marco? I don't have sausages for fingers, but I do seem to have left my spectacles behind at the hospital this morning."

"Yes, Daddy."

Catgut isn't that much different from working with heavy embroidery thread. At least that's what I keep telling myself so that I won't be disgusted by its origins. I step up next to Marco. I have the needle threaded in seconds.

Marco lets out another exasperated sigh. "It's a wonder women aren't the surgeons in society. They certainly have more experience."

When Marco reaches for the needle, I pull it and the tray even closer to me. "Teach me, too, Daddy."

I push out my elbows so that Marco has to move over another step. Daddy snips Marco's single stitch and pulls the small piece of catgut out.

"Alright then…start from the top again and see if you can close the wound," Daddy says, oblivious to the dark cloud forming over Marco's head. "Use the forceps to pass the needle through the flesh from hand to hand."

I look down at the pig's foot. The gaping wound Daddy's scalpel inflicted on the pig is fresh, but thankfully most of the blood must have drained away during the butchering. I stab the pig's flesh and pass the curved needle up under it, across the small divide, and pick up the other side. I pretend like I am mending a glove for a doughboy. I pull the catgut smooth, and the pieces of flesh ease slightly closer together.

"You've got it, Ginny." Daddy pats me on the back. I give Marco a smug grin. "Keep going."

The first few stitches are easy. It's near the middle of the gash when things become a challenge. It's hard to imagine a glove when faced with layers of cartilage, fat, and blood vessels. I stop to take a deep breath and steady my hand.

"Shall I fetch the smelling salts, Miss Jackson?" Marco says.

A fire burns in the pit of my stomach. "Shall I fetch a darning needle, Mr. D'Orio, so that you can practice threading it while you wait for your turn again?"

"Enough. What has gotten into you today, Virginia?" Daddy puts a warning hand on top of mine. "Surgeons can't be distracted. Patients die when doctors make mistakes."

That deflates the hot air out of Marco. Daddy didn't intend to be unkind, but there is a painful truth to his statement. Though Dr. Porter would emphatically deny it, I once overheard Daddy telling Mama that Mr. D'Orio would still be alive if he had attended to him instead of Dr. Porter. Marco retreats from the table and silently rolls bandages while I sew.

"Watch your pinky finger, Virginia. You don't want to contaminate the field." Daddy gently pushes my draping pinky finger back against the others. A few minutes later, I'm at the end of the gash. "Admirable job, Virginia. Now pull the needle and thread taut. Spin it around the forceps a few times." Daddy mimes for me. "And now with a whisk of your talented fingers, voila, the perfect knot."

My French knots in embroidery are much neater, but I can't complain too much about my first endeavor on skin. Meanwhile, Marco stops rolling bandages so that he can peer over my shoulder. He nods his head in reluctant approval. Before I have a chance to savor my accomplishment, Daddy slices his scalpel down the stitches ruining them.

"Pull them out and do it again. And again. And again. Until either your hands cramp or luncheon is served."

Daddy sits down at his desk and shuffles through his papers. "And give Marco a turn."

"Yes, the Italian boy who has sausages for fingers needs all the practice he can get," Marco jokes before returning to the bandages.

Instead of gloating, I say, "Would you like me to show you a threading trick I learned from Granny Jackson?"

Marco's face softens. "Yes, please."

Before I have a chance to show him, Kit stampedes into the room.

"I'm done." Kit smacks the ledger on Daddy's desk before noticing the pig's foot. "How repulsive." She beats a hasty retreat, but stops at the door. "Also, Mother telephoned. She's been detained at the dentist and says to eat luncheon without her. I already informed Angelina. She'll serve it momentarily."

"Well, then, let's stop for the morning. Go wash up, Ginny." Daddy deposits his doctor's coat on his chair and herds me toward the door. "Marco, give the pig's foot to the Walters' dog. We're done with it. And clean off the exam table. Mr. Carstairs comes at half-past one today to have his leg cast removed." Daddy pauses at the doorframe. "Are you hungry, Marco?"

"Always," he says.

Daddy lets out a chuckle. "Ah, I remember those days."

An odd spark lights in my empty stomach at the thought of having luncheon with Marco. In some ways, I feel like I know him better than many of my classmates. In other ways, I feel like I don't know him at all.

"Then have Angelina make you a sandwich," Daddy says, knowing full well that our expansive dining room seats twelve. "We have a busy afternoon ahead of us."

"Thank you, sir," Marco says, his tone cool and

professional. "I'll have your office tidied by one."

"Good lad," Daddy says completely missing or perhaps simply ignoring the disappointment on Marco's face.

WHILE WAITING FOR Angelina to serve our usual three-course luncheon, Daddy and Kit read their correspondence. I slide into the table last after washing my hands. Twice. Both times with Kit's bar of lavender soap to help wash the image of piggy parts out of my mind. I genuinely feel guilty about not asking Marco to join us. I'm about to broach the subject when Daddy waves his letter at me.

"Ah, finally some good news. It seems I now have a new nurse," Daddy announces, and my heart sinks. "A Miss Julia Brighton from Pittsburgh. Her fiancé is in the service but makes his home here in Philadelphia. She will live with his parents until they are married. Splendid. She will arrive on the Saturday evening train, and report for duty on Monday morning." Daddy tucks Miss Brighton's letter back into its envelope. "Looks like you are now officially relieved of your duties, Ginny. Thank you for your service over these last few weeks. I'm sure your mother will be thrilled to have your schedule open again."

My heart sinks down into my stomach.

Angelina pokes her head around the swinging door leading to the kitchen. "May I serve luncheon now, Doctor Jackson?"

"Yes, Angelina. I'm famished!" Daddy says.

Angelina carries in a tray filled with Mama's delicate wedding china. My stomach rumbles and then lurches when Angelina sets my plate in front of me.

Deviled ham salad tea sandwiches.

"May I be excused? I'm not hungry after all," I say as soon as Angelina leaves the room.

Daddy laughs. "Did the suturing lesson turn your stomach a bit?"

It wasn't from the pig's foot, but I nod anyway.

EIGHT

NOW THAT NURSE Brighton has taken over all of my duties, Mama is determined to fill the hole in my schedule with every war-related charity function she can find. If I have to spend another long afternoon at the Vaughns' participating in a "knit your bit" I will scream. I would rather help Daddy amputate toes than spend another hour with Margaret Vaughn. I get enough of her company now, back at school.

"Charles, please bring Katherine and Virginia over to the Red Cross by four today," Mama instructs over another sterile breakfast in the Jackson household. "We received a new shipment of supplies from the national headquarters on Saturday to make comfort kits. Since I wasn't able to convince the ladies to work on Labor Day, now we only have four days to complete the task. We will need all the women we can get to finish on time."

Kit and I groan in tandem and complain over top of each other.

Kit: "Mother, I need to go to the library today. I will try to come at the end of the week if you still need me."

Me: "Mama, I have school all day and then homework to do afterward. Couldn't Kit go in my place?"

Kit shoots me a wicked look.

"The Jackson Family always does their patriotic duty," Mama's voice crescendos and hardens. "I will see you girls at the Red Cross promptly at four all this week, end of discussion."

"Did you not see the note I left on your desk, Eleanor?" Daddy peeks over the top of his newspaper. "I am leaving for Boston this morning. Henry telephoned last night. He asked me to come to Boston for a second opinion. Several of his patients are exhibiting similar symptoms to the ones Virginia had in July, only worse."

"Is that even possible?" The memory of my head striking the parquet floor of the Bellevue-Stratford Hotel is still fresh in my mind. "I thought I was going to die."

"That's just it. Henry's patients *are* dying. Young men. In the prime of life. It makes no sense."

"Take me with you." My heart leaps at the thought of seeing Anna. "I can catch up with my school work easily when we return."

Now it's my parents' turn to complain in tandem:

Daddy: "Your lungs are still susceptible. I'm not going to give this influenza a chance to finish what it started."

Mama: "Absolutely not. Now is not the time for a vacation. Besides, the Red Cross needs us."

"It's not a vacation." I set my china tea cup down so forcefully that I'm surprised it doesn't chip. It does make Mama give me her full attention though, even if it's because she's worried about her prized china. "I have basic nursing skills now. And, I have a better bedside manner than Nurse Brighton."

"Now, now, let's give Nurse Brighton the benefit of the doubt," Daddy says. "This is only her second week here. Cecelia was my nurse for almost twenty years. We will need some time to adjust to each other."

I soften my tone and pat Daddy's hand. "Daddy, please. Take me to Boston with you. I can be of service. You know that we make a good pair. And I promise to follow your orders to the letter."

Daddy's will begins to crumble, but as always, he defers to Mama. "Eleanor?"

"I said no, and I don't want to hear another word about it. You are needed here, Virginia." Mama puts her reading spectacles back on and picks up her pen. "I presume that you will be going by train to Boston, Charles? I will need the automobile. Marco can deliver me to Mrs. Vaughn's for luncheon and later return home to pick up the girls—or at least Virginia—after school."

Daddy nods. "That seems like an agreeable arrangement."

I finish my last few bites of toast. They scratch all the way down my throat and stick behind my sternum. A last gulp of tea eases the pain of breakfast, at least internally.

"Would you like for me to bring something special back from Boston for you, girls?" Daddy says like we are America's most contented and congenial family. Before I can respond, he's already made up his mind. "I'll ask Anna to pick something out as I'm sure she will be just as put out with me as you are for not bringing you along."

Oh, I'm sure Anna—never one to shy away from her feelings—is going to give him an earful when he arrives in Boston solo.

"You are going to be late for school, Virginia," Mama says.

"Be safe, Daddy." I push away from the table and kiss the top of his head. "Hurry home."

"Come straight home today, Virginia," Mama nags me

one more time.

"Yes, Mama," I say, though I am already planning to have a headache or maybe belly pain from my monthly or something else appropriate for the situation.

MY SCHOOL DAY is such an utter chore that I honestly do have a headache by the time I return home. Apparently, I'm not the only one who is in a foul humor today. I loiter in the hallway outside of Daddy's office listening to Marco and Nurse Brighton's argument go from a slow simmer to a rolling boil.

"You are the hired help," Nurse Brighton snaps at Marco. "I am in charge while the Doctor is away and you will do as I say. Now, take them all out and count them again. The *correct* way this time."

I duck into the parlor when I hear Nurse Brighton's leather booted heels tap-tap-tapping toward the door.

"And instruct Angelina that I will take my tea in the parlor today," Nurse Brighton says.

"Tell her yourself!"

Nurse Brighton harrumphs and heads toward the kitchen. I count to ten before going into Daddy's office. Marco paces the small room, gesticulating wildly and grumbling to himself in Italian.

"Sounds like quite the dust-up going on in here," I say from the doorway.

"That woman…." Marco wisely drops his voice, and I come deeper into Daddy's office. "That woman is insufferable."

"Indeed. I miss Cecelia something fierce, especially on days like these." I flop onto Daddy's leather chair. "I wish we could go to Mr. Borrelli's for some *gelato di limone*. That would add some sweetness to this otherwise sour day."

Marco corrects my pronunciation, but with a smile on his face. "I wish. But per Mrs. Jackson, we must inventory all the medicine before we leave for the day. And of course, by we, I mean me. Guess I'll be missing school tonight."

"You go to night school?"

"Yes. I need this job...my family needs this job, but I want to finish high school, too. Who needs sleep anyway?" Marco runs a hand through his hair and puffs out his cheeks in fatigue. "And then there's my homework which still hasn't gotten done. Why do I need to study Shakespeare? I want to be a doctor. Give me a microscope or a test tube or at least a pig's foot and some catgut."

Marco does look more tired than usual. One by one, Marco pulls the bottles of medicine off of the shelf and puts them back on Daddy's desk. Nurse Brighton startles when she finds me sitting in Daddy's office.

"Oh, Miss Virginia, you're home." Nurse Brighton looks down at her tea guiltily. "I was just making myself a cup of tea before Marco and I resume our work. Please tell your mother that the papers will be on the sideboard before we leave. I know she was quite...adamant about that."

"Is there a lot left to do?" I feign ignorance.

"Oh, not much at all. I should finish within the hour."

"Splendid. In that case, Marco, I wish to depart for the Red Cross immediately."

"You do?" Nurse Brighton and Marco say in unison.

"He *is* my family's chauffeur, is he not?"

"Yes," Nurse Brighton says with a haughty sniff at Marco.

"Well, then, let's go, Marco. You do your job, and we'll leave Nurse Brighton to do hers." I stand up and hover near Daddy's desk. I pick up a bottle of digitalis and pretend to read the label. "Mama is so fastidious with her work. She likes every I dotted and every T crossed." I turn on my heel and head toward the door. "Also, please inform Angelina, that Marco won't be back until late. I have several deliveries he needs to complete while I am at the Red Cross. I'm sorry if that makes you late going home tonight, Marco, but there are things that I must have done."

Nurse Brighton's mouth opens and closes. I glance over my shoulder.

"Don't dawdle, Marco. I will be ready to depart momentarily," I say.

Marco looks just as confused as Nurse Brighton but answers, "Yes, Miss Jackson."

When I come back downstairs a few minutes later, Marco stands in the hallway with his chauffeur's coat and cap on. He pulls me by the elbow into the parlor and whispers, "I thought we were going to Little Italy?"

"We are." I pull the bottle of digitalis—which I had sneaked out of Daddy's office in my palm—out of my handbag. "I'm out of pocket money for the month, but perhaps Mr. Borrelli will trade with us?" When Marco frowns, I add, "I will tell Daddy upon his return. I'm certain he won't mind."

I'm not sure if that statement is completely truthful, but the crackle of lightning it causes down my spine makes the potential consequences of my rash actions suddenly seem worth it.

Marco takes the bottle of digitalis from me and slides it into his vest pocket. His impish grin is contagious. "You know this is going to throw off her numbers."

"Now that is none of your concern, is it? You are simply

the chauffeur."

"What errands did you need me to do?" he says.

"What errands…oh, that was part of the ruse. After you deliver me to the Red Cross, the rest of the afternoon is yours. You can go to a café or the park or the library to do your homework before bringing the Cadillac back. Maybe not the library. You might run into Kit."

When I reach up to straighten Marco's cap, he places his hand over mine. We pause there. A warmth rises in my cheeks.

"As you wish, Miss Jackson." Marco squeezes my hand before we both let go.

Suddenly, some of Mr. Shakespeare's works have a new meaning to me.

⚓

"YOUR MOTHER IS going to fire me for certain," Marco says as traffic crawls near City Hall.

"It's my fault. I will deal with my mother."

Of course, I'm not going to mention to my mother that I went to Little Italy, much less that I was having a spirited debate about *The Merchant of Venice* with our chauffeur.

"Shakespeare is much more palatable when delivered with *gelato di limone*," I say, savoring the memory. I knew I wanted *limone* going in, but that didn't stop me from having Marco read down the entire list of choices again in Italian for me. "At least you will receive high marks for your essay."

"Which you wrote."

"No, I told you what Literature teachers like to hear. You must still write it."

"Which I am happy to do if we can ever deliver you to

93

the Red Cross."

We both glance up at the giant clock. It's already gone four. Marco swears in Italian.

"What is taking so long today?" I roll down the window and poke my head out. "There's a crowd of people around City Hall. Lots of hats and cloth banners. I think they are picketing."

Marco bangs on the steering wheel and honks the horn as some of the picketers pour into the street. He slams on the brakes to avoid a woman wearing an expensive, blue, ostrich-plume hat. I know that hat. Mother says that it is both out-of-fashion and too ostentatious to wear while our country is at war. So, Kit wears it every chance she gets.

"Watch where you are going, lady! Why are these women in the street? Stay on the sidewalk!" Marco opens his hands to the sky like he is asking for divine help.

As our car moves forward again, the woman turns around. Our eyes lock. It's Kit.

❦━━━❧

"YOU'RE LATE," MAMA snaps under her breath at me when I finally make it to the Red Cross at four-twenty-five.

Mama looks around the room where all the dutiful society women sit packing boxes with comfort items for our doughboys. Their daughters—many of whom are my classmates—do the same. Mama marches me over to our designated table. She gives the ladies at our table a pleasant smile as if she's glad to see me.

Make no mistake. I am going to get it later.

Mama leans into me, smiles, but then hisses under her breath, "Where have you been?"

"I needed to borrow a book from the library. For school."

I regret that lie as soon as it comes out of my mouth.

"Where is your sister? Didn't you pick her up while you were there?"

I gulp.

"I'm right here, Mother." Kit appears behind me. She pulls out the chair on the other side of Mama and flops into it. She announces to our table as she removes her gloves, "Traffic was horrific. It was all our driver could do to get through the snarl. We almost went home, but I said, 'No, no, the Jackson Family always does their patriotic duty.' So, better late than never, right, Mother?"

Mama's hands vibrate with rage. We are in so much trouble when we get home.

"I heard those suffragettes were marching on City Hall today to stir up trouble." Mrs. Vaughn looks pointedly at Kit.

"Were they?" Kit rolls up a pair of socks and tucks them in a box. A fox-like smile fills her face. "Was your dear sister-in-law there? I haven't seen Harriet since last winter. Wasn't she one of the Silent Sentinels arrested in front of the White House? Such shocking treatment they received at the Occoquan Workhouse. Just shameful. Please do give Harriet my regards. And bring her to tea with you sometime. She's such a delight."

Mrs. Vaughn's face turns a very unflattering shade of scarlet. Margaret drops her head in shame. There is no great love between Margaret and me, but I feel badly for her. I know that stomach-clenching feeling of public humiliation she is feeling. Intimately, in fact, thanks to Kit's unbridled tongue.

"Would anyone care for some tea?" Mama jumps to her feet. "We've been working hard. Let's take a break. Mrs. Vaughn, Margaret, would you assist me with the refreshments?"

Margaret and her mother fairly bolt from the table. Soon our table empties as the others drift toward the back of the expansive room where Mama and the Vaughns pour cups of tea and pass out cookies.

"Why, Kit, why?" I say in exasperation.

"One day you'll understand." Kit smiles like a fox full of chicken dinner as she rolls socks. "Besides, you should thank me."

"For what? Shaming our mother?"

"No. For keeping your secret."

"What secret?"

"Whatever it was that you were doing with our chauffeur this afternoon that made you so late."

I stammer. "It's not what you think. I was assisting Marco with his essay."

"Mm hmm." Kit doesn't look convinced. "I don't see why you are so infatuated with that boy."

"I am—" I look around us and then lower the level of my voice. "I am not infatuated with him."

"Mm hmm."

Kit throws a pair of rolled socks at me. They bounce off my chest. I catch Mama's eye as I contort myself to retrieve them from the floor. It's a wonder that Kit and I don't burst into flames with the heated stare Mama is giving us from across the room.

"Tell me—so we can keep our story straight—where did we go this afternoon with our chauffeur?" Kit says.

"To the library."

"And where did you actually go?"

I look around the room. The women continue to congregate and enjoy refreshments at the other end of the room. Today, I am glad to be excluded from their prattle.

"Little Italy. I was assisting Marco with his essay on *The Merchant of Venice* over *gelato*...it's like ice cream. Nurse Brighton was being a complete beast, so I wanted to get away."

"I see." Kit's voice drips with disapproval.

"You can tattle to mother if you want, I don't care," I say, praying Kit won't call my bluff. "I miss nursing. I miss being truly useful. There must be more to life than...this." I gesture at the women milling around, gossiping, and complaining.

"I want to be useful, too, Ginny. How I wish I was at Radcliffe right now immersed in my studies, but I am needed here more. The suffrage bill goes to the Senate again this fall, but even after that, our work won't be finished. It still has to go to the House of Representatives and then to the states to ratify. We have to keep pushing. My schooling will have to wait. I need more time here."

I pause. I'm not sure whose secret is more scandalous: Kit being a suffragist or me gallivanting all over Little Italy with our handsome chauffeur unchaperoned. They are probably equal offenses in Mama's book.

"Then let's make a truce. I won't tattle on your suffrage work, and you won't tattle on my occasional clandestine trip to Little Italy for *gelato*," I say.

"How about I try to talk Father into allowing you to start nursing again? In return, you support my work. Or at least stay out of my way while I do it. Deal?" Kit puts out her hand.

"Deal." I shake Kit's hand.

"Oh, for pity's sake, Ginny. No wilted, limp handshakes. Shake like a man."

I grab Kit's hand again, squeeze it, and pump it up and down like Daddy does when he sees Dr. Carter. We both giggle.

"Again. These things take practice." Kit puts her hand out a third time. "Good afternoon, I'm Katherine Jackson, journalist and suffragist. It is a pleasure to make your acquaintance."

I pump her hand. "And I am Virginia Jackson, future surgeon. The pleasure is all mine."

We continue to shake hands and laugh until Mama breaks our hands to sit down.

"Stop that!" Mama settles into her chair. "Comport yourselves like ladies."

Which of course, makes Kit and I dissolve into giggles until Mama pinches us both on the thigh under the table. Hard. We are most definitely going to get it later. When I glance over at Kit, she gives me a wink. It's worth it though.

NINE

BY FRIDAY, DADDY still hasn't returned from Boston. Things must be dire. Unfortunately, no one seems to notice or care except for me. And maybe Marco.

Marco pokes his head out of Daddy's office when I walk in the front door after school. "A telegram came for you today, Miss Virginia. I didn't open it. *She* did."

Marco comes out into the hall, wiping his hands on his work apron. He pulls out a creased telegram from his vest pocket and hands it to me. The paper is warm. So are the fingers that brush mine as he passes me the telegram.

"I'll be in your father's office with *her* if you need me." A small smile spreads across his face, and he whispers, "Please need me. I mean, to drive you somewhere, anywhere, of course."

"Of course." The heat is rising in my face, so I duck into the parlor and bury my nose in Daddy's telegram.

INFLUENZA MUCH WORSE THAN EXPECTED STOP HOPE TO RETURN SUNDAY LATE STOP SENDING MARCO AND BRIGHTON TO DEVILS POCKET ON SATURDAY STOP INFORM ELEANOR OF PLANS

Based on the amount of stomping coming down the hallway from the kitchen to Daddy's office, Nurse Brighton is not pleased by this news.

"I most certainly am not spending my Saturday afternoon attending immigrants," Nurse Brighton's voice echoes across the hallway.

"But the telegram instructed—" Marco says.

"To the Devil with what the telegram said. I was hired to work Monday through Friday."

"It's three patients. It will only take two hours, possibly three."

"No. I've decided. I'm not going. In fact, the whole thing has given me a splitting headache. I'm going home." Nurse Brighton bursts out of Daddy's office to find me standing at the foot of the stairs with my telegram. The hardness of her face immediately melts into the pantomime of a benevolent caregiver.

"Oh, Virginia, dear. I didn't realize you were there," her voice softens to a treacle tone. "If your mother asks, please tell her I've gone home ill. A splitting headache." She rubs her temples as part of her act. "That's a good girl. Now, off you go."

Nurse Brighton gently pushes me up the first couple of stairs before ducking her head back into Daddy's office, where Marco is pacing and muttering in Italian.

"I'm not going," she snaps. "The decision is final."

"As you wish." Marco slams the door closed.

I slowly climb the stairs until I hear the front door slam, too. Then I circle back to Daddy's office and crack open the door.

"What now?" Marco turns around and colors. "Miss Virginia, I apologize." Marco falls into Daddy's big leather chair and lets out a frustrated sigh. "I can't wait for your father to return."

"Me, too." I walk over to Daddy's library and pull out a book on respiration, my self-study of the week. Granted, I have a textbook on respiration upstairs already, but I need another one. Or another book. Or simply a few more minutes in the place I wish I were the most.

Marco is so quiet as I ponder my reading choices that I wonder if he's fallen asleep. I get up the courage to peek back over my shoulder. Marco sits slumped forward in the chair until his knuckles are the only thing holding his head up.

"You look like you are carrying the weight of the world on your shoulders today," I say.

Marco releases another heavy sigh. "Some days, I feel a hundred years old."

I had planned to take my book upstairs, but instead, I sit down at Daddy's desk. I pretend like I am looking for a specific chapter until I settle on an arbitrary page.

"Why?"

"There is a rumor going around Little Italy that Uncle Sam is so desperate for men that the draft age is going to be dropped. To eighteen."

I inhale sharply and look at Marco. The peacock is gone. The crease between his bushy eyebrows tells me how much this is weighing on his mind.

"I'm not a slacker or a coward." Marco glares at me.

"Who implied that?"

"You did. In the kitchen. Earlier this summer. Over the peaches."

My stomach clenches.

"I want to do my patriotic duty," Marco says. "I do. But I also have many commitments here. Too many people depend on me. And I don't want to take lives. I want to save them."

"Me too. So, what if *we* went to Devil's Pocket on Saturday."

The idea tumbles through Marco's mind until the crease between his eyebrows relaxes. "I could deliver you to the cinema or a museum or maybe both. I only require a few hours to complete the tasks."

"No, I'm going to Devil's Pocket with you."

"We can't. It's not proper."

"Either both of us go or neither of us do." I hold up my hands. "These hands want to save lives, too."

Marco sits back in the chair. The peacock doesn't argue with me. "Then what do you propose?"

"Mama leaves for New York City in the morning. I'm sure my sister has some suff—business of her own to attend to. Come right after luncheon. We can go and be back before dinner without anyone being the wiser. If Mama asks, I'm going to a chamber music concert and then having tea with my new friend from school. We'll call her…Clementine. No, Charlotte. Completely new to Philadelphia. Not connected to high society yet."

"A chamber music concert?"

"Yes, because if Mama asks I can honestly say I don't know what the musicians played. She knows I can't tell Bach from Beethoven."

"I should warn you that Mr. O'Connor was on your father's list of patients to see," Marco says. "There's not much we can do for him besides change his bandages and rinse the necrotic skin."

My stomach rolls every time I think of Mr. O'Connor and his rotten toes. Blood doesn't bother me, but the smell of rotting flesh…. How am I ever going to make it as a surgeon?

"There is one patient I will need you to attend to. Your father specifically asked Nurse Brighton to do it." Marco digs at the collar of his shirt. "It's Mrs. Carnes."

"The lady with the new baby?" I clarify.

"Yes."

I remember her name from earlier in the week when I overheard Nurse Brighton gossiping about her. *Seventh child! No wonder they can't get out of poverty. Reproducing like rabbits.*

It still makes me pause, because Anna says the same thing, only without such a haughty demeanor. At least Anna offers a medical solution to the problem, whereas Nurse Brighton offers nothing but scorn.

"Something is wrong with the baby?"

"No."

"Then what?"

"Here." Marco hands me Daddy's telegram addressed to Nurse Brighton and points to a specific section.

VISIT MRS CARNES ALSO STOP HISTORY OF MILK NOT COMING IN STOP CHECK BREAST FOR POSSIBLE INFECTION STOP MAY NEED TO FIND WET NURSE AS BEFORE

Marco clears his throat and stands up. He pulls a book from Daddy's library. "Perhaps you should read this. It has a…um…section…on…um…nursing. The mother and child kind. I don't think Mrs. Carnes would feel comfortable discussing her…um…symptoms with me."

Marco hands me a blue cloth-bound book. The gold lettering on the spine reads *Obstetrics and Gynecology Nursing* by Edward Davis, M.D.

The thought of discussing one's bosom with another

woman is mortifying, but I have to do it. There will be much worse things in the future. All of my limited knowledge about marital things currently comes from Anna, who delights in informing me of such things whether I want to know them or not. Then again, she helped deliver her stillborn brother when she was thirteen.

"Thank you. I'll read it. Later." I slide the book under my respiratory one.

Marco jumps when the grandfather clock in the hall strikes half-past three. "We've got to get you to the Red Cross, or the Missus will have my hide."

"Wait. Let me put this upstairs." I tuck the book under my arm—spine facing down—and rush upstairs. The book won't fit in the hidey hole, so I slide it under my bed for safe keeping.

"IS THERE SOMETHING you'd like to tell me?" Kit says from the overstuffed chair in our bedroom when I return from my bath later that evening.

She tips up the book she's reading. It's a blue cloth-bound book. Oh no.

"Where did you get that?" I towel dry my hair like nothing is wrong.

"I stubbed my toe on it while I was coming around your bed."

"I wonder how it got there."

"Don't play dumb with me, Virginia." Kit snaps the book closed and gives me a withering look. "I can try to answer some of your questions if you are too embarrassed to ask Mother. I have learned quite a few things this evening."

My face burns.

"So…who is in a family way?" Kit says conspiratorially.

"Nobody."

"Alright then, who is trying *not* to be in a family way?"

"Pardon?"

"There is a woman in Brooklyn. A Mrs. Sanger. I met her while I was in New York City for the march. She believes that women can have a better lot in life if they don't have so many children. She has…ways…to prevent such things." Kit sits up straight. "Do you need to know these things, Virginia?"

"Absolutely not."

"Good." Kit settles back down into her chair and opens up the book again.

I sit down at our vanity and pull Granny Jackson's silver-handled brush through my hair. I wonder if I should tell Kit that I already know who Margaret Sanger is.

Kit snorts. "Oh dear Lord, please tell me it wasn't Margaret Vaughn who put you up to this research. That would be too rich. Horrible of course, but rich."

"Katherine!" I remain silent for another moment before deciding to clear Margaret's name and trust Kit with my secret. "No, I may have promised Marco that I would go with him on Saturday to Devil's Pocket to see three of Daddy's patients. Nurse Brighton refuses to go, and Mrs. Carnes's milk isn't coming in. There may be an infection in her breasts."

"What do you know about bosoms? You barely have a bosom yourself."

I grab the needlepoint pillow off of my bed and hurl it at Kit. It bounces quite satisfactorily off her head.

"That's why I'm doing research, Kit. So I can do something to ease Mrs. Carnes's suffering until Daddy gets back. He'll know what to do."

After a few moments, Kit stands up. I block Kit's path to the door.

"Please don't tattle on me."

"I'm not an imbecile." Kit pushes the book into my chest. "Just know that you are playing with fire. Make sure it's worth the risk."

I take the book. "It is."

"Then read fast. I want to go to sleep as soon as I'm out of the bath."

I flop down on my bed with the book. When Kit gets to the door, she looks back.

"I highly suggest that you put that book back tomorrow morning before Angelina tidies up our room. I have a feeling that she might jump to the wrong conclusion. And we definitely don't want *that* getting back to Mother."

TEN

"GIRLS, I AM leaving on the nine-oh-five today." Mama doesn't look up from her social diary.

"Have a pleasant trip." Kit doesn't look up from her newspaper either as she nibbles on a piece of toast.

"It must be a great honor to be asked to come to New York to meet with the chairman of President Wilson's special War Council," I say.

"Wilson...." Kit stabs at her poached egg with animosity. President Wilson is no friend to the Women's Suffrage Movement. "How I despise that man."

"Stop making everything political." Mama puts down her pen and takes off her spectacles. "Our country is at war, Katherine. We are fighting for the American way of life. *That's* our priority right now. Not women's suffrage."

"No, Mother, that is *your* priority. Not mine. Not my sisters'. It says right here—"

"Tell me about New York, Mama," I cut Kit off before she can ruin yet another meal.

Mama—undoubtedly stunned that I have been listening to her veiled boasting at the Red Cross events recently—closes up her social diary and gives me her undivided attention. "It is a great honor. President Wilson has been so pleased with our war effort work that he asked the chairman to arrange a caucus. I will be representing our chapter and sharing some of our ideas with other chapters that aren't as organized and efficient as ours."

"How wonderful, Mama. I thought you were the treasurer of the Philadelphia chapter though, not the president?"

"I am. For the last three years." Mama sits up straight. "They keep asking me to be president, but I find being the treasurer so much more rewarding. I will be discussing cost-saving measures during my speech."

I pour some more tea into Mama's empty teacup to ransom a few more minutes of her time. "Like when you used to work in your father's store?"

Mama pauses, probably wondering when she told me about working in the store. "Yes. Not everyone appreciates my cost-saving measures though. Then or now. But for the last three years straight, our budget has been accounted for down to the penny. Our home account, too."

"Yes, I can attest to that," Kit says.

I step on Kit's foot to silence her. "Mrs. Maguire told me that you used to work in Grandfather Fisher's store every day when you were younger."

"I did." A whimsical smile passes over Mama's face. "Father started me checking his figures at ten years old simply to keep me quiet and out from underfoot while he attended to customers and Mother attended to my younger sisters. When I proved to Father at fourteen that his dry goods supplier routinely overcharged him for 'womanly goods,' Father started paying me to double check his accountant's work."

Kit puts down her newspaper. "You had a job? A *paying* job?"

"I did. A small pittance to fund my hat collection. But I enjoyed my work." Mama stares off into the room, a small smile on her face.

"I wish I could have met your father. Sadly, I barely remember Grandmother Fisher either," I say.

Mama, in a rare moment of tenderness, wraps her hand around mine. "I wish you could have known them, too."

"Family lore says that Grandmother Fisher was quite a trying woman." Kit looks at us. "A trait passed down from mother to daughter."

Instead of reacting with anger, Mama only chuckles. "Yes, and from mother to daughter again, I'm afraid."

Before Kit ruins our moment of peace, I prod a little more. "Mrs. Maguire mentioned that you once had a favorite blue dress."

"You will have to be a little more specific, Ginny. I've had many a blue dress in my forty years."

"Cornflower blue with lace on the collar," I say, but Mama's face doesn't show any recognition. "Mrs. Maguire said that you probably couldn't sit down for a week after your mother saw how you spilled ink all over it. Goodness knows, Kit has ruined plenty of dresses with her sloppy penmanship."

Mama jerks her hand back from mine. "I wasn't a little girl. I was about your age."

"Mrs. Maguire said she tried every trick she knew to get that stain out, but it wouldn't lift."

Mama looks panicked. "Don't listen to one word that addled old woman says. I doubt she remembers that night any better than she does last night."

"Night? So what—"

Mama looks at the clock on the sideboard. "Goodness, look at the time. I won't be home until very late this evening, girls. Don't wait up for me. Katherine, you will be in charge of watching your sister."

Kit dips her newspaper down. "Mother, Ginny isn't five. She hardly needs a nursemaid."

"All the same, I'm counting on you to look after each other. Also, we have thirty invitations to address for our upcoming party after the Liberty Loan Drive parade," Mama says. "Angelina is ill-equipped for this task. So I need the two of you to do them instead. The invitations must go out in Monday's post."

"Yes, Mama."

Kit snaps her newspaper until she can hold it in one hand. She places it on the table between us.

"Mother, I'd like to take Virginia to a chamber music recital this afternoon," Kit says.

"I don't want to go to a dull concert," I say. "Daddy's telegram instructed Marco to take Nurse Brighton to Devil's Pocket this afternoon. I will go with them instead."

"You most certainly will not," Mama says.

"Only to report back to Daddy. I'll let Nurse Brighton do all the work."

"My dear friend from Radcliffe is playing." Kit taps her index finger on the paper. I look down. All I see is an article announcing the arrival of 300 sailors from Boston at the Philadelphia Naval Yard. "She is very accomplished. And if she should insist that we join her family for dinner...."

I raise my eyebrow in confusion at Kit. She points to another specific, but tiny, article down the same page. The headline reads:

LOCAL SUFFRAGISTS PLAN TO MARCH ON CITY HALL TODAY TO PROTEST MAYOR'S LACK OF SUPPORT FOR WOMEN'S SUFFRAGE AMENDMENT

The proposed march time, two o'clock.

"Go with your sister, Virginia. I don't want you home alone all day."

"I'm seventeen, Mama. I can stay home by myself."

Mama pauses. "Please send my regrets to the hostess. Let her know of my trip to New York City. Otherwise, I would escort you girls myself. Maybe Widow Clark could —"

"No!" Kit and I say in unison.

"Mother, I am almost twenty-one, I don't need a chaperone for an afternoon recital. Queen Victoria is no longer on the throne. We can be modern women now."

"It's not proper," Mama says.

"Neither is you traveling by yourself to New York City and returning home late. Should you turn down President Wilson's request because your husband isn't here to escort you?"

Mama's mouth opens and closes several times. "You are your sister's keeper, Katherine. Please make sure her activities are fitting and appropriate for a girl of her age and status. Am I understood?"

"Yes, Mother. And don't worry so much. I promise Ginny will have an edifying afternoon." Kit smiles sweetly.

I am both impressed and horrified by how convincingly Kit can lie.

"May we have Marco drive us to the event or would you prefer we take the trolley?" I add. "Father is paying Marco for the afternoon anyway."

Mama pushes away from the table and collects her things. "I'll inform Marco that he may need to work late if you are invited to stay for dinner by your hosts."

Before Mama leaves the room, she stops for a moment to kiss the top of my head.

"Take care of each other." Mama squeezes Kit's shoulder. "Don't wait up."

"Have a grand adventure, Mama," I say. "Sounds like you haven't had one in a very long time."

Mama gets that wistful look in her eyes again. "No, I haven't. Not for a long time."

As soon as Mama is out of the room, I whisper to Kit, "I wish we could drive ourselves."

"Me too. That adventure, however, will have to wait for another day. It looks like the rain clouds are here to stay. Driving is hard enough on a dirt road in the spring sunshine. I don't want to try it in the rain in a congested city."

"Grayson taught you to drive?"

"Shh. And, yes, we went driving in his automobile a few…dozen times." A mischievous grin pulls across Kit's face. Is there no end to my sister's scandalous behavior? "We will have to leave the driving to Marco today, but one day, little sister, one day we will learn to drive. I promise."

ELEVEN

"IT'S RAINING CATS and dogs today." Marco slides into the front seat of the Cadillac after we deliver Kit and an umbrella to her suffragist sisters at the Mayor's office. Marco shivers, sending water droplets flying off his slicked hair.

"What are you doing?" Marco startles when I climb into the front passenger seat.

The howling wind slams the passenger door closed behind me. "Learning how to drive."

"First, you are on the wrong side of the automobile to drive it, and second, no, your father would kill me."

"Not today, silly. I'm simply observing."

"It's not proper," Marco says. I give him a scathing look. He throws his hands up in defeat. "As you wish, Nurse Jackson."

I readjust one of Nurse Cecelia's crisp, white nursing caps on my head hoping to make us look a little more respectable. We drive in silence all the way to Devil's Pocket.

"Are you sure you want to do this?" Marco says when we arrive. "You don't have to, you know. I can...ahem... talk to Mrs. Carnes, if necessary."

"Though you may find it hard to believe, you aren't always the best tool for the job, Mr. D'Orio. I am, however, happy to allow you to attend to Mr. O'Connor's bandages. It will be character building for you."

Marco grimaces. "We should probably do that one first."

THANKFULLY, WHAT'S LEFT of Mr. O'Connor's toes stay attached to his foot as Marco unwinds the dirty bandages. I breathe through my mouth as Marco rinses the oozing sores with a water-and-carbolic-acid mixture. Mr. O'Connor hisses in pain.

"I hear you are a Philadelphia Athletics fan." I put a hand on Mr. O'Connor's shoulder to make him look up at me. "You must have been disappointed that the season ended early this year. Who did you put your money on since the A's didn't make the World Series?"

Marco makes a surprised sound.

"I do read the *Philadelphia Inquirer*, Mr. D'Orio," I say. I also overheard Daddy say the same thing while on the telephone with Dr. Carter who is a fervent Boston Red Socks fan.

"Red Socks, of course." Mr. O'Connor's face lights up. "I got two whole dollars ridin' on 'em. I'm no fool. That Babe Ruth. Arm of gold. Hope them boys all make it back. Baseball is one of the last pleasures in my life." Mr. O'Connor hisses as Marco binds what's left of his foot. "Aye. I know I don't have much time left." Mr. O'Connor looks up at me. His eyes are glassy. "If only I could make it to Shibe Park for one more game. Maybe see The Babe pitch against my A's. Then I would die a happy man."

A lump forms in my throat. I pat Mr. O'Connor's

shoulder. "Maybe you could buy an invalid chair like the injured soldiers use?"

Mr. O'Connor puts his hand over mine. "With what money, m'dear?"

"The money you win when Babe Ruth and the Red Socks win the World Series?" I suggest.

Mr. O'Connor laughs, though I was quite serious. "What about you, boy? Who'd you put yer money on?"

"I'm not a gambler," Marco says, and then softens his tone. "But if I were, I'd put two dollars on the Red Socks, too."

"That's right. You know how to pick 'em. You American, boy?"

Irritation telegraphs across Marco's eyes, but he answers cooly, "Yes, sir. Born here in Philadelphia."

"When you gonna go fight them damn Huns?"

"When Uncle Sam calls my number. My older brother is already there. He's with the 315th. Machine Gun Company."

"The 315th." Mr. O'Connor nods his head. "Philadelphia's Own."

"Yes, sir. Philadelphia's Own."

"Who knows? Maybe you'll find yerself stationed next to The Babe in the trenches one day. Wouldn't that be somethin'? You get me an autograph if you are ever stationed with any of them important people, won't ya, boy?"

"Yes, sir." Marco's voice is tight as he ties off the clean bandages.

"I'm afraid, that's all we can do for you today, Mr. O'Connor," I say as Marco cleans his hands and loads the remaining supplies back into the cherry crate. "My father will be back from Boston soon. He was disappointed that he had to miss his regular visit with you today."

"Thank you, Miss. You and yer Da always take good care of me."

Marco grits his teeth but tames his tongue.

"Whenever you are ready to take your leave, Miss Jackson." Marco yanks the box off the floor and tucks it under his arm.

"Take care, Mr. O'Connor. I'll visit again soon." I loop my drawstring handbag over my wrist and give his shoulder one last squeeze.

"Aye. Always a pleasure to see a pretty face."

Marco makes it to the door in three long strides. He waits in the hallway scowling.

"Always a pleasure to see a pretty face," Marco mocks in a terrible imitation of an Irish accent as we climb back down the stairs. "I'm the one who attended to what's left of his foot. But do I get even a simple 'thank you'? No. I'm just that Italian boy. That slacker not doing his patriotic duty."

"Thank you," I say sincerely, but Marco still looks at me with daggers in his eyes. "I hope Uncle Sam never calls your number. And, you *are* doing your patriotic duty. We need skilled medical personnel here, too." I pop open my umbrella as we step back outside into the rain and hold it above both of us. "Besides, maybe the pretty face Mr. O'Connor was referring to was yours."

"Don't be ridiculous."

"I don't know," I tease. "The girls in the *gelato* shop would probably agree."

"Are you jealous?" Marco leans in so close that I can smell his spicy hair tonic.

"Now who is being ridiculous?" I say though the butterflies in my stomach might disagree.

It's only a few minutes' drive to Mrs. Maguire's home.

As Marco parks the Cadillac a second time, I pat my handbag and hear the tell-tale sound of coins jingling. I plan to leave a few behind. Not as charity, but as payment for information.

I knock on Mrs. Maguire's door and then a second time. "She's a little hard of hearing."

Marco tries the doorknob. "She must be out. We should move on to Mrs. Carnes. No sense putting it off any longer today."

I hope my disappointment doesn't show. I follow Marco down the hallway and one set of stairs.

"Wait. I dropped my handkerchief." I rush back up the stairs before Marco can offer to fetch it for me. When I get back to Mrs. Maguire's door, I open up my handbag, push my handkerchief out of the way, and pull out the coins. I dip down and slide them under her door. I would leave her an anonymous note, but she wouldn't be able to read it. Some days, the Miss Mildred Franklin School tries my patience, but overall I am thankful for my education. If I had been born into Devil's Pocket instead of Rittenhouse Square, I might be spending my day doing laundry instead of suffering through Shakespeare.

"Silly me. It was in my handbag," I say when I meet up with Marco again.

Marco tucks Daddy's telegram into his vest pocket. "Mrs. Carnes lives across the street."

The glass bottles in the cherry crate tinkle together as Marco and I jog across the street through the ever increasing rain. Marco raps on the door.

"Since I am not the right tool for the job, as you say, I'll be in the kitchen trying to get a spoonful of Castor oil into her other children while you attend to Mrs. Carnes," Marco says.

Honestly, I'm not looking forward to the task either, but I won't let Marco see that. After a quick introduction, I follow Mrs. Carnes's only daughter—who can't be more than ten years old—through the kitchen and into her mother's bedroom. Mrs. Carnes lies listlessly under a skillfully-stitched quilt, her newborn swaddled in a light blue blanket beside her.

"Hello, Mrs. Carnes. I'm Virginia Jackson." I still can't refer to myself as Nurse. "My father, Dr. Charles Jackson, is away in Boston, but he asked me to come see you today."

"Aye, undoubtedly at Granda's request." Mrs. Carnes turns her head to look at me. Dark circles frame her blue-green eyes. "My grandfather always speaks so highly of Dr. Jackson. I know there isn't much more he can do for Granda, but he appreciates the regular visits nonetheless."

"Mr. O'Connor is your grandfather?" I ask, though now I can see the family resemblance.

"Yes." Mrs. Carnes, who is probably in her late twenties, looks me over from head to toe. "How old are you, Miss?"

"Seventeen, ma'am."

"No offense, Miss Jackson, but what could a young girl like you possibly know about babies?"

Thanks to Anna, more than any respectable debutante should, but I can't say that. I clear my throat to steady my nerves.

"Do you have any redness or heat in your...breasts, Mrs. Carnes?" I can hear Anna in my mind mocking me. Then again, she uses the word breast with the same ease as saying elbow. Much to our teacher's displeasure. Last term both of us had our knuckles rapped on more than one occasion for such "indelicate talk." I clear my throat a second time.

"Yes." Mrs. Carnes pulls at her faded nightgown. I

glance away. Then I pull my eyes back. The baby attaches to her breast with ease and sucks with vigor. A moment later, his face red, he breaks away and howls in frustration.

"I believe you have a clogged milk duct." I hope I sound convincing, quoting back what the medical book said.

"I know. In a day or two, I won't have any milk left at all. It's always the same," Mrs. Carnes says more to the wall than me.

"I'm sorry. Shall I fetch you a hot compress and some aspirin for the pain?"

"Yes, thank you."

"Have you tried Mellin's Infant Food?" I repeat back Daddy's suggestion to Miss Shannon.

Mrs. Carnes rolls her head back to the other side and gives me a scathing look. "I'll be certain to ask the housekeeper to buy me some when she arrives with the cook and nanny later today."

I wince. I'm not the right tool for this job either. Mrs. Carnes squeezes her eyes tight and lets out a frustrated sigh.

"Ask my sister-in-law," Mrs. Carnes says in a softer tone a moment later. "She lives down the hall. Her baby is almost weaned, but maybe she has enough milk to feed Colin here until I can find another wet nurse."

"Of course. You take a few moment's rest."

After a steadying breath, I slide my hands under the tiny baby. His howl settles into a hungry whimper. I pull Colin to my chest—careful to keep a hand behind his head like Daddy always does—and tuck the hand-me-down blanket around him. Lord, please don't let me break this child with my ineptitude.

When I arrive back to the kitchen, I find Marco's task hasn't been any easier.

"C'mon, boys. It's not so bad." Marco holds a spoonful of Castor oil in front of the eldest boy. Five boys lined up in stair-stepped formation all stand with grimy hands latched firmly over their mouths.

"It must be hard being the only girl in the family," I say to the little girl rocking herself in the corner. "May I send you on a special errand? Could you fetch your aunt for me? The one who lives down the hall. The one with the baby. Your baby brother is so hungry. Perhaps she can nurse him a little bit."

The little girl nods and bursts out the door.

"Let's act like soldiers now, boys. Down the hatch," Marco continues to wheedle without success.

"You seem to be working very hard over there, Mr. D'Orio. Would you care for a piece of candy?" I catch Marco's eye. "I brought too much candy with me. I am happy to share with you."

Marco lets out an exasperated sigh and pours the Castor oil back into its bottle. "I would love some."

I dip the baby back until his tiny body rests on my forearm, his head tucked in my elbow. With my free hand, I open my handbag and pull the paper cone of sweets out. I pour the contents out on the table.

"I have some lemon drops, a few peppermint buttons, and even one chocolate kiss. Which do you prefer?" I say, hoping that my plan works.

The boys' mouths have dropped open at the sight of my bounty. Marco walks over, picks up a lemon drop and pops it in his mouth.

"Mmmmm, lemon drops. My favorite," Marco says. "*Gra*—thank you, Miss Jackson."

"Mine, too." I pop one in my mouth. "Mmmmm."

Marco and I ignore the boys and discuss the treatment

options for Mrs. Carnes. Marco lights the stove to boil water for Mrs. Carnes's compress.

"Does your mother like candy?" I ask a moment later when the compress is ready. The boys nod in unison. "A piece of candy might help her get this medicine down. Which kind do you think she would prefer?"

"The chocolate," the eldest boy says. "Da always buys her chocolate for her birthday. We aren't allowed to touch it."

"Would you help me deliver it to her? My hands are a bit full at the moment." I pick up the glass of water with my free hand.

The boy scoops up the dainty, foil-wrapped candy and falls in behind me. Marco brings up the rear with two steaming rags in a bowl and the near-empty bottle of aspirin. The three of us crowd around Mrs. Carnes's bed.

"Mam," the boy's voice wavers. "You have to take your medicine. You have to get better. Here's some chocolate to help you get the medicine down."

Tears well up in Mrs. Carnes's eyes as her son places the chocolate in her hand like he's presenting her a diamond ring.

"And here's some aspirin, ma'am." Marco hands Mrs. Carnes a tablet of aspirin after putting the steaming bowl on her bedside table.

"Be brave, Mam," the boy urges as I hand his mother the glass of water.

Mrs. Carnes swallows the aspirin before unwrapping the silver foil. She slides the chocolate between her dry lips and smiles. The boy throws himself across his mother's chest. Mrs. Carnes winces but hugs him tightly.

"God bless you, Sean. This makes me feel so much better." Mrs. Carnes strokes Sean's hair. "Now go help with your brothers. I need you to be the man about the house until your Da gets home. Can you do that for me?"

Sean stands up straight and wipes his eyes with the back of his hand. Marco herds Sean out the door so that I can help Mrs. Carnes put the hot compresses on her red, rock-hard breasts.

"There are only four aspirin tablets left in the bottle, but I'll leave them for you. Take them as needed for pain." I quote the book some more even though Mrs. Carnes probably knows more about the treatment than I do. "The milk will cease in a few days. Then your breasts will go back to normal."

"Thank you. You've done all that your father usually does. Though I do appreciate the chocolate this time. I'm just so tired. More so than ever."

I feel an inner tug at my conscience. Just because I have the knowledge—thanks to Anna—doesn't mean I want to share it. But maybe I need to.

"You know that there are…ways…ways to prevent pregnancy." I regret the words as soon as they are out of my mouth.

"It's a sin," Mrs. Carnes says matter-of-factly.

"With due respect, ma'am, is it? Especially within the confines of marriage? To space your children a little more and give your body a rest in between. Women die during childbirth every day, ma'am. There are new ways to protect your health. To protect your other children from losing their mother."

I wait for Mrs. Carnes to chastise me or worse, promise to have a word with my father about my impertinence. Instead she says, "You sound like that red-headed girl."

"Anna?"

"The one down here passing out pamphlets. Haven't

seen her in a while now."

"Anna and her pamphlets moved to Boston with her father at the beginning of the summer. Please don't think ill of her." This isn't the first time—and probably won't be the last either—that I am called to defend my passionate friend. "Her mother died during childbirth when Anna was thirteen. That's why she is so ardent about this issue. She doesn't mean to upset people with her unconventional views. She just doesn't want any other girl to lose her mother."

"Aye. I lost my mam the same way when I was five. My Da remarried soon after though, and his new wife gave him seven more children. I wish we had more midwives in Devil's Pocket. There aren't enough to go around. We have scholarly men who try to help—no offense to your father— but they can't replace the intuitive wisdom women have passed down from generation to generation."

"That's why Anna and I plan to attend medical school one day. We need more women doctors."

"God bless you both, Nurse Jackson. I hope you succeed. And maybe I'll take a look at the pamphlet. I'm sure my sister-in-law still has one. Heaven knows she never throws anything away."

I hear the front door open, and a woman's voice echoes through the living room.

"Speak of the Devil. There she is now." Mrs. Carnes groans and attempts to sit up.

"Please, rest. It's the best thing you can do for your family right now."

Mrs. Carnes melts back down into her bed and closes her eyes. "Maybe just for a little while then."

Her breathing lengthens as I back out of the room and gently close the door. I tiptoe back toward the kitchen, careful to not wake the baby still asleep in my arms.

In the kitchen, I find that Sean has his brothers and sister lined up like soldiers, mouths open. Marco delivers a spoonful of Castor oil—followed by Sean with a peppermint button—to each of the children.

"Here, let me take him from you." Mrs. Carnes's sister-in-law scoops the baby from the crook of my arm. His nap disturbed, the baby immediately begins to howl. "Aye. Aye. Just a moment, wee one."

The woman whisks the baby into the only other bedroom. The baby stops howling, so I presume they are successful at the task. I pick up the few remaining pieces of candy to return them to my handbag but change my mind.

"Why don't you keep the rest of the candy, Sean, as payment for your service?" I say, and the children squeal in delight. "Perhaps your auntie would care for a piece?"

The little girl scoops up a peppermint button and races to the other bedroom. I follow behind her.

"How is he nursing?" I say to the aunt, though the baby looks contented.

"Like a piglet. My, this child is hungry." She kisses his tiny fingers. "Don't you worry none. I can nurse him for a few days at least. We take care of our own."

The rumpus coming from the living room interrupts our conversation. I look back over my shoulder at Marco who stands in the middle of the living room with two of the littlest boys stuck to his legs like monkeys. A third boy jumps on his back.

"We should go, Nurse Jackson. It's late." Marco walks toward the bedroom door, the children still stuck to him. "Your sister will be worried."

"Boys. Boys!" the auntie says. "Get off Marco this instant!"

But they don't obey her. We are halfway down the hall before the boys finally give up their game and run home. Marco takes the cherry crate from me so that I can open my umbrella.

"Does the auntie know you?" I say as we step out onto the street. I put the umbrella over both of us. It doesn't help much.

"We are acquainted." Marco tugs at his collar which is getting wetter by the second. "I've been coming to Devil's Pocket with your father for a while now."

"Not that long."

"As you said, it must be my pretty face. I do make a striking impression with the ladies."

I remove Marco's half of the umbrella.

"Ayyy." Marco wraps his hand around mine and pulls the umbrella back toward him. "I used to come to Devil's Pocket with Dom sometimes. Some people were glad to see the D'Orio brothers. Some people, were not. Hmpf. You don't have to walk around with your birth certificate to prove how American you are. Why should I?"

"And I shouldn't have to fight to be a surgeon or to vote."

Marco starts to complain but stops himself. "You are not wrong."

I look up at him. "You are not wrong either."

Marco and I let out a frustrated sigh in tandem. We slide into the Cadillac, and both of us shiver from the dampness. My hand continues to shake as I place my handbag into the cherry crate between us.

"So, how much money did you leave behind at Mrs. Maguire's when you *dropped* your handkerchief earlier?" Marco fires up the Cadillac. "What? You were jingling like a horse pulling a Christmas sleigh when we left. Now you are silent."

"Am I that obvious?"

"Only to those paying attention."

"Are you paying attention?"

Marco stumbles over his words before settling on, "I'm paying attention to the road. I don't want to have an accident. Especially with you here."

Marco grips the steering wheel with both hands and keeps his head facing forward. I study the side of his face. There's a light scar underneath his chin.

"What happened to your face?" I say.

Marco wipes his cheek. "Where?"

"Here." Nothing has been appropriate today, so I use my index finger to touch the spot.

"Oh, that. That was Marco versus Dom, battle number four…hundred or so. I lost. Dom and the kitchen table won. I'm pretty sure it was your father who put in the stitches. I think it makes me look roguish. Like Douglas Fairbanks, no?"

I want to tell him the truth. That I think he's even more handsome than any of the actors I've seen at the cinema, but instead I say, "I think you should pay attention to the road."

The heat from my index finger continues to travel down my arm and into the pit of my stomach. It stays there smoldering during the entire drive across town.

"What a splendid day, even if the weather is frightful." Kit, her banner, and her completely ruined hat slide into the back of the Cadillac. "What the devil are you doing, Ginny?"

"I'm learning how to drive."

"By watching," Marco clarifies. "Only watching."

"I should say. I'm all for adventures and learning, but

there are some things we must be rational about." Kit unpins her hat and shakes the water off it. "Ohhhhh, my poor hat. You have served me well. Alas, sometimes we have to make personal sacrifices in the name of progress."

Kit pulls the wilted, stringy ostrich plume from the hat's band and blows on it to try to fluff it back up. "Mother will be glad of its demise. I think she is still put out over Cecelia buying it for me. Cecelia was right though. It has been as much a part of my suffragist's uniform as her nursing hat is part of hers."

"Have you heard from Nurse Cecelia since she joined the Army Nurse Corps?" Marco asks.

"Yes, but only a single postcard from South Carolina." Kit pushes her hat back into shape, but it doesn't hold. "She apologized for being such a coward about saying good-bye. She was afraid that we would attempt to talk her out of her decision."

"And we would have," I say.

"True. She said she likes her work at Camp Wadsworth, that her roommate from West Virginia was young enough to be her daughter, and that she didn't know when they would ship out for France."

"I hope never." My stomach clenches thinking about Cecelia being in harm's way. "I'm sorry, I know that it's unpatriotic and selfish but I want Cecelia home."

"I understand." Marco looks over at me. "I want my brother home, too."

TWELVE

"WELCOME HOME, MISS Katherine. Miss Virginia." Angelina reaches out to take Kit's dripping Mackintosh.

"Why are you still here, Angelina? It's Saturday." Kit unfastens her rubber overshoes and kicks them off. A small stream of rainwater runs out of them. "I thought you only worked half-days on Saturdays."

"I was baking for Mrs. Jackson's tea party tomorrow after church." Angelina adds my Mackintosh to the pile over her arm. Though she looks weary, Angelina says, "You will want dinner, yes?"

Marco pops out of Daddy's office. His trousers are wet all the way up to the knee, and his hair is flattened to his head. "I want dinner."

"Later." Angelina tut-tuts Marco. "When we are home."

A pang of guilt stabs at my empty stomach. "Since we've had the most unconventional day and Mama isn't coming back until late, shall we eat dinner together tonight? You always make enough to feed a small army, Angelina."

"Oh no, we couldn't," Angelina says.

"Oh yes, we could," Marco says.

"*Mio Dio*, Marco! You are raining on Mrs. Jackson's good floor. Go to the kitchen."

"Dripping. Not raining. People can't rain." Marco leaves a trail of water down the hall.

Angelina smacks Marco in the back of the head as he passes her.

"Yes, let's eat in the kitchen tonight. *All* of us. Mama's not here. There's no need for such antiquated formalities." Kit sneezes three times in a row. "But first, some dry clothes."

Thirty minutes and two dry dresses later, Kit and I arrive at our dinner party. I tuck a damp tendril of hair back into my slapdash hairstyle. I wish I had time to create something better, but Kit was already complaining that I was taking too long for such an unceremonious event. But it *is* a ceremonious event. I've never eaten in the kitchen before, much less with a boy who outshines Douglas Fairbanks.

Marco stands up as we enter. He pulls out our chairs like we are dining at The Ritz.

"I hope you do not mind. Marco insisted you won't mind." Angelina places a large bowl of pasta in a red sauce in the center of the table next to a loaf of crusty bread and a heaping platter filled with balls of meat. "If you do not like it, I will make another dish."

"Italian food. How exotic!" Kit claps her hands together in delight.

"Mamma says this is American food. Not Italian food." Angelina sits down. "Marco doesn't know Napoli, but I do."

"Remember. Marco doesn't *remember* Napoli," Marco corrects her English. "Angelina and Domenico were born in Napoli, but the rest of us are Americans."

"I *remember* when Mamma would make *polpette*. There was much bread and little meat inside the ball. But now in America, we can eat meat every day."

"Until the war broke out," Marco interrupts.

"My father was happy to eat much meat like this, but Mamma says this is not *polpette*. This is meatballs. Too much meat."

"I prefer meatballs to *polpette* too, but don't tell Mamma that," Marco says. "Also, don't tell Mamma we are ruining this pasta by putting tomato sauce on it. She would be scandalized."

"Well, I think it all looks delicious." I put my arm across my stomach to muffle the rumbling.

We all look at the food and then at our respective sibling. Who is going to lead the blessing? An awkward silence hangs in the air.

Marco clears his throat. "Papà always said the blessing. Then Dom. Now that I am the man of the house, it's my job."

I take a deep breath, waiting for Kit to start in on Marco. Instead, she dips her head at him. I jump when Marco takes my hand, but then notice he has Angelina's also. After a moment, I take Kit's hand, and she takes Angelina's. Marco does the blessing entirely in Italian. At the end, Angelina and Marco cross themselves with their right hands.

"Amen," Kit and I say in unison.

Marco squeezes my hand before releasing it. "I would offer to make a toast to unconventional dinner parties, but alas there is no wine."

"You drink wine?" I say, astonished.

"It is the Italian way," Marco says with a shrug.

Angelina gives Marco a reproachful look. "Only one glass and with dinner. Mamma is very strict about that."

"I do so enjoy a nice bottle of Chateaux Margaux with dinner. Especially with venison." Everyone looks at Kit.

"Now, shall we?"

I eat until I am sure my corset will burst at the seams. Kit makes it through the entire meal without arguing even once. She even laughs off some of Marco's gentle ribbing.

"What did you put in this sauce?" I dab at the last bit of sauce on my plate with my bread. "It is delicious."

"A little oregano, some basil, fresh garlic," Angelina says as if Kit and I know how to make anything more complicated than a sandwich.

"You should put this on all our food," I say.

"Oh no. Mrs. Jackson does not like spicy food. She says Doctor Jackson must have plain food because his stomach hurts often. I only make the recipes the old cook left behind."

"We really must bring Mother up to the twentieth century." Kit lines up her silverware on her plate as though we are dining at the Bellevue-Stratford Hotel.

"Who wants coffee?" Marco hides a yawn behind his hand. "I do. Especially as we have to take the trolley all the way home in this foul weather. One day, I will *own* an automobile."

"Mama doesn't allow me to drink coffee," I say.

"Mama isn't here." Kit dabs at the corners of her mouth daintily with her napkin. "I would enjoy a cup, also."

Angelina jumps to her feet.

"Show me how to make coffee, Angelina." Kit pushes away from the table. "Please. A modern woman should know how to make coffee. Ginny, pay attention. You need to learn, too."

"What's for dessert?" Marco leans back in his chair and rubs his stomach. "*Nonna* D'Orio would turn over in her grave if we ended this exceptional meal without something sweet."

Angelina lifts the cover off a plate sitting on the counter. "I made *baba* this afternoon. There are many."

I let out a little squeal of delight at the teacup-sized cakes piled together on top of Mama's best cake plate. Marco looks over and turns up his nose.

"They're dry. Where is the rum syrup? It's not *baba* without the rum," Marco says.

Kit's mouth pulls up into a devilish smile. "We have rum."

"No, we do not. Mama poured it out when she joined the Women's Christian Temperance Union." I don't care if the cakes have rum on them or not, as long as I get to eat one. Possibly two. Maybe a third after Marco goes home.

"This Prohibition legislation is a foolish idea. It will never pass Congress, and even if it does, we Italians will find a way around it." Marco's hands flutter around until he catches himself. He tucks them back in his lap. "We've been drinking *vino* for centuries. We aren't about to stop now."

"In that case. Wait here." Kit scurries out of the room. She's back a moment later with a decorative bottle. She unplugs the stopper and takes a whiff. She winces. "Yes, it's still good."

"Where did you procure that?" I say.

"Never you mind, Ginny." Kit hands the bottle to Angelina. "And you don't need to mention this to Mother either."

This is possibly the best dinner party I've ever attended.

"AH, *NONNA* D'ORIO would be pleased," Marco says when I present him with a cup of rich, dark coffee and a mushroom-shaped cake swimming in a sweet, rum-laced syrup. He takes a tentative bite of the cake, nodding his head as he chews. After washing it down with some of the coffee, Marco presses his index finger into the dimple of his cheek and twists it back and forth.

I raise my eyebrow at him. "You don't like it?"

"Pardon?" Marco says, and I imitate his gesture. "Oh, no, that means 'delicious.' This *baba* is...." Marco pinches his index finger and thumb together and pulls it horizontally across his body. "perfect. In fact, it is...." He kisses his fingers and flowers them out. "the best. A good ending to a dreary day."

"How fun. It's almost like we are playing charades," Kit jokes and my stomach clenches. "Oh, do teach us some more."

"That's all," Marco says, suddenly self-conscious. "Just a few gestures."

I know that is not true. When Mr. Borrelli and Marco talk to each other, their hands move as much as their lips do.

"Would you care for sugar in your coffee, Marco?" I jump up to fetch the sugar bowl before he even answers affirmatively. "Can you fetch the cream, Kit?"

Two pots of coffee and a second round of *baba* later—because I needed to practice making the rum syrup, of course—we are all groaning. Angelina pulls herself to her feet with the vigor of a snail.

Kit must see the bone-weariness in Angelina's eyes, too, because she says, "Allow me to clean up the kitchen tonight." Angelina protests, but Kit takes the coffee cups from Angelina's hands. "I insist. You've been here way past schedule because of us. Please, go home."

"We aren't completely helpless, you know." I pile the dessert plates gently on top of each other, the rum syrup sticking to my fingers.

Angelina looks at her brother who yawns despite the multiple cups of coffee he drank. He shrugs and mumbles something to her in Italian.

"Thank you," Angelina says.

Marco pushes away from the table. "I need to put the medicines and things away before *she* sees them on Monday morning."

"Oh, I left my handbag in the cherry crate." I deposit the dishes in the sink and lick my sticky fingers.

I follow Marco up the hallway to Daddy's office. My handbag is where I left it, tucked in between the bottles of Castor oil and carbolic acid. Our fingers brush when we both reach for it, sending a crackle of lightning between us. Marco stares at me. The lamplight dances off the bits of hazel in his brown eyes. Eyes that telegraph he is conflicted about telling me something. Oh dear Lord, do I have rum syrup on my chin?

Angelina pokes her head in the door, startling us. "Good night."

"Good night. And thank you for the most delightful dinner," I say, rubbing my chin just in case while Marco hastily places the medicines back in their appropriate spots. "I hope we shall have another opportunity to dine on spaghetti and meatballs."

Marco lets out a snort. Angelina smiles before she leaves, politely pretending as I am, that there is a real possibility that we could repeat tonight's conviviality. Marco puts the cherry crate away, and I turn off the desk lamp. When Marco gets to the office door, he stops so abruptly that I have to put my hand on his back to keep from running up on his heels. Marco turns, his face inches from mine.

"Miss Virginia, I wanted to say…*Si nu baba*." Marco

pulls at his collar. "You are *baba*."

"Thank you, I think." I guess there are worse things he could compare me to.

"No, it's a phrase we use a lot. It means, 'You are a real treasure.' Your father would have been proud of you today. You are a fine nurse, Virginia." Marco leans in and kisses me on both cheeks. "Good night."

As I stand dumbfounded, Marco turns on his heel and leaves.

"I think you are *baba*, too," I say too late.

Marco pokes his head back around the door. A cocky smile lights up his face. "*Grazie, bella.*"

Just as I work up the courage to return Marco's kiss on both cheeks, Angelina calls his name with a tinge of warning in her voice and holds out his coat. I mutely follow Marco and Angelina out onto the front stoop, cursing my missed opportunity. I watch the pair walk exhaustedly arm-in-arm, huddled under a worn umbrella until they turn the corner.

I close the front door and rest my head against it. My cheeks still register Marco's kiss. I pinch my index finger and thumb together and pull them across my chest horizontally. *Perfect.*

"VIRGINIA!" Kit's bellow from the kitchen bursts my spell.

I float into the kitchen to see Kit up to her elbows in dirty water. Undoubtedly another first for Kit today.

"These dishes aren't going to wash themselves." Kit must be regretting her offer already. "Grab a dishtowel and dry them off. And don't you dare chip one. Or Mama will have your hide."

"No, she would dock Angelina's pay."

"True. So we can't breathe a word of this to anyone.

Ever."

"Why is it so scandalous to eat dinner in your own kitchen?"

Kit stops and stares at the pile of dirty dishes. "I'm not sure. It does seem quite ridiculous now, doesn't it?"

I walk behind Kit and wrap my arms around her corseted waist like I used to do to Mama when I was eight years old. I give her a tight squeeze.

"Thank you, Kit," I mumble into her shoulder blade.

"For what?"

"The coffee. The rum-soaked *baba*. For helping me break the rules today."

I can feel Kit's breath catch in her lungs even with her corset on. "That's what older sisters are for. Tonight, we eat in the kitchen with the help. Tomorrow, we chain ourselves to the White House gate together in protest."

"Please, no."

"I make no promises." Kit wipes her hands on the apron she has borrowed from Angelina and turns around. "I do promise to keep helping you on your journey wherever, whenever, however I can. No matter what anybody else says, Ginny, follow your dreams. Be your own woman."

"I promise."

Kit wraps her arms around me and squeezes me tightly. "Ah, you are growing up so fast. Just wait. Soon you can escape this place. Escape this life. Escape Philadelphia."

Kit turns back to the sink and scoops up a soap bubble in her hand. With a gentle puff of air, Kit sends the bubble aloft. We watch it float away and sigh in tandem when it bursts on the edge of the kitchen table.

"But first...the dishes." Kit releases an irritated sigh. "I must say, I don't enjoy this part of being a modern woman."

"Shove over." I roll up my sleeves. "This modern woman isn't afraid to get her hands dirty."

THIRTEEN

A BREAK FROM each other was just the soothing balm my family needed, but it also lit a fire in my belly. Now that I've seen all of the exciting things outside of my tiny, sheltered world, I don't want to go back into it. Especially if it means that I only see Marco for a few minutes each day.

"Ask him," Marco whispers on Monday morning when he intersects me in the foyer before school. "Philadelphia needs more skilled nurses. Your father even said so. Ask him to let you assist again, even if it is only in the afternoons."

"I am not a skilled nurse though," I say, putting on my coat.

"But you learn quickly. And you already have more bedside manner than *she* will ever possess. Sometimes the thing that can heal the most is a kind word...." Marco reaches out and tucks a lock of stray hair behind my ear. "And maybe the pleasure of seeing a pretty face."

Marco starts when I wrap my hand around his.

"Your hands are skilled, too," I say, holding Marco's stare. "We can work circles around Nurse Brighton when we are a pair."

Marco rotates his hand until he can lace his fingers through mine. "Then, let's be a pair."

A whoosh of cool air rushes down the hallway. Nurse Brighton is on time for work now that Daddy is back home from Boston. Her lips purse together when she sees us. Marco drops my hand like it's a snake and sprints toward the kitchen.

"I'm going to be late for school." I snatch my school books off the sideboard and dart around Nurse Brighton without so much as a greeting.

I lumber off to school thinking about what Marco said. My mind drifts away to us standing in the foyer together, Marco's fingers entwined with mine. Marco leaning in to kiss my cheeks. My mouth. Unfortunately, I stay in this heady state all day long. It is so bad that Miss Douglas makes me stay inside at recess after she catches me daydreaming. Also, in my irritation, I may have mumbled how pointless studying *King Lear* is.

On my walk back home at the end of the day, I steel myself to confront Daddy. I must be allowed to go back to work with him even if it is for only a few hours each afternoon. Maybe not even every afternoon. These hands are eager to work. Eager to learn. My resolve pops like a soap bubble as soon as I open the front door.

"That was not our agreement!" Kit's voice echoes through our home.

I tiptoe toward Daddy's office.

"I want him fired!" Mama's shrill voice freezes me in my tracks.

"Now, let's not be rash, Eleanor." Daddy uses his calm, your-toe-is-going-to-have-to-be-amputated voice.

"I am not being rash, Charles. It appears that in my absence on Saturday, our family has suddenly become a rich source of gossip. Between Katherine's *hobby* and Virginia gallivanting all over Devil's Pocket, I can scarcely show my face in public. I have never been so ashamed of my family in my whole life!"

"How is having an opinion and a voice ruining our family's name?" Kit says.

"You were arguing in the middle of the street with Reverend Brill."

"He said I should be ashamed of myself. That women's suffrage goes against God's plan."

"Katherine, your father and I have been more than patient with your little…hobby. This is not Radcliffe College. Your behavior has consequences here. For all of us. I will not stand idly by while you tarnish our family's name. If you are going to stay in this house, then you will follow our rules. If you need something to do, join the Red Cross with me. We could use more intelligent women there."

"Yes, you most certainly could."

I hear a smack, and Kit rushes out of Daddy's office with her hand to her cheek. She barrels past me, taking the stairs two at a time.

"Kit, wait!" I rush up the stairs behind her.

Kit already has her travel bag open and is hurling her belongings into it by the time I make it through the door.

"Kit, please, wait."

"I'm leaving. I'm tired of living in such an oppressive, backward, ignorant household."

"Where are you going? Radcliffe?"

"No, to my dear friend's home. She has been begging me to come stay with her for ages. I'm sure she won't mind an impromptu visit."

I put my hand on top of the dress Kit is folding. "Please

don't leave."

Kit looks at me. Her eyes are glassy. "I must. And someday you will too, Ginny."

I rush back downstairs and burst into Daddy's office. Daddy slumps in his favorite leather chair while Mama continues to pace and squawk in front of him. I hold onto the doorframe for support.

"Why are you doing this? I don't want Kit to run away." I stuff a sob down deeper into my chest.

"And you!" Mama jabs her index finger at me. "You are *not* to go to Devil's Pocket or Little Italy or anywhere with that boy again. Do you hear me, Virginia? The vile words and insinuations...you will go to school, come straight home, and go to the Red Cross with me. That is all."

"But Mama—"

Mama silences me with her icy glare before turning back on Daddy. "I want him gone, Charles. Today."

"He's a good man, Eleanor." Daddy runs a hand through his rapidly receding hairline. "A little misguided and impetuous, but—"

"You have a nurse now, Charles. You don't need that boy anymore. Chauffeurs are a dime a dozen. Hire a new one."

"Please, Daddy, don't," I say.

"Be quiet, Virginia," Mama says.

I step deeper into Daddy's office and put my hands on my hips. "No, I won't. Marco is more of a healer than Nurse Brighton will ever be."

"To your room, Virginia. Now!" Mama points at the door.

I turn on my heel and head toward the door, hot tears stinging my eyes. As I step out into the hallway, I see Marco and Angelina standing outside of the kitchen door. Marco stands like a statue, his protective arms around his sister who is silently sobbing into his chest. Marco's eyes pierce all the way through my body, down to my soul. I turn around and barge back into Daddy's office.

"Nurse Brighton—" Mama continues to lecture Daddy.

"Is a good-for-nothing, gossiping cow and should be fired." The venom flows out of my mouth freely. "She is jealous of Marco, and is doing everything in her power to have him fired."

"I said to your room, young lady."

I let Mama's words hang in the air. The poisonous viper curls back up in my stomach before it makes its second strike.

"No," I say.

"Pardon me?" Mama's voice is granite hard.

"I said, no, Mother." I push past Mama and collapse on the floor next to Daddy's chair. I grab his hand and make him look at me. "Please, Daddy. Don't send Marco away. He's going to be a wonderful doctor one day. I've seen what he can do. Give him another chance. Let Marco show you what he can do."

"Virginia...sweetheart." Daddy pats my hand with his.

"I was the one who insisted on going to Devil's Pocket. I was tired of being left behind. He protested, but I made Marco take me with him."

"Virginia Marie Jackson, you will go to your room at once, and you will not come down for dinner," Mama says.

"Enough, Eleanor," Daddy says with a weary sigh. "Leave her be. I will deal with my disobedient daughters."

Mama harrumphs and exits the room.

"Your mother is right, I'm afraid." Daddy continues patting my hand. "You know I don't listen to gossip, but I can't ignore Nurse Brighton's report. How you and Marco sneaked off to Devil's Pocket together, stranding her here, so you could steal 'precious romantic moments' alone."

"Daddy, changing the fetid bandages of what is left of Mr. O'Connor's feet is hardly a romantic moment."

"True." Daddy chuckles. "I should have never asked you to help me this summer. I opened that Pandora's Box and now I can't get it closed again."

"Daddy, Marco and I make a good pair. You should have seen us with Mrs. Carnes," I say. Instead of looking proud, Daddy looks horrified. "So, we should have let Mrs. Carnes suffer until you returned? No. You instructed Marco and Nurse Brighton to attend three patients on Saturday. Nurse Brighton refused, so I took matters into my own hands. I am not going to let someone suffer because your nurse is lazy, inept, and has an abysmal bedside manner. She wasn't here on Saturday as instructed, so I took her place. I am not sorry for that. I refuse to be sorry for that."

Daddy is silent for a few minutes. The air coming in and out of his lungs has a slight wheeze to it. He's tired. Worn down.

"I won't fire Marco," he says finally. "But he won't be anything but the chauffeur for a while, and you will be nothing but your mother's dutiful daughter until otherwise notified."

"Daddy—"

"Please, Ginny, I'm tired. Oh so, tired. Please be the one woman in this household who gives me peace. Just for a little while. Until your mother's pride is repaired."

"I will. But know that I *am* going to medical school."

"Yes, I know. Anna filled my ears with your plans every chance she got. If you want to attempt medical school, I won't stand in your way. But if you change your mind and want to settle down with a nice boy—a nice Rittenhouse Square or Main Line boy, I should clarify—then I would be just as happy."

"But I wouldn't."

I hear Kit coming down the stairs. Daddy doesn't follow me when I race to the door.

"Please don't leave, Kit." I grab her elbow to keep Kit from opening the front door.

"I am going to my dear friend's home. Please tell Mother and Father that I will return in a few days or maybe a week or so."

I follow Kit outside and down the front stairs to the sidewalk. I hear Daddy call Marco's name from inside.

"Wait, you don't have to do this," I say.

"Yes, I do. Not only for me but for you, too." Kit puts down her traveling bag and hatbox to embrace me. "Be strong. Stand up for yourself. Never apologize for who you are or what you want."

Kit releases me and scoops up her belongings. She squares her shoulders, lifts her head, and marches down sidewalk. I trail after her. We aren't ten feet down the street when the Cadillac pulls up beside us and stops.

"Miss Katherine." Marco jogs around to the passenger side. "Your father has instructed me to take you to the train station or wherever in Philadelphia you wish to go."

Kit stands there, mentally debating her choices. She looks down at her fashionable, but uncomfortable, shoes and sighs.

"I will allow you to take me to the Broad Street Station." Kit holds out her traveling bag and hatbox toward Marco.

Marco opens the door and collects Kit's belongings from her. After giving my hands a final squeeze, Kit slips inside. While Marco tucks the traveling bag and hatbox into the trunk, I look up at my home. Mama watches from her bedroom window and Daddy from the window of his office. Neither of them tries to stop Kit. Kit has "run away" from home on multiple occasions over the years, but has always returned. Usually within a few hours after her pocket money has run out and her temper has cooled down. This time though, I think she means it.

"Excuse me, Miss Virginia," Marco says because I am blocking the open door.

"Of course." I take a step back.

When Marco passes me, he slides a tiny scrap of paper into my hand. I clamp the note to my hip. Tears sneak out the corner of my eyes as they pull away, especially when Kit looks out the back of the Cadillac's window and waves a gloved hand at me. My heart shatters. I take the front steps two at a time and slam the front door closed before retreating to my bedroom. Only when my door is securely locked, and my pillow soaked do I look at the piece of paper crushed in my fist.

Apple tree. 9 p.m.

FOURTEEN

I STAY IN my room the rest of the day. And even though Mama relents and invites me to dinner, I refuse. With the storm raging in my stomach right now, I don't think I could keep anything down anyway. I unfold and refold the tiny scrap of paper a hundred times while willing time to move faster. Though the house is silent, I know my parents are still awake. I open my bedroom door a crack and peek down the hall. Light filters out from under the door of Mama's boudoir. She'll be up for hours completing correspondence or rectifying the household accounts or whatever she does to help fill the hole in her heart. I close my door when I hear my parents' bedroom door open. Daddy's cane-foot-foot gait passes in front of my door a moment later and down the stairs, undoubtedly on his way to the parlor with a pillow in his hand. Part of me feels badly for him. The never-ending tempest in our home is wearing on his body more than ever. But he also chose to allow Kit to walk away from our family. He's made his bed tonight, and it's on the settee in the parlor.

The grandfather clock downstairs chimes nine o'clock. It's now or never. I rush to the window, slide open the sash, and climb out onto the limb. Soon after, I settle into the crook of the tree and trace my finger over the initials carved into the bark a long time ago. The wind picks up, rustling the thick layer of leaves and fruit around me. I take a deep breath. The air rushing in smells like wood smoke, ripe apples, and anticipation. My heart skips when I hear the sound of booted feet echoing through our brick courtyard.

"Virginia?" Marco whispers from the base of the tree. "Are you there?"

"Shh. Yes." I glance toward my open window. If Mama checks on me, the small amount of light from my room will give away my hiding spot.

I hear a grunt and the rustling of leaves as Marco ascends the tree. A moment later, Marco is halfway up but on the opposite side.

"Ow!" Marco rubs the top of his head after it collides with the branch above him. "This was easier when I was younger and shorter."

Marco continues to scramble around until our heads are of equal heights. He hooks one arm around the trunk and swings his upper body around the tree.

"I brought you something to sweeten this sour day." The faint light of my room bounces softly off Marco's face. "You are going to have to get it though. Because if I fall out of the tree while retrieving it, my arm won't be the only thing broken, if your father catches me. Check the left inside pocket of my coat."

I pause, both intrigued and slightly mortified at the same time.

"I know, it isn't proper," Marco says. "Never mind, I'll get it."

I put my hand on Marco's shoulder to stop his retreat back around the tree. With my left hand anchoring me to the tree trunk, I reach my right hand out and slide my fingertips underneath the collar of his hand-me-down coat. Marco's heart hammers against my thumb as my hand drifts down his chest to his ribs. When I lean in closer, trying to find the pocket sewn inside his coat, the edge of my sleeve pulls back. Marco's lips suddenly brush my temple, and my body ignites. My fingertips quickly abandon their task. Instead, they cup the side of Marco's face. Marco dips his head and presses a warm kiss on the inside of my wrist. I'm sure he can feel my racing pulse. When my hand doesn't leave his face, Marco's lips continue to trail up my exposed skin until they meet the fabric of my sleeve. Marco's dark eyes look up at me. Waiting. Wondering. Wanting.

I press my lips gently on Marco's right cheek and then his left. But it's not enough. Before I lose my nerve, I press my lips against Marco's.

His eyes slowly open when I pull away. "May we please get out of this tree so I can kiss you back properly?"

"Yes."

Marco swings back around the tree trunk. His booted feet hit the ground seconds later. Meanwhile, I carefully slide down the tree one branch at a time. I have never fallen out of my beloved tree. Tonight will not be a first. Finally, I make it to the lowest branch and hang most unlady-like preparing to jump to the ground. Marco steps up in front of me and places his hands on my waist. I let go of the branch and float gently toward the ground like I'm Anna Pavlova at The Met. Marco's hands don't release my waist even after my boots touch *terra firma*. My heart slams around inside my ribcage, my corset the only thing keeping it from bursting out of my chest. Marco leans down and presses his lips against mine.

His lips travel from my mouth to my ear. "I have a confession. I've wanted to do that since Saturday."

"I have a confession," I whisper back. "I've wanted you to do that since long before Saturday."

"Then we should make up for lost time."

As this will probably be the first and last romantic moment we will ever share, I pull Marco in closer to me. His lips find mine, and this time they are not chaste. They are brazen and hungry. Heart flutters and butterfly wings quickly transform into bolts of lightning from my lips to the pit of my belly.

"Thank you," Marco says when we finally must take a breath. "For earlier today."

"I'll never get to see you again. Mama will make certain of it."

"Yes, you will." Marco pulls me into him until my cheek rests against his chest. His heart races as the heat flows from his body to mine. "I don't know how yet, but I will think of something. Don't give up on me."

"Never."

Marco steps back and reaches deep into his inner coat pocket. A moment later, he deposits a paper cone into the palm of my hand. I unroll the top and pull out what I knew would be inside.

"*Grazie*," I say, and Marco doesn't even correct my pronunciation this time.

I bring a lemon drop up to Marco's lips. He takes the candy from me, kissing my fingertips in thanks. Marco's lemon-flavored kisses sweeten my day more than the entire contents of Miss Nan's Confectionary could ever do. The faint sound of the grandfather clock striking ten filters out my bedroom window.

"As much as I would love to stand out here all night

with you, I guess I'd better let you find the warmth of your bed." Marco rubs his warm hands on my upper arms. "I don't want you to become ill again."

"Goodbye, Marco."

"Not goodbye, *bella,* but good night. You wait and see."

"I'm going to hold you to your promise." I tuck the paper cone of lemon drops back into the inner pocket of Marco's coat. "Save these until our next rendezvous. As a promise that there will always be some sweetness in our lives no matter how sour the rest of the world is."

"I promise." Marco kisses me one last time. "Do I need to give you a boost?"

"No, but I would like one anyway."

Marco squats down and laces his fingers together. I put my booted foot in his palms. He hurls me heavenward with so much force that I almost overshoot the tree limb. I hook my toe in the knot and slowly pull myself up the tree. Marco stands under me with his arms spread just in case. I should probably hold my skirts close to my legs, but I don't. I stop to pluck a ripe apple from our tree before climbing back through my window.

"*Buona notte, bella,*" Marco whispers after I am safely back inside.

"*Buona notte,* my Romeo." My heart fissures as I close the window sash and watch Marco disappear into the darkness.

I flop back onto my bed and put my cool fingertips against my still warm, tingling lips. Is this what it means to be a modern woman? I wonder for a long time until my empty stomach growls in a most undignified manner. I polish the apple on the bodice of my dress before taking an enormous bite. The sweet juice drips all down my chin. Oh, how I wish Kit were here for one of our late-night tête-à-têtes. Or even Anna, though despite her interest in Mrs. Sanger's work, finds long discussions about boys frivolous and tedious. One day, my friend. One day, someone will catch your eye, and I will have to listen to your tales of heart flutters and butterfly wings and all that ridiculous rot.

FIFTEEN

MONDAY CIRCLES BACK around again, and my mood is as dark as the stormy morning sky. The thought of walking to school in the deluge adds salt to my wounds. I'm just pulling my umbrella out of the canister when Daddy blows through the front door.

"It's not fit for man nor beast today." Daddy wipes his wet face with the handkerchief I made for him last Christmas, the one with the looping J in crimson in the corner.

"May I stay home then?"

Daddy pats my head. "No."

I groan and gather my books off the sideboard.

"The Cadillac is all packed, sir." Marco's honeyed voice washes down the hallway from the kitchen, and a ray of sunshine penetrates the darkness of my morning. I turn to drink in the sight. Marco stands outside the kitchen door with a Thermos flask in his hand. "Angelina made some hot tea for you, sir. She wondered if you would like a slice of freshly-made apple cake to go with it."

"That would be delightful." Daddy shuffles through the pile of out-going correspondence on the sideboard. "And, Marco, telephone the hospital and let Dr. Porter know that

I've been delayed by a half hour, but that Nurse Brighton should arrive shortly."

Marco's eyebrows knit in confusion, but he immediately answers, "Yes, sir."

"Be ready to leave in five minutes, Ginny. We'll take you to school this morning."

There is a spring in Marco's step as he returns to the kitchen. Suddenly, I feel lighter, too.

We drive in silence the short trip to school, Marco and I not daring to say a word to each other. While Daddy reads his newspaper, I spend the time studying Marco's countenance. Remembering the spicy scent of his hair tonic. The feel of his taut chest muscles under my fingertips. The taste of lemon on his lips. It's only been a week, yet it feels like a lifetime ago. Daddy yawns, interrupting my heated thoughts.

"Don't wait up for me tonight, Ginny. It's going to be a long day, I fear. Dr. Porter telephoned early this morning. He said there are six hundred sailors at the Navy Yard down with the influenza now and yesterday the first civilian was diagnosed with it."

"Daddy, let me come with you to the hospital. I can help. I can—"

"Go to school," Daddy finishes for me. "End of discussion."

Marco's shoulders slump. Lightning streaks across the sky and a thunderous boom announces my arrival at the front gates of school. The heavens continue to pour like a personal message to Noah. Marco opens the car door for me, an umbrella at the ready.

"There is a large puddle here, Miss Jackson," Marco says as I step out onto the Cadillac's running board. "May I assist you over it?"

I nod. Marco slips a strong arm around my waist and helps me leap across the puddle that he straddles. A puddle, I notice, that could have been avoided if he had pulled the Cadillac forward a few more feet. Marco immediately releases me when my booted feet hit the sidewalk, but an impish smile crosses his face. As he delivers me to school, Marco makes sure that the umbrella completely covers me even though it means water is pouring off the brim of his cap. Several of the upper-level girls loiter near the front door, witnessing my escorted arrival. Margaret Vaughn's jaw fairly hits the floor.

"Thank you, Mr. D'Orio," I say, stepping from underneath the umbrella.

"My pleasure, Miss Jackson." Marco tips his cap at my classmates who are giggling and gossiping behind their hands. "Ladies."

The giggles turn into mocking laughter as I head down the hallway. A stray drop of water makes its way through my hair and down the side of my cheek. I reach into my coat pocket to retrieve my handkerchief, but my fingers tangle in something metallic. I pull out a chain necklace with a matching pressed silver heart pendant attached to it. I flip it over in my palm. The words *Ti Amo* are etched into it.

"What have you got there, Virginia?" An arm suddenly grabs mine.

I pull the necklace tight inside my fist. "Nothing."

"Nothing? Nothing at all?" Margaret says, her eyes like daggers. I have avoided Margaret as much as possible since the Red Cross incident. She grabs my wrist with her free hand. "Then what is this?"

Margaret squeezes my wrist so tightly that my hand opens in pain. The necklace drops to the floor. Margaret and I both scramble to grab it. A black leather boot stomps down on it first though, smashing the tips of both Margaret's and my fingers.

"To whom does this trinket belong?" Miss Douglas says, her foot still firmly on my necklace.

"It's mine, Miss," I say, shaking the pain out of my fingers.

"Then you will kindly put it away." Miss Douglas removes her foot. I snatch the pendant and plunge it deep into my coat pocket. "You are dismissed, Miss Vaughn. A moment, Miss Jackson." When the hallway clears, Miss Douglas opens the book in her hand and pulls out an envelope. She holds it out to me. "Against my better judgment, I am going to honor my dear cousin Beatrice's request."

I take the letter with my name written on the front. It's not written in a stranger's hand though. I recognize Kit's loopy handwriting immediately. "Thank you, Miss."

"Virginia," Miss Douglas's voice is quiet but firm. "This is a fool's game. I want suffrage as much as Katherine and Beatrice do, but this isn't the way to do it. Now, go, read your letter and be back before class commences."

I duck into the lavatory to have a few moments of privacy.

September 14, 1918
Wynnefield

Dearest Ginny,

I wasn't quite honest with you recently, and it has weighed heavily on my mind. I'm not sure what will happen over the next few months, but I am bound and determined to do my part to the fullest this time. I won't shy away from conflict even if it means my own comfort is at stake. Though I had Marco take me to the Broad Street Station, I never left Philadelphia as I may have implied. Instead, I am preparing over in Wynnefield at the home of my dear friend Beatrice Douglas. We will leave for our new adventure soon, though it may be another month before we are settled in Washington. If you see my face on the front page of the newspaper, know that I chose this path willingly and with no regrets. I don't wish to harm our parents or cause embarrassment to you, but if that is the price to pay, so be it. I apologize in advance. I wish I could send correspondence to our home, but instead I will send you updates on my adventures through your English teacher

Miss Douglas who is Beatrice's cousin and sympathetic to our cause. My dearest Ginny, I wish so much that I could be there with you now to guide you on your own adventure. Know that my work will ripple into yours. Please be patient with me.

Your loving and devoted sister,
Kit

I ignore the polite tapping on the lavatory door as I try to make sense of Kit's letter. My sister is leaving. For good this time. As many times as I have wished that she was gone, this is not what I meant. I want to take it all back.

I tuck the letter into my pocket and pull out the necklace. *Ti Amo.* My fingertips trace the engraved letters. I don't know what the words mean, but I can guess. This day is so full of conflicting feelings that they threaten to pull me apart at the seams.

A persistent tapping begins again on the door.

"A moment, please," I say to whoever is in need of the lavatory. I put on the necklace. The chain is so long that the heart pendant sits appropriately over my real one. I contemplate wearing it back to class just to aggravate Margaret. I sigh and tuck it into my bodice instead.

The tapping turns into fevered banging. I open the door, and an underclassman yanks me out the door.

"Rude!" I say as she slams the door in my face.

To her credit, Miss Douglas doesn't make me stand in the

corner for being tardy to her class. There are mumbles of "teacher's pet" from Margaret as I slide into my assigned desk next to hers. I place my hand on my chest and the cool metal of the pendant presses into my skin. I wish I could announce my secret to the world—or at least to my nosy classmates—, but instead, I will have to keep it and the promise of more lemon drop-flavored kisses to myself.

The irony that Miss Douglas would choose Tennyson's poem *In Memoriam* as our in-class assignment is not wasted on me.

"'Tis better to have loved and lost, Than never to have loved at all." Even Margaret's nasal, monotone recitation of the famous poem sends me wildly digging for my handkerchief.

"This poem seems to resonate with you, Miss Jackson," Miss Douglas says as I dab at my eyes.

I nod. Tennyson may have been writing about his deceased friend, but my mind travels back to Kit...and to Marco.

"In that case, why don't you come to the board and write a line for our class poem." Miss Douglas holds out her chalk to me.

I sit frozen, everyone's eyes on me until Miss Douglas clears her throat changing her request to a demand. As I walk to the blackboard, scenes from the apple tree and of Kit driving away flash back and forth in my mind. Nothing comes out of the end of the piece of chalk though when I put it against the blackboard. As I stand frozen, I can hear the stagnant air rushing in and out of my lungs. Whatever Margaret whispers to the girls sitting around her causes them to snicker.

I don't apologize for the *screeeeeeing* sound my nails make against the chalkboard when I write with the tiny nub of chalk:

Losing someone you love is like having a puncture in your heart so deep that no amount of catgut can ever close it. Slowly you hemorrhage to death.

Miss Douglas reads my stanza aloud and winces. "Well, that is certainly inventive—if a bit repulsive—imagery." Several of my classmates chuckle and Margaret continues to shoot daggers at me. "You may be seated. Miss Scott, front and center. You may add the next line."

I return to my desk, as Miss Douglas coaxes her dullest student into producing something of value that is also spelled correctly. When Miss Douglas turns her back to us, Margaret leans forward and stage whispers to her lackey Lucretia, "Just when you think the Jackson sisters can't possibly be more outrageous, one of them has an affair with her chauffeur."

"I am *not* having an affair with our chauffeur," I say from between gritted teeth, keeping my head held high and facing forward.

"So you weren't joyriding with that boy through Devil's Pocket recently?"

"No, well yes, but no."

"So which is it?"

"We were not joyriding. We were attending to patients."

"That's what you may call it, but we all know the truth. Don't we?" Margaret says, and the girls around her concur.

That's it. Margaret wins. I completely lose my composure. "You…don't…know…*anything*."

"I know that your sister was arrested."

Lucretia and some of the girls gasp. Whether they truly didn't know or are simply playing their part in this theatrical display, I don't know.

"And so was your Aunt Harriet, I'd like to remind you. So put that in your pipe and smoke it, MARGARET VAUGHN!"

I look around to see the whole class—including Miss Douglas—staring at us, mouths agape. Anna always says that honesty is the best policy. This frequently blows up in her face, but I do see why it is occasionally helpful. I stand up and glare at all my classmates. I take a deep breath to steady my voice and bring it back to a more lady-like volume.

"Since everyone is so interested in my private life today, allow me to set the record straight. One, my sister Katherine is a suffragist. Two, she was arrested in February 1917 for demonstrating in front of the White House as one of the Silent Sentinels but released to my father without being charged. Three, I aspire to attend the Woman's Medical College of Pennsylvania and train to become a surgeon. Therefore, when I travel with my father, chauffeur, or any other man into Devil's Pocket, know that I am attending to patients and not joyriding. And furthermore, what I do with my leisure time is none of your damn business."

Some of my classmates gasp. Others giggle. Miss Douglas looks ready to throttle me.

"Ladies! And I use that term loosely today. Ladies, you will cease immediately." Miss Douglas whacks her desk so hard with her ruler that it breaks off, which of course makes the other girls laugh even harder. "Miss Vaughn, you will stay in at recess and write 'I will not interrupt class with my gossip' one hundred times. Miss Jackson, you will also stay in and write, 'I will comport myself as a lady while at school' one hundred times. If anyone else would like to join them, then I dare you to make a peep. Those who would like to enjoy their recess will silently compose their own poem until I call time. Am I understood?"

"Yes, Miss," we say in unison though a few muffled giggles continue to sneak out during the remainder of class.

At the end of class, I catch Miss Douglas's eye. She gives me a small smile and a head nod. Unfortunately, she still makes me stay in at recess and write lines on the blackboard until my hand threatens to dislocate from my wrist.

THE WALK HOME is dry, but both the sky and my thoughts are filled with black clouds. As I pass the parlor, I see Nurse Brighton is already having afternoon tea including a generous slice of apple cake. Does this woman ever work? I hang up my coat and deposit my books on the sideboard, determined to enjoy my tea and cake in the kitchen with someone much more agreeable. Plus, maybe Angelina will have some news about Marco for me.

"Angelina, may I have some hot tea and—" My breath catches in my chest.

Angelina is nowhere to be found, but Marco is asleep at the kitchen table on top of a pile of books and papers. A dog-eared copy of *Romeo & Juliet* lays flat on the table beside Marco's head. I tiptoe behind Marco so that I can read over his shoulder. Tucked underneath his head is a piece of paper. Up in the right-hand corner it reads:

As I lean in closer, Marco twitches. I don't want to wake him, but the ink from his essay is beginning to make a mirror image on his left cheek. I gently tug the paper from under Marco's head.

Marco jerks straight up in his chair. "I'm sorry. I didn't mean to—"

"Good afternoon, Mr. D'Orio." I use my fingers to comb out some of the matted curls stuck to the side of his head.

After confirming that we are alone, Marco wraps his fingers around my wrist and gently pulls me onto his lap. "Good afternoon to you, too."

I pull the necklace out of my bodice and cradle the pressed silver heart in my palm. "Thank you for your most thoughtful gift."

"You're welcome, *bella*."

"You know if Nurse Brighton or my father walk in on us, our goose is cooked," I say, but Marco wraps his arms tighter around my waist anyway.

"Dr. Jackson stayed at the hospital. He asked me to bring Nurse Brighton back here so that she could attend to any patients he might have. We've had a grand total of… none."

"At least you've had time to work on your schoolwork. What are you working on so industriously today?"

"Nothing." Marco turns his *Romeo & Juliet* essay over.

"Marco, I already saw it. In fact, I can read some of it on

your cheek." I use my thumb to wipe the ink off.

"It's hard to think today. My mind is everywhere except my work."

I finger the necklace. "Mine, too."

Marco takes a deep breath and wraps his hands around mine. "Did you see today's paper?"

I shake my head.

"The rumors were true," Marco continues, and my heart sinks. "Uncle Sam is so desperate for men for his War Machine that the draft age is being dropped to eighteen. They could draw my name as early as next month."

"No, oh no, no, no." I grip Marco's hands tighter.

"I mean, I did pray to see my brother again." Marco lets out a rueful chuckle. "But I meant in Little Italy, not in a trench somewhere in France."

"Don't say that. I couldn't bear it." I wrap my arms tightly around Marco's neck.

The sound of clinking china and booted feet echoes down the hallway. I jump up, straightening my skirt.

"I should go, Marco. No, you should go."

The footsteps come closer. I grab Marco by the hand and drag him into the pantry with me. I place my finger over Marco's smiling lips as we cram into the narrow pantry like sardines in a tin. Marco's foot hits a can of something making it topple over, but there is no room for him to bend down to right it. Meanwhile, the ropes of onions hanging up bang into my head. In the dim light sneaking around the edges of the door, I can see Marco biting his bottom lip to contain his laughter. I hush him. He snorts. The ridiculousness of our situation overtakes us until Marco pulls me in tight to his chest to muffle my giggling.

Nurse Brighton bursts through the swinging kitchen door. "Angelina? Angelina! Where is that girl? I finished my tea a quarter hour ago."

I hear Mama's tea things clatter against the counter. I pray that none of them chip, knowing who would get the blame and have her pay docked if they did.

"Those lazy Italians. Always shirking their duties," Nurse Brighton says.

I pull Marco closer to me to keep him from exploding out of our hiding place. Instead, he presses into me and whispers in my ear, "That's certainly the pot calling the kettle black."

"And where is that useless boy? Up to no good, I'm certain."

Marco tips my chin up and kisses me with enough passion to prove Nurse Brighton correct.

"No good at all," Marco whispers.

We continue with our clandestine kisses long after Nurse Brighton crashes back out the kitchen door. A stab of guilt punctures my heart as the same lips that denied my 'affair with the chauffeur' earlier now hunger for his kisses.

My heart clenches when I hear Mama's muffled voice mixed with Nurse Brighton's in the hallway. I drag Marco out of our hiding spot back into the kitchen.

"Hurry! Out the back door." I gather all of Marco's belongings into a hasty pile and press them into his chest.

"Your hair." Marco pushes my hair, which somehow came undone in the pantry, over my shoulder and pulls a stray piece of onion skin out of it.

"Don't worry about me. Go, quickly, before Mama catches you."

Marco pulls me across the floor with him to the back door, depositing multiple kisses along the way.

"*Ti amo, bella.*" Marco kisses me one last time before slipping out the door.

I don't have time to respond, and I'm not sure I can anyway. Marco is barely around the corner of the house when Mama bursts into the kitchen. I pick up Nurse Brighton's teacup like it's mine.

"There you are. Where is Angelina? The Clarks are coming at four." Mama's eyes spot the still open pantry door.

"I was hungry," I say before she can ask and close the pantry door with my foot.

"You didn't eat the tea cakes, did you?"

Mama pulls the lid off her best cake plate and counts. A dozen mushroom-shaped *baba* sit in perfect symmetry on top. They are dry. Nonna D'Orio would be horrified.

"You know, I hear that in Little Italy they top their *baba* with rum sauce." Oh, what I would give to be sharing rum-soaked *baba* with Marco again tonight.

"Rum sauce? Honestly, Virginia. Not in this house. And this is exactly why you will not be going into the immigrant neighborhoods again. I do not even want to know what other improprieties you witnessed in Little Italy."

If Mama only knew the improprieties the onions just witnessed in her pantry. My heart flutters at the memory.

"Don't stand there lollygagging. Go dress for tea." Mama shooes me out of the kitchen. "Goodness gracious, Virginia, what has happened to your hair?"

Since "I let Marco run his hands through it" will most certainly be the wrong answer, I choose to answer truthfully, "It's been a tempestuous day. I seemed to have popped a few pins along the way."

"Well, go freshen up. The Clarks are bringing their nephew with them. I hear he is quite the head-turner at Villanova."

Unless he is a certain Italian boy, I doubt I will even

notice that he is in the room, but I also keep that comment to myself.

Mama leans in and sniffs me. "And use some of my toilet water. That will mask a multitude of sins in a pinch, including dirty hair."

SIXTEEN

NURSE BRIGHTON'S INEPTITUDE is now a well-known fact in Rittenhouse Square. With Daddy away at the hospital all day almost every day now, many of his regular high society patients have turned to Dr. Lakes for their routine care. He hasn't been to see Mr. O'Connor or Mrs. Maguire in weeks. The one good thing: Out of necessity, Daddy has allowed Marco to be his assistant again. Not me though. Even when Nurse Brighton feigned sickness to get out of going to Devil's Pocket to change Mr. O'Connor's bandages, Daddy still denied my request. Instead, I "knit my bit" and roll bandages. I'm sure I've rolled enough bandages to stretch to France and back. Mama has canceled three dinner parties in the last two weeks using the excuse of Daddy being away. There is a truth to that. He has been away. His paying patients have also been away. And to top it off, Nurse Brighton is eating through our sugar ration with reckless abandon thanks to her non-stop cups of tea during her workless days.

This, of course, makes me madder than a wet hen when I come home from school to find Nurse Brighton napping in Daddy's leather chair, a scandalous, dime novel slipping from underneath one of Daddy's medical journals.

I clear my throat. "Good afternoon, Nurse Brighton."

Nurse Brighton jumps to her feet. "I'll finish this article later. It was giving me a headache anyway."

She puts the journal—the book still poorly hidden inside—back on Daddy's desk.

"Another busy day," I say facetiously.

"Oh, yes. Would you care for a cup of tea?"

I do, but not with her. "No, thank you."

"Before I forget, your father wanted you to read this book." Nurse Brighton hands me a brown leather book with a frayed spine. The gold embossed lettering reads *Lectures on Surgery*.

"My father wants me to read this?" I highly doubt it, but I take the book from her anyway.

"I'm only repeating what *that Italian boy* said. Something about you studying the chapter on heart surgery. You know what, I bet that boy was playing a joke on me." Nurse Brighton goes to take the book back from me, but I snatch it to my chest.

"Yes, I remember now. Daddy and I were discussing this topic…um, at breakfast…yesterday. So glad he finally remembered. I'll leave you to your tea."

Thankfully, Nurse Brighton is easily distracted by her stomach. I whisk the book upstairs and flop down on my bed. I flip through the musty textbook until I find a piece of paper poking out.

Tonight. 9:00 p.m. Apple tree.
Ti Amo, Marco

My nervous system buzzes with anticipation. I wrap my arms around my pillow and pretend like it's Marco. I don't need one of Nurse Brighton's dime novels. My mind can construct its own romantic story just fine.

An insistent rapping on our front door interrupts my daydream. A moment later, the rapping turns into banging. Booted feet too fast to be Nurse Brighton's scurry up the hallway.

"I'm sorry, the doctor is not here, Mrs. Grant." Angelina's voice travels up the stairs.

"But my husband is bleeding!" a shrill voice follows up behind it.

Angelina continues to apologize as the woman becomes more hysterical by the moment. I wait for Nurse Brighton to step in. She doesn't. I tuck Marco's note under my mattress and go downstairs to investigate.

"May I help you…Mrs. Grant, was it?" I say to the woman who is berating Angelina.

"Finally." The woman pushes past Angelina into our home. A man, his arm bundled up tight, steps in behind her. "My husband. He's ripped the stitches Dr. Jackson put in a few days ago. I told him not to go back to work so soon, but did he listen? No, he did not. A nail head hooked the stitches in his arm and ripped them clean out."

"Bring your husband into my father's office. I'll fetch Nurse Brighton." I walk toward the kitchen, Angelina on my heels.

"She is not here," Angelina whispers when we get to the kitchen door.

"It's barely gone three o'clock. Where did she go?" I say, and Angelina shrugs. "Now what are we going to do?"

"I can telephone your father at the hospital. Maybe he can return. Or Marco."

"Yes, Marco." My heart flutters at the opportunity both to see Marco and to give him a chance to show Daddy and our community what he can do. "Don't bother my father with this request. Ask Marco to return instead. I'll clean the wound and prepare for new sutures."

When I return to Daddy's office, I find the giant of a man sitting on the examining table cradling his arm. Blood seeps through the tea towel at an alarming pace. Meanwhile, his wife flutters around him in a tizzy.

"I'm afraid Nurse Brighton has gone home for the day. My father's assistant, Mr. D'Orio, will be here shortly to stitch you back up." I wash my hands in the basin in the corner and put on my apron. "In the meantime, let me clean the wound and check for sepsis."

A concerned look telegraphs between the man and his wife. I know that look. It's the reason why Daddy insisted on hiring Nurse Brighton to attend to his blue-blooded patients.

"Mr. D'Orio is quite skillful. My father has been personally training him since so many of our doctors are overseas presently."

I pull the tea towel away. The J-shaped gash looks like an untied shoe, with blood oozing around the reopened part of the wound. The catgut suture thread hangs off the man's arm in a trail. I take a deep breath. The wound is deep, but it isn't dirty or maggot-infested.

"Mr. Grant, let me find you something to ease the pain before I rinse the wound."

I open the medicine cabinet to find it nearly empty. Even the staples—aspirin, laudanum, bicarbonate of soda, and Castor oil are depleted. There are a few bottles left near the back, but I don't know how much to give or even what they do.

"It seems my father is out of laudanum at the moment." I close the door. If Daddy isn't seeing patients here, why are we so low on medicine? Is Nurse Brighton falling down on this task, too? Or has Mama cut off the funding in an attempt to rectify our household budget? "I could fetch you a leather strap to bite down on like the olden days."

The man jams his hand down into his pocket and fishes out a flask. He takes several gulps.

"Then again, spirits can work in a pinch too." I bring the basin and pitcher of water over to the examination table. "You should put that away. My mother is a member of the Woman's Christian Temperance Union."

The wife takes the flask—and a swig herself—before slipping it into her coat pocket. I pull the tea towel back again, rinse the area, and bandage it back up again.

"Please keep pressure on the wound while I see what is delaying Mr. D'Orio." I walk calmly out of the room but then race down the hall to the kitchen. "Where is Marco? He should have been here by now."

Angelina looks up from where she is shelling peas and winces. "I do not think he is coming. I could only send a message to him through a nurse at the hospital."

I let out an exasperated sigh. Be careful what you ask for. God may give it to you. And in ways that you never intended. I need Marco. Or Anna. Or even Mama, though the mere sight of blood gives her the vapors. As I head back down the hall, I catch my reflection in the mirror next to the coat stand. The blood-splattered apron may belong to Nurse Brighton, but it is this debutante whose trial by fire begins today.

"Mr. and Mrs. Grant, I'm afraid Mr. D'Orio and my father have both been detained at the hospital. I will change the bandage one more time, and then you may go to the hospital for stitches."

"With that influenza goin' round. No, thank you, Missy."

Mrs. Grant takes her husband's meaty hand in hers. "He'd go in for stitches and come out in a pine box. I just know it."

"I ain't goin' to no hospital," Mr. Grant slurs. I suspect he's been self-medicating while I was gone.

"Or," I say, putting my hand to my breast, pressing the silver heart into my chest. "I could do it."

"A young girl like you? You got stitching experience?"

"Yes. Lots." On cloth and one pig's foot, but they don't need to know the details.

"Well then." Mr. Grant holds out his hand for the flask. "Let's get to it."

I gather the supplies slowly and methodically, part of me hoping that Marco will still suddenly appear. He doesn't. I poise the catgut-threaded needled over the prepared arm. Mrs. Grant presses her husband's face into her bosom, stroking his hair and whispering encouraging words into his ear. Mr. Grant is so inebriated that he doesn't even flinch when the needle pierces his skin. I use Daddy's previous stitches as my guide. I pull the wound together stitch by stitch, careful to keep my pinky from dropping into the field. Soon you can't tell my new stitches from Daddy's old ones. The telephone rings just as I make my final stitch. I don't let it distract me. Within minutes, I have the wound tied off, the field cleansed one last time, and the arm bandaged.

"I think that will about do it, Mr. Grant." I rinse my hands off with the last of the water from the pitcher and dry them on my apron.

Mr. Grant is in a stupor and has drooled all over the front of his wife's dress, but Mrs. Grant nods her head.

"Thank you, Miss. Your pa couldn't have done much better." Mrs. Grant pulls a silver half dollar out of her pocket and holds it out to me. "For your services today. Go on now. Take it. I would've paid your pa the same. Equal pay for equal work, I always say."

"Thank you." I take the coin and slip it in my pocket.

Before I can ask Mrs. Grant if she is acquainted with Kit or Beatrice Douglas, a crash and wailing comes from the kitchen. I burst into the kitchen a moment later to find Angelina on the floor with peas spread all around her. Angelina looks up at me. Tears stream down her cheeks.

"*Mio fratello*." Angelina rocks herself. "My brother. He's dead."

I sink to my knees on the floor and whisper, "Marco?"

"Domenico," Angelina says between sobs.

I wrap my arms around Angelina. "We need to tell Marco. But first, we need to take you home. Your mother must be devastated."

"Is everything okay, Nurse Jackson?" Mrs. Grant says from the doorway.

"My...friend, Miss D'Orio has received some distressing news. She needs to return to her family in Little Italy immediately."

"We can drive her home. It's the least I can do after you helped my husband."

With that Mr. Grant weaves down the hallway toward us, crashing into the sideboard as he comes.

"No, thank you. We'll hire a cab." I stand and pull Angelina to her feet. "Should I call one for you also, Mrs. Grant?"

Mrs. Grant pulls herself up tall. "I am a modern woman, Nurse Jackson. I know how to drive our automobile just as proficiently as Mr. Grant does. Better, in fact, I'd argue."

"Well then, would you be so kind as to drive us to Little Italy?"

"I will." Mrs. Grant turns on her heel and starts back up the hallway, only stopping long enough to grab her husband by his good arm. "Come along now, darling."

Angelina and I climb into the back of the Grants' Model T as Mrs. Grant takes the wheel. Meanwhile, Mr. Grant falls into a sodden stupor in the passenger seat, his loud snores punctuating our drive from Rittenhouse Square to Little Italy.

"It's right there." I point to the D'Orios' home at the end of the street. "The row house on the right with the yellow roses underneath the window."

"You're not going to stay here, are you?" Mrs. Grant whispers to me when I follow Angelina out of the automobile.

"I'm not certain yet."

"Then I will wait for your return, Nurse Jackson." Mrs. Grant strips off her driving gloves and places them in her lap. "You yell if you require assistance. Mr. Grant was a champion boxer in his day."

I look over at Mr. Grant, perched on the passenger side window, mouth open wide and snoring. I don't expect him to be capable of defending anybody's honor for at least several more hours, but I thank Mrs. Grant anyway.

Angelina takes my hand and squeezes it when we arrive at the front door. A wave of grief crashes over me as soon as we step foot into their tiny home. Mrs. D'Orio sobs from her favorite chair, a telegram in her hand. Giorgio perches on the edge of the chair, patting his mamma on the back and whispering comforting words to her in Italian. Isabella sits at the foot of the chair, her braided head resting in her mamma's lap.

A sob lodges in my throat for a man I never knew. Angelina seems to forget that I am still attached to her as she stops in front of the small Catholic shrine tucked in the corner of their living room near the front door. Next to the statue of Jesus on the cross is a photograph of a man in uniform. My breath catches in my chest. It's like looking at a future Marco when all the traces of boyhood are gone.

Angelina looks at me, eyes wet with unfathomable grief. "Our brother. Our Domenico."

Angelina releases my hand so that she can light a candle at the shrine. She takes a circle of rosary beads off the top of the family *Bible* and loops them over her hands. I shift from foot to foot as she prays quietly. When Angelina finally crosses herself and puts the beads back down, I add an "amen."

"Mamma," Angelina says, and the sobbing begins all over again.

"Mrs. D'Orio, on behalf of my family, please accept our most humble condolences." The words don't register with her, or for me either honestly. I clear my throat. "I am sorry. I am so very, very sorry."

"*Grazie*," Mamma D'Orio says as tears continue to tumble down her cheeks.

"May I telephone Marco for you? He is at Pennsylvania Hospital with my father."

"We already did." Giorgio, a spitting image of Marco at thirteen no doubt, says. "He will be here soon."

"Thank you, Miss Virginia. You are too kind." Angelina squeezes my hand but pulls me toward the door. "Marco and Domenico were very close. The news will be difficult for him."

I want to stay. I want to pull out the necklace and show them that I belong here. I want to be the one who comforts Marco. But I don't belong here. Maybe one day, but not today.

"Of course. Please call on me, on my family, for anything," I say.

"Thank you."

I open the door to find a young woman on the other side. A young woman with peaches-and-cream skin holding a baby with big hazel eyes and an unruly patch of dark hair. I know her.

Before I can exchange any pleasantries with Miss Shannon, Angelina says, "You should come back later. This is not a good time."

"We are family, Angelina." Miss Shannon enters the D'Orio home anyway. "Marco asked me to come."

Mrs. D'Orio pushes out of her chair. A stream of Italian words—and gestures—flow out of her. Giorgio grabs his mother's arm to halt her charge to the front door.

"You're not welcome here, Miss Shannon," Giorgio translates, though he doesn't need to.

"Marco is heartbroken." Miss Shannon—and her now screaming baby—press further into the D'Orios' home, pushing me backward into the altar alcove. "I want to comfort him."

I bump into the shrine causing Domenico's picture to slide off the small shelf. I barely save it before it hits the floor.

"I want to comfort him," I say, knowing that no one can hear me over their heated quarrel. "I want to help put his shattered heart back together."

"What of your grandchild?" Miss Shannon yells at Mrs. D'Orio. "When are you going to stop denying that we exist? We are *la famiglia* too! Why can't you listen to Marco?"

"Please, Miss Virginia, please…." A mortified Angelina takes the picture frame from my hand and looks at the door.

I know I've overstayed my welcome. I have no right to be here at all. I am not Marco's only *bella*. I am not *la famiglia*. I will never be *la famiglia*. I rush out the front door, pulling it closed behind me. I rest my forehead against the roughhewn door, drawing in deep breaths of the cool early-autumn air and pushing the tears down deep in my chest. Neighbors peek out of windows and doors as the D'Orios' dirty laundry is aired in front of the entire community. I pull the silver heart out of its hiding place. With one quick yank, the chain snaps. I leave the necklace on the doormat, so Marco can tread on it as much as he's tread on my real heart.

"Are they all right in there?" Mrs. Grant says when I get in her automobile.

"I need to go home."

I can't help myself. I look back one last time. The front door opens, and Miss Shannon and her baby stumble out before it slams behind them. Miss Shannon openly cries, her foot resting on top of my necklace. I bite my lip to keep a sob from breaking through.

"Were you sweet on that Italian boy? The one who works for your pa," Mrs. Grant says when we are halfway back to Rittenhouse Square. My silence must be damning because she snorts in disgust. "You keep away from them immigrant boys. Nothin' but trouble, I tell you. Keep to your own kind, I say. I'm sure those Rittenhouse Square and Main Line boys are lining up for a moment of your time."

Keep to your own kind. I squeeze my eyes tight to keep the tears inside, but they slide out anyway.

SEVENTEEN

Knit your bit.
Step into your place.
Are YOU doing all you can?

THE POSTERS PLASTERED all over Rittenhouse Square shout at me as Mama and I walk the short distance home from church Sunday morning. Mama insists on stopping and chatting with a few of our well-heeled neighbors, especially ones with sons Kit's age. Appropriate conversations with the appropriate parents of appropriate young men. They should plaster another poster in Rittenhouse Square: *Stick to your own kind.*

"Mama, was Daddy your first love?" I say as we stroll through the park.

Mama stumbles a bit. "My word, Virginia. Where did that come from?"

"I'm simply curious. Now that I've had my debut, isn't it expected that I start meeting young men?"

"No. Well, yes, but no. We don't have to be in such a rush. Katherine is our priority right now. Presuming that she is in a much better humor when she returns from her little *adventure*." Mama shakes her head in exasperation.

"When Katherine returns, we will start hosting dinner parties and such again. Maybe this year we could even progress to a second meeting. Surely there is a young man out there for Katherine."

There is, but he can't be Kit's as much as Marco can't be mine. What a dismal state we are in. I hook my elbow through Mama's and we stroll in silence for a while.

"You didn't answer the original question," I say.

Mama looks out into the park, her eyes not focusing on anything in particular. "There was a boy before your father. Though I'm not sure I would say he was my first love. Maybe first reciprocal infatuation."

"How romantic," I tease. I pull Mama down onto a park bench near the statue of the Lion Crushing a Serpent. "Please continue. I want us to talk. Woman to woman."

Mama's forehead wrinkles in concern.

"No, not *that*." Plus, I probably already know more about that than Mama does anyway, thanks to Anna. "So, reciprocal infatuation…unless you would rather talk about the other matter, of course."

"No, I most certainly would not. Now then, when I was about your age, I worked in Grandfather Fisher's store after school and on Saturdays, so I didn't have time for many teas and dinner parties."

"Lucky."

"Don't be sassy. Anyway, I met a lot of different types of people while working in the store. Customers. Deliverymen. Craftsmen. Some of them tried to curry favor with my father through false flattery. As if their proclamations of my beauty or an invitation to dinner would somehow garner them better trading rates with Daddy."

Mama looks over at the young couple across the way

from us. They sit the prescribed distance away from each other on the park bench, but you can see the attraction flowing between them. That never happens at our home despite the continuous parade of sons, grandsons, nephews, and cousins that circle through our parlor when Kit is at home.

"And…," I lead Mama.

"There was one boy. He often came with his father to sell us goods for the store. We used to play checkers together every Tuesday while our fathers haggled over goods."

"Wait, you play checkers?"

"Yes, not in a long time, but I used to be quite skilled at it. Tuesday, their delivery day, became my favorite day of the week."

"That doesn't even sound like reciprocal infatuation. That sounds like friendship."

"That's what I thought, too. Then when we were about sixteen, he started leaving behind little gifts. A hair ribbon. A tea cake. A flower. Every Tuesday a little something would magically appear."

It's hard enough to picture Mama as a young woman, much less with someone who isn't Daddy. "Did he court you?"

"Oh, my, no." Mama puts a hand to her chest. "No, we were simply friends playing checkers. Nothing more."

"Why not? I'm no expert, but isn't a boy leaving you gifts considered courting?"

"It was a different time then. We were too different. Sometimes love doesn't conquer all." Mama closes her eyes, sealing away what must be a painful memory based on the depth of the wrinkle between her eyebrows. "Charles was the better match for me. For my family. Your heart thinks it knows best, but it doesn't. Feelings cool.

Being a proper match is much more important."

A figure suddenly blocks the sun.

"Mrs. Jackson. Miss Virginia." Everett Franklin Winthrop the Third tips his hat at us. "Fancy meeting you lovely ladies here."

"Hmm, it is the shortest route from church to both our homes, Everett. I believe the likelihood is pretty high," I say, and Mama pinches my upper arm. "I mean, it's always a pleasure to see you, Mr. Winthrop."

I stand up before Mama pinches me a second time. Behind Everett several paces back, his parents wait near the head of the lion statue. His mother catches my eye and then immediately ducks her head like she hasn't orchestrated everything that is probably about to happen.

"Mrs. Jackson, would you mind if I took a short stroll around the park with Virginia before we all head home for luncheon?" Everett smiles at Mama, and she melts.

Before I can decline, Mama says, "That would be lovely. We were just talking about you."

Everett's face lights up and he offers me his arm. "Shall we?"

"I would hate to disappoint my mother." I step off, but refuse to take his arm.

Everett trots up to me a moment later. He prattles on about himself—his school, his rowing team, his awards—until we are almost at the park gates nearest to my home.

Everett puts his hand on my arm to stop me from continuing straight home. "Are you angry with me?"

I stop. "No. Why?"

"You go out of your way to avoid me at church and social functions. Have I offended you? If so, I sincerely apologize and would like to make amends."

Everett's wounded puppy dog face catches me off guard.

I put my hand on his arm.

"No, you haven't wronged me." You simply don't ring my bell, as Anna would say.

Everett's pained expression relaxes. "Oh, thank heavens. I have been contorting myself into knots for months wondering what stupid thing I may have said or done to earn such ire from you."

His assessment surprises me. I thought I had handled our limited interactions with indifference, not anger. Guilt stabs my gut.

"And I am not angry with you. I apologize if I gave you that impression."

"I'm doing this all wrong." Everett drops his head and shifts from foot to foot. "No wonder you don't want to associate with me. I am the complete clodhopper Father says I am."

Laughing at his confession was probably inappropriate. Everett looks up through his dark eyelashes at me. A smile tugs at the side of his mouth.

"You are not a *complete clodhopper*," I say. "However, you can be a little too…."

"Attentive? I understand. I'm smothering you." Everett takes a step backward. "I apologize."

Everett's parents will soon be upon us. His father wears a disappointed look.

"Let's stroll some more." I turn on my heel and head back into the park. Before we pass his parents, I slip my hand into the crook of Everett's elbow. The disappointment on his father's face disappears. At least for the moment.

When we are out of their earshot, Everett clears his throat and blurts out, "Are you in love with him? That Italian boy. The one you allow to call you by your Christian name."

"Everett."

"I apologize. Complete clodhopper, I know. I only ask because I would like to court you. But if you've already given your heart away, I will give up my futile pursuit before I embarrass myself any further."

My heart—bruised and battered—is firmly back in my chest. "Mr. D'Orio is my father's assistant. That is all."

Everett fairly skips off the path pulling me with him to a secluded park bench. He sits down too close, catches himself, and slides away to a respectable distance.

"Well then, if you're not spoken for...could we...start over?" he asks.

Everett's smile is sweet and shy. It still doesn't ring my bell, but I decide to take a chance.

"I am Virginia Jackson." I offer Everett my hand to shake. "It's a pleasure to meet you."

"Everett Franklin Winthrop the Third." Everett squeezes my hand instead of shaking it, but at least he refrains from kissing it. "The pleasure is all mine."

"What is it that you do, Mr. Winthrop?"

"I am in my final year at Chestnut Hill Academy. I have already been accepted to the University of Pennsylvania for next fall, where my father informs me that I will be studying law." Everett's eyes drops. "Or I could be drafted before then."

"That is terrifying."

Everett shrugs. "At least I wouldn't have to study law."

"You could simply tell your father that you don't wish to study law."

"And break the tradition? Six generations of Winthrop men have become lawyers. I would be kicked out of the family tree so fast my head would spin." Everett puts his hand on mine. "May I ask a favor of you? I know it is completely impertinent, but, would you write to me if I am drafted? Would you be my anchor? My something to come home to?"

I hem and haw. Everett releases my hand.

"I apologize for being so forward." The tips of Everett's ears turn bright red.

My brain says that Everett could be a good match for me. Maybe there is an ember inside me that could be fanned into a flame. There is only one way to find out. I look around. Our chaperones are nowhere to be seen, so I slide down the bench closer to Everett and open my hand to him. It takes a moment for him to understand. He slips his hand in mine. When I don't pull away, he leans in. I close my eyes. My lips wait for several breaths before Everett's lips brush my cheek. I put my hand on his face to stop his retreat. Emboldened, Everett leans back in until his lips press against mine.

When he pulls away, I say, "You don't have to stop."

Everett takes me up on the invitation, his lips warm and inspired. I wait for heart flutters and butterfly wings and all that ridiculous rot. It doesn't happen. At all. Now I know why Kit's gentlemen callers invited to dinner rarely make it to the dessert course. If there are no sparks to begin with, how can you ever ignite a fire? If the divide is too deep between Marco and me, maybe I can find a Grayson of my own. But he's not here today. He may not even be in Philadelphia.

I jump to my feet, but Everett stays attached to my hand. "I must go. Mama will be worried."

"Does this mean I may court you now?" Everett laces his fingers through mine.

I don't want to be cruel, but I also don't want to lead him on. "I promise to write you letters if you are drafted. I will even knit you socks to go with my letters. All the doughboys deserve as much."

"Thank you." Everett's reply is more of a question than an answer. "So, next Saturday—"

"Is the Liberty Loan Parade and the party at our home after." I break our connection and back away. "I hope you will come."

"Of course. I wouldn't miss it."

"Splendid. Good day, Mr. Winthrop." I rush away, embarrassed by my cowardice.

At some point, I will have to tell Everett that my heart is a piece of coal and that no amount of attention or affection from him is ever going to ignite it. I will have to amputate his aspirations to be my husband. Mama is wrong. I feel like such a heel, but this isn't 1818. A modern woman shouldn't be yoked to a man that her heart has no connection to. I just hope that I haven't committed myself to a life of spinsterhood.

EIGHTEEN

ON MONDAY MORNING, I walk into the dining room out of habit before remembering that Angelina won't be there waiting with our breakfast. My heart clenches thinking about her collapsed on our kitchen floor surrounded by spilled peas. Since I am unable to do anything to help her situation, the least I can do is prepare my own breakfast. In fact, I'm going to make coffee. I am even going to drink it in front of Mama.

I jump when Daddy, disheveled and unshaven, hobbles through the dining room door.

"Daddy, you're back."

"I am. For a few hours at least." Daddy kisses the top of my head before collapsing into his usual chair. "I have missed you, Ginny."

Mama suddenly bursts through the servant door, startling all three of us. She places a plate of burnt toast in the middle of the table before retreating to the kitchen again. Daddy raises a questioning eyebrow. I shrug. Mama returns a moment later with the tea tray. She walks to Daddy's side of the table and pours him a cup of weak tea.

"Thank you, Eleanor." Daddy takes a sip of tea and winces at the results. He adds a spoonful of sugar before passing the sugar bowl to me. And, for once, Mama doesn't remind us of our sugar ration.

"Would you care for butter or apple butter on your toast, dear?" Mama says. Daddy and I look at each other in confusion until she clarifies. "Charles?"

"Apple butter," Daddy answers after a pause. "Please."

Mama slathers a thick layer of apple butter over two pieces of burnt toast and places them in front of Daddy. "Ginny?"

"Apple butter, please," I say.

After Mama serves probably the first breakfast she's ever cooked—and I use that word loosely—in her forty years of life, she takes her usual seat but leaves her social diary closed. Daddy and I gnaw at our toast in stunned silence.

"I am giving Angelina the week off to take care of…her family's personal business," Mama says a few minutes later. She lifts up her equally charred toast and winces. "Perhaps we should dine out once or twice this week. We could try a new restaurant."

"I'm afraid you will have to go without me." Daddy gives up on his toast. "I am only home for a quick bath and a nap. Then I must return to the hospital."

"Charles, you work too much," Mama says with genuine concern. "You aren't a young man anymore."

"I know. Oh, how I know." Daddy sighs and rubs his bad leg. "I guess we are both going to have to make do this week." Daddy rummages in his vest pocket and pulls out a letter. "I found this slipped through the mail slot this morning. Marco has gone to New York City to retrieve his brother's body and take care of his affairs."

Affairs. The word is a fresh stab to my tender heart. Still, I don't envy the task Marco has in front of him. What if

I had to go collect Kit's dead body? My eyes sting even thinking about it.

"We should probably cancel the party after the Liberty Loan Parade on Saturday," I say to change the subject. "Since Angelina will be absent."

"Absolutely not. We'll put on the party ourselves," Mama says, and I choke on my tea. "Don't worry. I'll ask to borrow Mrs. Whitmore's cook and maids for the evening. I'm sure those Irish girls will be happy for the extra work."

Those Irish girls. Like Miss Shannon? I shake the image of Miss Shannon crying on the D'Orios' doorstep out of my mind.

"Speaking of work. Daddy, I implore you to bring me to the hospital with you. The article on the front page of the *Philadelphia Inquirer* yesterday said the Spanish flu is spreading across America like wildfire. They are asking for all able-bodied women to work as nurses."

Daddy shakes his head, but I won't give in that easy.

"At least let me help out here in the afternoons," I press. "Nurse Brighton is driving away our livelihood with her ineptitude and poor bedside manner. I'll only serve our neighbors here in Rittenhouse Square. Anything beyond a sprain or Chicken pox or simple laceration, I will send directly to the hospital. I promise."

Daddy swirls the rest of his tea around in his teacup. "Yes."

I sit up straight in my chair, convinced I'd misheard Daddy. "Pardon me?"

"Yes, you may attend patients. But only after school and *only* when Nurse Brighton is present. That would free up some of the non-urgent cases at the hospital. By the way, I heard what you did in my absence."

My stomach clenches.

"Well done, Virginia." Daddy beams, but then his face hardens. "But don't you *ever* do that again."

"I had no choice, Father. The patient refused to go to the hospital, and Nurse Brighton had already left for the day. Who else could do it?"

Daddy gnaws on his toast searching for an appropriate answer. There isn't one, so he changes the subject. "Eleanor, would you recheck my books? I thought I put aspirin on my purchase order recently, but maybe I didn't." Daddy rubs his temples. "I surely could use some this morning, and we are fresh out."

Mama flips open her social diary and jots down a note. "Of course, Charles. It would be my pleasure."

"Thank you." Daddy sighs. "I wouldn't be able to keep doing this without my girls back home keeping things running."

"Then bring Kit home." There will be hell to pay later, but I spill Kit's secret. "She never left Philadelphia."

Mama's teacup clatters against the saucer. "Pardon me?"

"She's in Wynnefield. At Beatrice Douglas's home. But only for a short while longer. Until things are sorted." In the name of self-preservation, I decide to allow Kit break her plans to move to Washington to our parents herself. "Daddy, allow us all to assist you, especially while Marco and Angelina are away. I'll tend to your patients. Mama can tend to your business affairs. And for the love of all things holy, please let Kit hire another nurse for you."

"Virginia!" Mama says.

"It's all right, Eleanor. In trying times like these, it's time to dispense with the niceties." Daddy ponders my suggestions through the rest of his tea before answering. "Bring Katherine home. It's time for us to be a family again and support each other. I know some of Katherine's ideas are unconventional, but times are changing. I see young women filling all kinds of roles that would have sent my mother to her fainting couch. Doctor Porter even said his youngest daughter is now an electric welder on Hog Island."

"Scandalous," Mama says.

"Fascinating," I say.

"After the horrors I witnessed in Boston and what's happened with the D'Orios, I just want all my girls safely home." Daddy gives Mama a pleading look. "Please, Eleanor. I want my daughters here. Safe and sound."

WHEN I WALK out of school that afternoon, I hear a high-pitched whistle. A second whistle makes me, my classmates, and everyone else on the sidewalk, look across the street to discover its source. I know that whistle. It's my sister's. The one that makes Mama apoplectic every time Kit does it, especially when we are in public. I jog across the street before she can hail me a third time.

"I am not a cow. In the future, a simple 'Yoo-hoo, Virginia' will suffice," I say, my face burning.

Kit laughs, causing the brim of her new burgundy hat to flap up and down. The hat isn't the only new thing adorning my sister. There is also a handsome young man attached to her.

"Ginny, I would like for you to meet someone." Kit's slate blue eyes twinkle as she takes my hands and squeezes them.

I already know who he is. I remove my hands from Kit's so I can offer one to the man who has captured my sister's heart. "You must be Grayson Reynolds."

The young man blinks and looks at Kit. "I am indeed. It is a pleasure to finally make your acquaintance, Miss Virginia."

Grayson shakes my hand. I am dumbstruck. My sister's taste is impeccable, and I'm not talking about her hat. Tall, blond, blue-eyed, dapper, and a firm supporter of the suffrage movement, it is no surprise why Kit has fallen head-over-heels for Grayson. My heart bubbles for my sister, and then hardens to stone as an image of Miss Shannon standing on top of my necklace passes through my mind.

"I am quite cross with you, sister, for betraying my secret to Mother," Kit says, but her face immediately softens. "However, things have taken a turn for the positive. So, I shall forgive your loose lips."

"Say, would you ladies like to take some refreshment at the pharmacy before we walk Miss Virginia home?" Grayson says. "I hear they've created a number of new sugarless desserts that would tempt even those with a ferocious sweet tooth."

"Yes, let's celebrate my news with a treat," Kit says.

Grayson steps between us and offers an arm to each of us. "Well then, it would be my pleasure to treat two of Philadelphia's finest ladies to an afternoon outing."

I wince, expecting Kit's mood to sour and for her to insist that she is capable of paying for herself. And for her sister, who currently has no pocket money.

"We accept your most generous invitation, Mr. Reynolds." Kit's gloved hand pats Grayson's arm.

My shock turns to envy as I see the loving look that passes between the two of them. To my embarrassment, we enter the pharmacy to see several of my classmates, including Margaret Vaughn, sitting in a row at the pharmacy's soda counter, sipping on egg creams and making eyes at the soda jerk. With more and more shops temporarily closing their doors because of the Spanish flu, I guess the pharmacy is one of the few places left for people to congregate.

All eyes turn in my direction as I enter on the arm of this incredibly handsome man and in the company of my scandalous sister. I ignore their tittering as we pass the soda counter to a small cluster of tables. Grayson pulls out a chair for Kit and then one for me. I place my school books on the empty chair, and Grayson rests his hat on top of them.

"Now then, what decadence shall we indulge in today, ladies?" Grayson hands me a menu.

Kit removes her gloves and tucks them into her handbag. "I'm still recovering from luncheon with Mother. I'll just have a lime rickey."

Presuming that I should follow Kit's lead, I put the menu down. "I'll have the same."

"Now I feel like a glutton for wanting a banana split. Are you sure a boring old lime rickey is all you crave?" Grayson smiles conspiratorially at me. "Surely I can tempt you with an ice cream sundae?"

Kit chuckles. "If Mother is making dinner, I suggest you do."

I look over the menu again. There are so many creations I've always wanted to try that it's hard to make a decision. At least I can cross anything that has lemons in it off the list. I don't need any reminders of Marco.

"I'll have the Broken Hearts sundae." I finally decide.

It's twenty cents, but based on the expertly-tailored suit Grayson is wearing, I'm sure he can afford it. As soon as Grayson excuses himself to place our order with the soda jerk, I pounce on Kit. I grab Kit's sleeve so hard that I nearly pull her into the floor.

"He's so handsome," I squeal.

"Shhh. Did you think I was exaggerating?"

"Yes, no, well maybe a little bit. Isn't Grayson engaged though?"

"He was. But when his prospective in-laws discovered Grayson's commitment to the suffrage movement, they suddenly didn't want their family associated with such a man."

"A pity."

"Quite."

"Daddy wants you to come home," I venture while Kit is still in a good humor.

"So I heard." Instead of being thrilled, Kit's voice is flat.

"I talked him into letting you hire a new nurse for us."

"I know. Mama said as much when she came to Wynnefield this morning to pay me a visit."

"Kit, don't you see? You can come home now. We can be a family again."

"What if I don't want to?" Kit says sharply but then takes my hand. "Ginny, I'm too different from them. They want me to be the dutiful daughter. The socialite. The hostess. A decoration for some wealthy man's arm. I want to write. I want to march in protest. I want a husband who wants to change the world with me, not for me."

"Oh dear, you've broken the bad news, I see," Grayson says while simultaneously balancing all of our orders in his hands. He gives Kit a pointed look before delivering her lime rickey.

Kit releases my hand and takes a long drink of her fizzy treat before continuing in a much more civilized tone. "Ginny, I am happy to come home and assist Father with finding a new nurse. I am not happy, however, about assisting Mother with the party she's planned after the Liberty Loan parade, especially as it has now transformed into a twenty-first birthday celebration for me. I doubt my suffragist sisters outside of Philadelphia could arrive in time. Then again, maybe that was the plan. I shall endure it, however, with the utmost patience and grace."

"Excellent plan, darling. Now…." Grayson digs into his banana split with vigor. "This is delicious. Would you care for a bite?"

"No, thank you." Kit sits in silence for several moments, deep in thought.

Despite its name, my Broken Hearts sundae makes my heart—or at least my taste buds—happy. Three small balls of vanilla ice cream sit in my heart-shaped glass dish. I drag one of the two wafer cookies through the whipped cream and mashed strawberries. Strawberries! In late September! Such decadence.

"Oh my, this is heavenly. Thank you, Mr. Reynolds," I say.

"Please, call me Grayson."

I can see my classmates over the top of Grayson's shoulder. Margaret, in particular, is pea-green with envy. Over my decadent treat or the handsome man at my table or the fact that I don't have to lie to my mother about going to a soda fountain or maybe all of the above. I smile at Margaret. She immediately ducks her head.

"Broken hearts, hmmm?" Kit raises an eyebrow at me. She reaches toward one of the three whole, hulled strawberries decorating the top of the dessert.

"They do look like hearts." I scoop up one of the whole strawberries in my spoon. "Though not in the anatomical sense, of course. Human hearts aren't so symmetrical.

The right atrium is larger and more muscular than the left atrium. It—"

Kit blanches and pulls her hand away.

"Never mind," I say. "This is delicious. Thank you, *Grayson*."

"It sounds like both of the Jackson sisters have been blessed with sharp intellect," Grayson says. "So, you'll be attending Radcliffe College next fall, also?"

"No, I plan to attend Bryn Mawr College with my dear friend Anna first. After two years of study, then we will apply to the Woman's Medical College of Pennsylvania." I use the edge of my spoon to cut off a respectable-sized bite of ice cream. "Unlike Kit, my goal is not to attend college as far away from our parents as possible."

Grayson chuckles. "A shame. For Radcliffe."

Oh please, let Kit marry this man!

An hour later, Grayson pops open his gold pocket watch and startles at the time.

"My, it's grown quite late. I'm sure your mother will be concerned," Grayson says. "I'm pleased she agreed to our outing at the soda fountain. Katherine tells me some Philadelphia matrons are strongly opposed to them."

"Mrs. Vaughn," Kit and I say at the same time.

"Though that doesn't seem to keep her daughter Margaret from frequenting this establishment, I see." Kit looks around Grayson, making eye contact with a guilty looking Margaret who sheepishly licks the last of her sundae off her spoon.

"May I escort you ladies home?" Grayson stands and offers an arm to Kit.

"Let's walk Ginny home, but I am returning to Wynnefield tonight. Beatrice and I have some things to attend to." Kit shares a knowing look with Grayson.

"Of course." Grayson dips down for his hat before hooking out his other elbow. "Shall we, Virginia?"

There is more giggling and goggling from my classmates as I depart. The Jackson Sisters never disappoint. I'm sure everything from Kit's ostentatious hat to Grayson's countenance will be gossiped about at length for weeks during recess. Kit and I share a smug look. Let them talk.

"Oh no, I left my school books inside." I realize when we are a few steps out the door. "I'll only be a moment."

"Be careful, Virginia," Margaret says as I pass by her. "Or your Italian lover might become jealous."

Margaret's friends howl with laughter. My stomach tightens, but I ignore her barb. I snatch my books off the chair and storm back toward the door.

"Tie ammo, Virginia," Margaret mocks—incorrectly at that—as I pass her.

I pull up short. "Be careful, Margaret. I'm not the one at a soda fountain without a chaperone. What would your mother think? She is so old-fashioned about these things. I mean, she won't even allow you to attend the cinema. Even with her. Such a pity."

Margaret's face looks like she sucked on a lemon. Mama may be old-fashioned, but Mrs. Vaughn is stuck in the Dark Ages.

"And, by the way, it's *Ti amo*, not tie ammo. If you are going to mock me, at least do it correctly."

The girls around Margaret giggle, and she shoots them a dirty look. Margaret doesn't know my truth, and I don't know hers. But as long as she keeps her mouth shut, we won't have a problem.

NINETEEN

"IMBECILES!" MAMA BURSTS into the dining room Saturday morning. "It's spice cake. How difficult could it be? Read the blessed recipe. Mrs. Whitmore was wrong. I am never going to hire those Irish girls again. They are completely incompetent. I just pray we have enough sugar left now to make the icing."

Mama releases an exasperated sigh and collapses onto her chair. She pours herself a cup of tea, which someone has finally instructed her on how to make correctly.

"Now then." Mama opens her social diary and taps the page with her index finger. "The Liberty Loan Drive Parade. We need to leave for the festivities this morning by nine."

"I thought you were no longer attending, Eleanor?" Daddy snaps his newspaper closed.

"I changed my mind after reading yesterday's *Evening Bulletin* article." Mama adds some notes to her social diary without looking up. "It said this influenza poses no danger to most."

"Bullocks." Daddy bangs his fist on the table, making all of our teacups rattle in their saucers.

"Charles, such language." Mama closes her social diary.

"The article said that the influenza is usually accompanied by a great miasma, foul air, and plagues of insects. None of which have occurred in Philadelphia. Dr. Krusen and the Health Board suggested that everyone simply stay warm, keep their feet dry, and their bowels open."

"Krusen is a fool. I've seen it. First in Boston and now more and more cases here in Philadelphia. Provost Crowder even canceled the next scheduled draft call because of this influenza."

I breathe a sigh of relief for Marco—and Everett—but then let my heart harden again.

"Henry's telegram yesterday said they have 1500 soldiers and sailors down with the Spanish flu in Boston." Daddy rubs his graying temples. "That the morgue is at capacity, and they have resorted to stacking the deceased one on top of each other like cords of wood."

Kit puts her hand to her mouth. Even my stomach clenches at the thought.

"Charles, this is *not* appropriate breakfast conversation." Mama puts her piece of burnt bacon back down on the plate next to her charred toast.

"Eleanor, Pennsylvania Hospital is full of influenza patients, too."

"You said it was full of *sailors* with influenza."

"Yes, and 200 civilians."

"Charles, if Dr. Krusen didn't think the parade was safe, he would have canceled it." Mama pulls herself up tall. "Besides, everyone is going to be there. I don't want them talking badly about us. Again. If nothing else, the Jackson Family *always* does their patriotic duty."

"Do I have to go?" I say because I still have two more rosebuds to do on Kit's birthday present.

"Yes," Mama says.

"No, you mostly certainly do not," Daddy says.

"May I be excused?" Kit puts her napkin over her barely touched breakfast. "Grayson will be here shortly. Mama, are you sure you don't want me to go to the parade on your behalf. There is so much work to be done still before the party. I promise to be pleasant to the Red Cross ladies." Kit sniffs the air. "Is that my birthday cake burning?"

Mama sniffs, shrieks, and bolts for the kitchen.

"You will wear a nursing mask at all times at the parade." Daddy and Kit push away from the table at the same time. "And leave your gloves on."

"A lady always does, Father." Kit kisses Daddy's cheek before she flutters out of the room.

Daddy and I both raise a questioning eyebrow. Kit has never been this agreeable. Something is definitely afoot.

"I will be hiding in my office until the party. I highly suggest you join me." Daddy hobbles toward the door. He turns back to me. "Ginny, my right leg is on fire this morning. Could you fetch the business ledger off your mother's desk for me? She said she was finished with the inventory."

"Of course, Daddy." I take one last gulp of tea but abandon the rest of my breakfast.

THE SCENT OF rose soap fills my nostrils as I enter Mama's pastel-colored boudoir. Daddy's ledger sits precariously on top of a stack of correspondence on her desk. A small note pokes out of the ledger. I can only read part of it: *Missing items: 3 bottles of aspirin…1 bottle of morphine.* I open up the ledger to read the rest. Unfortunately, my sleeve bumps the stack of papers, sending half of the pile onto the floor. One letter slides underneath Mama's desk. When I drop down and pull it out, a photograph comes with it.

July 9, 1894
Alexei

The top part is in Mama's hand, but I can't read the symbols at the bottom. I flip the photograph over. We have several old photographs around our home of my father as a boy and a young man. This is not my father. 1894. Mama would have been about sixteen years old. Who is this handsome young man?

When I slide the photograph back under the desk, my fingertips hook another treasure. I pull out a ripped piece of cloth about the size of my hand. It's a little faded in places, but it's still blue. Cornflower blue but without any lace. A lock of hair the color of corn silk is wrapped in a faded white ribbon and pinned to the corner. All the members of the Jackson family have dark brown locks.

"Did you find it?" Daddy yells up the stairs.

I drop the fabric. "Yes. Just a moment."

I put the fabric back in its hiding place before piling Mama's correspondence neatly on her desk. Would Mrs. Maguire remember this boy?

As I come back downstairs with the ledger, I have to dodge around the parlor furniture currently littering the foyer. Mama is turning our parlor, music room, and dining room into one large room for the party.

"Over there. No, over here instead," Mama orders two of the Irish girls to carry the settee from one side of the room to the other. "Wait, I like it over there better after all."

I squeeze into Daddy's office and hand over the ledger.

"Where did the medicines go then?" Daddy says after reading down the list.

"I may have given Marco a bottle of digitalis for Mr. Borrelli one time to spite Nurse Brighton."

"Virginia," Daddy scolds me.

"I'm sorry. I won't do it again." I should probably confess my entire sin and tell Daddy about trading it for *gelato*, but Daddy looks so worn. Also, I am a coward. I grab a pencil off Daddy's desk and hand it to him. "Now we've accounted for the digitalis, and you broke the bottle of Dover's powders last week. But I don't know what happened to the morphine and three bottles of aspirin. Do you?"

"No. Count the bottles again. It must be a mistake." Daddy collapses onto his chair and props his right leg up on his desk. He massages his calf and knee through his pants leg. "Starting today, inventory is now your responsibility. And I will hold you, Marco, and Nurse Brighton accountable for every spoonful and every tablet of medicine that leaves this house. We have no medicine to waste."

"Of course, Daddy. You can count on me."

"I know." Daddy smiles and picks up the ledger once again. "Now, let's start counting. First up, Gebauer's Ethyl Chloride. We should have seven."

<hr />

AT FOUR O'CLOCK, after a mad afternoon of polishing silver cake forks, Mama sends me upstairs to nap and prepare for the evening's festivities. She threatens to dress my hair for me. I decline. Oh, how I wish Angelina were here. Now we will have ugly coifs and slightly burnt spice cake for the party.

At least my gift is above middling. I tuck the handkerchief decorated with a spray of pink rosebuds into a box and tie a white silk ribbon around it. I tuck the present under my bed as Kit's booted feet echo up the stairs.

"What a day. My feet ache so." Kit collapses onto our overstuffed chair. She digs through her handbag and hands me back my old nursing mask. "If Father asks, I wore it."

"How was the parade?"

"Do you want the version I gave Mother or the whole truth and nothing but the truth?" Kit unhooks her boots and slides them off. "Warning: I may end up on the front page of the *Philadelphia Inquirer* tomorrow."

"Katherine," I chastise.

"Should someone bring it up at the party, Grayson was well within his rights to punch that ugly man in his filthy mouth. He was defending my honor."

"Kit!"

"No one was arrested. It was a small kerfuffle." Kit unpins her hat and removes it. "Oh, I have something for you."

Kit digs back in her handbag, indifferent to the constant scandal that seems to follow her closer than her own shadow. She holds out a light blue box and cracks it open. Inside on a bed of black velvet rests a solid gold pocket watch with my initials engraved on it.

"A belated birthday gift. It was Grayson's idea, but I wrote the sentiment."

I pull out the little note tucked inside.

Your time is here.

Love always,
Katherine

"It's beautiful. Thank you. But it's your birthday, not mine." I retrieve the box from under my bed and hand it to Kit. "This hardly seems fitting compared to your gift, but Happy Birthday, Kit."

Kit unwraps it and squeals. "Oh my goodness, it's beautiful. What tiny intricate roses." Kit hugs me, her eyes glistening. "I will treasure it, Ginny. I will carry it with me everywhere I go. On every adventure I undertake with my sisters."

The wind leaves my sails. "Your sisters?"

"I misspoke. My dear friends. You are my only sister. My favorite sister in fact."

Kit gives me a gentle squeeze, but the damage is already done. Her words confirm what I've suspected for ages. Between these dear friends and her honor-defending Grayson, our home has become nothing more than a place for Kit to hang her fashionable hat. We are superfluous to her modern woman's lifestyle.

"Come, let's get you ready for my party." Kit sits me in front of our vanity, unpins my hair, and lets it tumble freely down my back. "Unless, of course, you'd prefer Mother to dress your hair."

"No!" I say though I can see Kit is teasing me.

Kit bites her bottom lip in concentration as she twists and tucks and pins my hair up into a womanly coif. Kit doesn't have Angelina's skill, but I am still pleased with the results. I lean into the vanity mirror and pinch my cheeks.

"Ah ah ah, stop that." Kit grabs her handbag and digs through it. She pulls out a shallow metal container and pops its lid off. "It's from Selfridge's. It's all the rage in London." Kit dabs her ring finger into the pot and then dabs the pink substance on my cheeks. "Not too much. Just a dab to give your face some color. Suck in your cheeks like this."

I laugh at Kit's imitation of a goldfish. "I didn't inherit Granny Jackson's high cheekbones like you did. I don't think any amount of rouge is going to help that."

Kit releases her face. "Trust me, Ginny. Now pucker. And voila…enviable cheekbones."

Kit also insists on adding a little color to my lips, dusting my face with powder, and dabbing a drop of her orange blossom perfume—not toilet water but actual perfume—behind each of my ears.

"Grayson brought it back from his recent sojourn in California and gave it to me as a twenty-first birthday present." Kit pinches the tiny, cut glass bottle, between her thumb and forefinger. "They say it's Mary Pickford's favorite scent. Or maybe it was Theda Bara. Lillian Gish? One of those cinema actresses. Regardless, I find it delightful."

Kit takes a long, pleased sniff before dabbing the perfume's stopper behind her ears. She even dabs it on her bosom. Kit makes up her face too before hiding her beauty products deep in our vanity's drawer.

"Go put on your corset while I dress my hair." Kit pulls Granny Jackson's boar's hair brush through her hip-length hair. "The good one. I loathe them, but they do produce such a nice figure. My friends give me grief about being a fashion plate, but I do so love a fetching hat. There's no reason why a modern woman can't be strong yet still fashionable."

"I wish we could be fashionable and yet still breathe," I

say later as Kit pulls the corset's laces tighter and tighter. "Enough Kit. I prefer my ribs without fractures."

Kit pours yards of lemon yellow silk over my head and then steps back to admire her handiwork. "Look, you even have an enviable bosom now."

When we are both suitably attired, Kit twirls around in her amethyst-colored dress. The delicate embroidery on the matching lace overdress catches the lamp light. I stare at Kit as she tucks a few pieces of stray hair back into place.

"I don't want you to go to Washington. I want you to stay here," I say to Kit's reflection in the vanity mirror. "At least until I leave for college."

"I have to. In fact, as soon as the ink is dry on my inheritance check, I will depart. I may be a modern woman, but at the end of the day, a woman without her own money has very little power. I can't move on to the next chapter of my life without funds."

"Where will you live? Who would rent an apartment to a single woman?"

"They do have boarding houses in most large cities, Ginny. My, you have lived such a sheltered life. We will have to remedy that. I promise to send for you as soon as I am established in Washington."

"Mama and Daddy will send the police after you. They can have you committed, you know."

"Then I shall disappear." Kit's voice has a stony reserve to it. "I will go to New York City. Or California. I will change my name, become someone else." Kit takes my hands in hers. "Please, don't tell Mother and Father. They won't understand, but I know you do, Ginny. And one day, you'll join me. We'll be the marvelous, cultured, educated, *voting* Jackson sisters of Washington. Be patient. I need to set some plans in motion first, and then I shall send for you."

"I don't want to live in Washington, Kit. That's your dream, not mine. I want to be a surgeon. I can't do that in Washington."

"You can't do that in Washington, *presently*." Kit tips my chin up. "Chasing your dreams requires sacrifices, Ginny. Sometimes, those sacrifices are painful. Incredibly painful." Kit uses her birthday present to dab at her eyes. "Now, none of this crying business. It's time to see what kind of circus Mother has produced on my behalf."

TWENTY

"AH, THERE SHE is, our birthday girl." Grayson beams with pride as Kit and I enter the party, arm in arm.

Philadelphia's finest fill our parlor, music room, and dining room to capacity, but they part like the Red Sea when Kit and I step into the room. I nod at Margaret when we pass, daring her to say a word. I'm sure she will dissect the evening for our classmates on Monday and present a laundry list of all the things we did wrong. Around the combined rooms we circle—my barnacle attached to Kit's ship—receiving insincere words of congratulations and veiled compliments.

"Virginia, sweetheart, would you come over here?" Daddy hails me from across the room.

I swish over to Daddy, who chats with a portly, bearded man who reeks of spirits.

Daddy draws me in closer by my elbow. "Dr. Porter, you remember my younger daughter, Virginia."

I offer my gloved hand and walk through all the required pleasantries with the enthusiasm of a dress dummy.

"I hear you are quite the little nurse," Dr. Porter slurs. I wait for him to pinch my cheek and offer me a lollipop. "Maybe I can spirit you away from your father to be my nurse after graduation."

Some of the scandalous gossip about Dr. Porter—including the way he changes nurses like other men change their socks—runs through my mind. I shiver.

"I intend to go to college after graduation," I say.

"To study what? How to land a wealthy husband?" Doctor Porter guffaws and elbows Daddy.

"Medicine," a melodic tenor voice says from over my shoulder.

I turn, and the most beautiful man I have ever seen is there. Did Grayson bring a cinema star back with him from California, too? The white shirt and matching bowtie of Marco's tuxedo make the skin above it appear even more golden. His sometimes wild curls are tamed into a slick, sophisticated wave.

I am completely dumbfounded. So is Daddy. Dr. Porter clears his throat waiting for an introduction to the boy who shouldn't be here. The boy who can't be here.

"Harry," Daddy says. "This is my...this is Marco D'Orio. Marco, Dr. Porter."

Marco lets Dr. Porter's hand hang in the air for a moment before grabbing it in a bone-crushing handshake. "Ah, the infamous Dr. Porter."

Daddy clears his throat. "I didn't realize you were back in Philadelphia, Marco. I assumed that you were still busy with your family."

"D'Orio?" Dr. Porter says. "I remember taking care of a D'Orio this past spring. I believe he was a mechanic or carpenter or such. Are you related?"

A fire lights behind Marco's eyes. "Yes."

"He was up and running soon after, I'm sure."

Marco's gloved hands pull into fists at his sides. "No. My father died from tetanus soon after. That happens when you don't clean your tools with carbolic acid in between patients. Even an ignorant Italian immigrant's son knows that."

Daddy clears his throat loudly and claps a hand on Dr. Porter's shoulder.

"Let's go get you another cocktail, I mean, some punch, Harry." Daddy herds a sputtering Dr. Porter away.

Marco vibrates like a tuning fork as he tries to control his temper. Meanwhile, from across the room, Everett catches my eye and smiles at me. As he tries to step away, his father pulls him back into the conversation with the bank president, Mr. Vaughn. I look back at Marco, and my heart melts. I may be a modern woman, but there are still things I can never have. I bolt for the door.

"Wait," Marco calls after me.

To the kitchen staff's surprise, I swoop through the kitchen, out the back door, and into the courtyard. I rest my palms and forehead against the smooth bark of the apple tree. I want Marco to stay. I want Marco to leave. I want this part of my life to be over.

"Virginia?" Marco's voice calls out softly in the darkness.

I stay silent, but a moment later a warm hand gently cups my shoulder and turns me around. The moonlight lights up Marco's perfect face.

"I clean up nice, no?" Marco adjusts his bow tie. "Maybe now I look like someone worthy of your acquaintance." Marco wraps his fingers around my wrist and pulls me gently toward him. I dig my heels into the soft ground. Hurt flickers in his eyes. "Virginia, what did I do?"

"Marco, your family needs you. *All* of your family."

"I know. I did a lot of thinking on my way to New York and back."

My heart sinks as thoughts of Miss Shannon, her foot

firmly on my necklace, passes through my mind.

"Marco, I—"

"I'm enlisting in the Army. As a medic."

I stumble back a step. "Pardon?"

"Why wait and have someone else pick my destiny. No, I'm going to be my own man. Make my own choices."

"But your family? Miss Shannon."

"It will be hard for them, I know, but I'm tired of going through the motions. Every day I wake up and wonder how I'm going to make it through one more day. Don't misunderstand. I respect your father and everything he's done for me, but it's time for me to move on. Call me haughty or acting above my station, but I don't want to be an assistant all my life. I want more. I want to be a doctor."

"Your mother just buried one son, and now you want to offer yourself up as Uncle Sam's next sacrifice?"

"The Army recruiter said I could be a medic with all the training I've already had, and move up from there. He said they might even pay for me to go to medical school. Think about it, Virginia. This poor, immigrant boy might finally be able to become a doctor."

"And Miss Shannon and Colleen? What about your promise to them?"

"They moved in with Mamma. I'll help provide for them, but that's all I can do." Marco lets out an exhausted sigh. "I'm only eighteen years old. I want to see the world. I want to do big things. I want to fall in love with a girl who is completely out of my league."

Marco leans in, his warm breath washing across my skin. He kisses my right cheek and then my left. I stand there emotionless. Despite his affections, Marco is not mine. He can never be mine.

"I want to court you," Marco says. When I don't reply,

he adds, "When I come back from the war, then. When I am no longer the chauffeur. When I am my own man."

"You belong to someone else."

"Not yet. Uncle Sam is too busy fighting the Spanish flu right now. I have a little more time before I leave for France."

"No, you belong to Miss Shannon."

"No, I'm *responsible* for Siobhan and Colleen. There's a difference."

"In the eyes of the church, you are married. Therefore, you cannot court me."

Marco looks at me confused. Then his eyes widen. A snort slips out. Then a chuckle. Then a belly laugh.

"You think *I* am Colleen's father? That Siobhan and I—"

"So, you are saying that I am mistaken?"

"Very, very, *very* mistaken." Marco's amused smile disappears. "Dom wanted to marry her, but Papà forbade it. All of Little Italy heard that fight, I'm afraid, before Papà kicked Dom out of the house." Marco puffs out his cheeks and blows out an exasperated breath. "Nine months later, Papà was gone, Dom was fighting in Europe, Colleen arrived with little notice, and here we are. So maybe your friend might be on to something."

"What friend?"

"The red-haired girl. The one passing out family planning pamphlets in Devil's Pocket."

"How do you know Anna?"

"You fine ladies go to the *cinema* and the *opera*," Marco feigns a blue-blood accent. "Poor Italian boys have to find their fun in other places."

"Marco!"

"No, that's not what I meant. Only that I went to Devil's Pocket so much with Dom that I made some friends along the way. That doesn't sound much better, does it? How about, I saw your friend there, and she lectured me on more than one occasion."

"Anna does have a reputation for butting into other people's business."

Marco leans over and grabs my hand. "I'm not perfect, Virginia. I haven't always acted honorably, but that reckless, stupid boy died the same day Papà did. Since then, I've tried to do better, be better. Be the man of the house while Dom is away. The truth is, I don't think your father will allow me to court you. At least, not now." Marco gently rubs his thumbs over the knuckles of my hand. "That's why I have to work twice as hard. I have to prove to your father that I am good enough."

"You *are* good enough. Right now. As you are."

"I have to get his blessing." Marco kisses the top of my hand. "I *will* get his blessing. Soon."

"My mother—"

"Doesn't like me, I know. But the doctor is the man of the house. If I can win him over, eventually she will come around."

I jerk my hand back from Marco. He's not wrong, and that makes me hate it even more. "I don't want to sneak around. It's not proper."

"Nothing about this—" Marco gestures to us and the tree. "has been proper. You said you are a modern woman. Maybe you can change things." Marco steps in closer to me once again but doesn't take my hand this time. "On the train, I also thought about that day I caught you sitting in this tree. The day of your party. I was sure you would fall to your death."

"You highly underestimate me."

Marco shrugs. "I do. Did. Not anymore. And if I am

honest with myself, that's the day I fell in love with you."

"Honestly?" I say, and Marco nods. "Because I did not share your infatuation."

"No? Surely you jest."

"I assure you. I did not. In fact, I found you nothing but a self-important peacock."

Marco sputters at my teasing. I pull him into me and kiss him deeply until his feathers are no longer ruffled. A warm wave ripples through my body when Marco's arms encircle my waist and his warm lips travel down my neck.

"And, yes, you do clean up nice," I say when we finally break apart again several minutes later. "You look very handsome in a tuxedo."

"It was Dom's." Marco pulls me against his chest and sighs. "He bought it for the wedding he never got to have."

"I'm sure he would have made a handsome groom." I wrap my arms around Marco's waist and hold him tight. I feel the hitch in Marco's breath.

"I saw Dom's death certificate in New York City. He died in a trench in France like so many of our boys have. But Dom didn't die from a German bullet or during a heroic battle in a French field. He died from Spanish flu. I haven't told Mamma that. I don't want to break her heart. She thinks her son died a war hero."

"He went to war. He is a hero."

Someone clears his throat. I look over Marco's shoulder to see Grayson standing a few feet away from us.

"I hate to interrupt, but you are missed, Miss Virginia."

I drop my head, but Marco simply smiles and doesn't let go.

"I shall stall them for another minute or two." Grayson turns on his heel and heads toward the kitchen door.

"We'd better go inside." Marco's fingers caress my

cheek.

"Only if you promise not to leave my side."

"I'm afraid I've already overstayed my welcome. Especially as I was never invited to the party to begin with."

"You are my guest. I insist."

"Well then." Marco offers his elbow to me. "Shall we?"

Kit gives me a wink when Marco and I enter the parlor. Daddy ushers Dr. Porter to the other side of the room, and Mama pounces on me.

"Virginia, where have you been?"

Mama's scolding is interrupted by Grayson tapping a fork against his punch cup. Finally, the room settles. Marco snatches a pair of punch cups off the tray one of the Irish serving girls is holding as she purposely dodges him.

"I would like to propose a toast," Grayson's smooth voice carries through the room. "To a courageous young woman who brings life and purpose to everything she does. You inspire me and motivate me and occasionally *exasperate* me." Grayson pauses as the room chuckles. "I look forward to witnessing your adventures in this new chapter of your life. To Katherine."

"To Katherine." Everyone lifts his or her punch cup, though some much higher than others.

Kit looks at me, and both of our eyes fill with tears. I have to look away. After a round of "For She's a Jolly Good Fellow," everyone receives a slice of spice cake—which is dry and has only a tiny smear of icing on top. Marco raises a questioning eyebrow at the sad example of birthday cake. Two bites in, I contemplate dumping mine into the potted plant in the corner.

"Angelina would have made a much better cake." I abandon my plate—and Marco does the same—on a side table and slink away.

Marco leans into me and whispers, "Come to Little Italy. I will take you to Falcone's for the best *cannoli* in—"

"All of Philadelphia?" I tease.

"Of course."

The small ensemble Mama hired resumes their performance of "Smiles" by the Joseph C. Smith's Orchestra. Grayson whisks Kit to the center of the room for an elegant but spirited—and completely scandalous by Mrs. Vaughn's standards—foxtrot. I sigh. I have never seen my sister look so beautiful.

"Would you care to dance?" Marco says once a few other couples have joined in.

I float around the room in Marco's arms staring deeply into those hazel-flecked, brown eyes. I stay attached to Marco long after the song finishes. Mama clears her throat bringing attention to my inappropriateness. Marco releases me, but I refuse to let go of his hand. So he twirls me around like a ballerina once and then twice before pulling me in close. Mama clears her throat even louder. Everett Franklin Winthrop the Third stands next to her looking like Marco ran over his dog with our automobile. Oh dear Lord.

"Thank you for allowing me one dance, Miss Jackson." Marco takes a step backward and bows.

"The pleasure was all mine. I didn't know you were such a skillful dancer."

"We do dance in Little Italy. Find me a tambourine, and I will show you the *Tarantella Napoletana*." Marco does a few jig-like steps.

"That is enough, Marco." Mama jerks Everett in front of her. "There are other *gentlemen* who would like to dance with my daughter."

I expect a flash of anger from Marco, but instead, he says, "But of course, Mrs. Jackson."

Marco kisses my hand and leads me over to Everett. He gives me one last cinematic smile before retreating to the punch table. I look from Marco to Everett to Kit, who has been attached to Grayson all evening, an enormous smile on her face.

"Excuse us, please, Mother." I take Everett by the elbow and lead him away from the dance floor to the quietest corner of the dining room. "Everett, I've been thinking. I am happy to write to you and knit you socks if you are drafted. But…."

"I see."

"I'm sorry, Everett. What I told you the other day was true. But tonight…things have changed."

Everett looks like I have stabbed him in the chest with a cake fork. "I will take my leave then and bother you no more."

I hold Everett's arm tight to prevent his escape. "Wait. Just because I can't give you my heart, doesn't mean you don't deserve one. In fact, I want you to trust me on something. Yoo-hoo, Margaret." Margaret can't pretend like she doesn't see me waving in her direction because she has been staring at me all evening. I whisper to Everett, "I've heard Margaret and the other girls talk about you at school."

"They do?" Everett says, puffing back up.

"Constantly." That may have been a slight exaggeration, but Margaret and her group do discuss boys and parties and dance partners during recess almost daily. I pull Everett by the arm to where Margaret stands looking bewildered in the corner of the room. "Margaret, dear, you mustn't spend the whole party holding up the wall.

Please, come dance. Mr. Winthrop is an excellent dancer. Come show him why you always take top marks in our dance lessons at school."

Margaret's mouth opens and closes as I fairly drag the two of them to our makeshift dance floor in the middle of the dining room.

I lean in and whisper in Everett's ear, "You are *not* a clodhopper. Show her what a true gentleman you are."

I attach Margaret's hand to Everett's arm before backing away. Mama scowls at my subterfuge, but Everett and Margaret have genuine smiles on their faces. I scan the room until I find Marco on the edge of the parlor. He smiles and raises his punch glass at me.

⁂

THE GRANDFATHER CLOCK strikes midnight too soon, and Marco's and my fairytale evening comes to an end. And like a mixed-up Cinderella story, it's time for Marco to shed his princely attire and return to his hardscrabble life in Little Italy. I drag my feet fetching Marco's overcoat and hat until only he and Grayson remain of our guests.

"Were these for Dom's wedding day, too?" I rub my fingertips over the fine fabric.

Marco chuckles. "No, not on Dom's wages. Let's just say Mr. Borrelli heard about my plans and didn't want me to shame my family or our community. There was a package waiting for me on my doorstep this morning."

"Mr. Borrelli bought these for you?" I say incredulously.

"No, but I'm sure he had a hand in its purchase. His youngest brother is a tailor. The unsigned note inside the box read: *In gratitude to one of Little Italy's favorite sons.*"

Tears prick my eyes as Marco's beam with pride. If only

my Rittenhouse Square neighbors could see Marco the way his community does. If only my parents could, too.

"Marco!" A tipsy Daddy pounds on Marco's back. "I'm expecting you back on Monday. Not sure Nurse Brighton missed you much, but to the Devil with her. We've got a full caseload at the hospital. This influenza is whipping us soundly. So get some rest tomorrow. You'll need it."

"Yes, sir," Marco says as Daddy herds him toward the door.

I trail after them, desperate for another moment or two with Marco.

"Dr. Jackson, a moment, sir." Grayson comes to our rescue once again. "May I discuss something with you in your office?"

"Thank you," I mouth at Grayson when he looks back over his shoulder.

Grayson winks at me before grabbing onto Daddy to keep him from crashing into the door frame.

"I like this fellow." Marco tucks my hand into the crook of his arm and pulls me in close to his side. We walk together to the front door. "I hope we will see more of Grayson in the future. He seems to tame Katherine."

"No one can tame Katherine."

"True enough. Complement her then. I have never seen her so happy."

Once we are outside, Marco closes the door behind us. In the safety of the shadows, I dare to wrap my arms around his neck.

"Kit's leaving. She's becoming a full-time suffragist as soon as the ink is dry on her inheritance check. She leaves for Washington as soon as her suffragist friend arrives from New York."

"*Mio Dio*. So much for peace in the Jackson household."

Marco shakes his head. He reaches into his coat pocket and pulls out the pressed silver heart necklace. "You lost this at my home. I hope you still want it."

I stare at the necklace. I want it. I want Marco. I want a life with him in it.

"Yes, I do."

Marco steps behind me and places the necklace around my neck. As I turn to face him again, Marco loops his fingers under the silver chain on my locket. His hand slides down the chain until he can cup the silver heart in his palm. The warmth from the back of his hand sears the skin on my chest. I shiver, and Marco pulls me close one more time for warmth.

"Go be with your sister. Tell her goodbye." Marco steps away and reaches for my hand. He kisses it. "*Buona notte, bella*. Thank you for a magical evening."

"*Buona notte*, Marco."

Marco descends the front stairs to the sidewalk with all the grace of a refined gentleman. He's only a few steps down the sidewalk when he looks back over his shoulder at me. With a laugh, Marco begins a little jig with an imaginary tambourine while whistling what must be a jaunty Italian tune. Even though I am shivering, I stay outside in the moonlight watching Marco slip away into the night.

In a few hours, the sun will rise on the infamous Jackson sisters, and our lives will never be the same.

TWENTY-ONE

KIT SAID IT would be easier this way. It's not. She had no idea the depths of Mama's unbridled fury.

"Of all the selfish things your sister has ever done, this one is outside of enough!" Mama shrieks from the hallway as I come down the stairs for a late breakfast. "She took me for a fool! Of all the spoiled, selfish people in the world. CHARLES!"

Daddy hobbles out of the parlor, still wearing parts of his tuxedo from last night. He rubs his temples.

"Charles, call the police." Mama crams Kit's letter in Daddy's face.

"That won't be necessary." Daddy takes Kit's letter but doesn't read it.

"Your daughter has run away. With *that man* undoubtedly. Our family's name will be ruined. Why aren't you doing something?"

"I already have. I gave Katherine my blessing. And half of her inheritance last night."

"You what?" Mama wavers before collapsing on the stairs at my feet.

"She will not receive the remainder until she is married. And if you haven't scared the young man off, Eleanor, I hope that will be soon."

"Kit is engaged?" I say, wondering why she would leave out such an important detail when she told me goodbye about four o'clock this morning.

"Not yet, but Mr. Reynolds asked for my blessing. He needs to take care of a few details first."

"A few details?" Mama's voice rises on an alarming note. "Such as traveling with an unmarried, unchaperoned woman? What will everyone say?"

"Absolutely nothing," Daddy snaps. "Katherine will stay with the Douglas family until Grayson's great aunt arrives from Cambridge to chaperone their trip north. Then Katherine will live with Mrs. Grayson and assist her with the war effort until the new term starts at Radcliffe in January."

Kit failed to mention the number of untruths that were part of her plan. I bite my tongue.

"No, this is completely unacceptable, Charles." Mama stands up and wrings her hands.

"Eleanor, it is my decision to make. The last time I checked, I am still the head of this household. Therefore, Virginia…." Daddy's hard stare turns on me. "Get dressed. You are coming to the hospital with me. We are desperate for nurses."

"Have you completely taken leave of your senses? Virginia might catch the influenza."

"You wanted Virginia to march in some fool parade—a cesspool of pestilence—yesterday to save your reputation, but now she can't attend to people who know her and need her? She's a damn fine nurse, Eleanor, and I want her with me."

"I forbid you to take her." Mama quivers with rage.

"I am your husband, and you took a vow to obey me."

"Mama, I want to go." I put a comforting hand on her arm. "I will take precautions. Please, allow me to go."

I grab the bannister to keep from falling down as Mama barrels past me up the stairs. The door to her boudoir slams closed soon after.

"We leave at the top of the hour." Daddy's voice contains no remorse for amputating Mama's heart. "And don't forget your mask."

A knot forms in my stomach as I climb the stairs. I can hear Mama's sobs through her boudoir door, but when I go to comfort her, I find the door locked.

I knock on the door a second time. "Mama?"

"Please leave me be, Virginia. Go, *obey* your father like a good girl. Meanwhile, I will pray for my daughters, since that is all I can do."

I'm just coming down the stairs again when there is a pounding on our front door. Daddy walks out of his office, freshly shaven and with his work clothes on.

"May I help you, sir?" Daddy says to the bedraggled young man standing on our porch.

I recognize him from Devil's Pocket. He lives in Mrs. Carnes's tenement.

"M' whole family has the influenza, Doctor." The man wrings his hands. "M' wife, all five kids. Burning with fever. And my brother's family, too. Please help us. All our pharmacies are closed. Dolores—Mrs. Carnes—said you have medicine."

Daddy looks over his shoulder at me. I immediately put on my mask.

"Did you come by automobile?" Daddy continues to block the door.

"Yes, sir. I borrowed m' boss's delivery truck. I know we aren't supposed to drive on Sundays, but to the de'il—I beg your pardon, Miss—with the gas ration. M' family's more important than this Godforsaken war."

"Please wait in your truck. I'll only be a moment."

"Thank you, Doctor."

Daddy closes the door and heads for his office. I follow behind him.

"Write these down," Daddy says as he adds a few bottles of medicine to his bag. He stops, pulls a few out and hands them back to me. "Take these ones upstairs. Put them in my bedroom. Now, new plan. Telephone Marco and ask him to come here."

"Daddy, it's Sunday. They are probably just coming home from mass."

"Marco knew my gift of a telephone for his family came with strings attached." Daddy scribbles down a list of medicines on the back of an envelope. "Telephone him. See if he can acquire these from the pharmacy at the edge of Little Italy. Then both of you meet me in Devil's Pocket, Mrs. Carnes's tenement building. We'll go on to the hospital together from there."

"You don't want me to come now?"

"No. You need to limit your exposure as much as possible. As much as it pains me to admit it, your mother is right. We need more hands at the hospital but know that I am still going to keep you away from the influenza patients as much as I can." Daddy pulls out the Cadillac's keys and puts them on his desk. "Call Nurse Brighton, too. You will need a chaperone to travel with Marco."

"Daddy, this is 1918. I am going to work, not strolling around Fairmount Park."

"It's looked down upon."

"So is working on the Sabbath and driving an automobile on Gasless Sundays."

Daddy puts up his hands in defeat before grabbing his bag and hobbling out the door.

———

"I HAD TO call in all my favors, but I got them," Marco says when he finally arrives. "But only one of each. I may be one of Little Italy's favorite sons, but even I have limitations." He points to each bottle in the cherry box, and I log them. "Dover's powders, aspirin, strychnine, digitalis, soluble caffeine salt, and Castor's oil."

I close up the ledger and go to grab my nursing apron from its usual spot, but it's not there. I look around Daddy's office until I remember. I put it in the laundry pile next to the other cloths and bandages soiled with Mr. Grant's blood. I'm sure it is still sitting there over a week later because Mama's laundry skills are even worse than her cooking ones. I'll borrow a clean one from the hospital.

"How did your parents take the news this morning?" My expression must say it all because Marco says, "*Mio Dio*, that bad, huh?"

"Mama is holed up in her boudoir. She wouldn't even let me bring her a cup of tea."

"Ah, well. That's good for me then."

"Why?"

Marco dips his head down to give me a tender kiss. "Thank you for helping me forget my troubles for a while. Being with you is like a bowl of *gelato di limone* on a hot summer's day."

I pull Marco into me until his strong arms circle my back. Our kiss is not tender. The scraping of furniture across the wood floor above our heads reminds us that we aren't alone. We break away from each other. I fix a few locks of Marco's hair that have sprung out during our stolen moment.

"Your mother already thinks the worst of me." Marco picks up the crate of medicines. "I probably shouldn't prove her right."

DADDY IS NOT thrilled to see me sitting in the front seat of the Cadillac next to Marco. In fact, he disappears from the first story window of the tenement and reappears on the sidewalk before Marco even has the medicines unloaded. Daddy pulls down his gauze mask and gives us such a stern look that Marco gulps.

"It's worse than I thought," Daddy says. "Some will make it, but some won't. I can only see a few more patients, and then we must leave. Bring the medicines in, Marco. Put your mask on first. Virginia, you will stay in the car."

"But Daddy."

"You will obey me, or you will go home. Am I understood?"

I cringe. "Yes, Father."

"Let's go, Marco." Daddy hobbles back toward the tenement with Marco two steps behind him.

I pull my coat tighter around me as I wait. And wait. And wait. I am catnapping when a sudden knocking on my window startles me. It's a little girl. It takes me a moment to place her. It's Mrs. Carnes's daughter. I open the car door and get out.

"Are you all right?" I ask the grubby-faced girl.

She shakes her head "no" before grabbing my hand and jerking me toward the tenement building.

"Is someone in your family ill?" I hold my mask up to

my face with one hand as the girl drags me up the stairs by the other one. We don't go to the Carnes' apartment though. Instead, the girl pulls me down another hallway.

"Please, Nurse. Please come to our home." A middle-aged woman with streaks of silver in her brown hair waves for us from down the hall, but the girl doesn't pause.

We don't stop until we reach the last door at the end of the hall. I follow the girl inside the cramped apartment which reeks of garlic and musty straw. In the corner, two little boys close in age huddle together each with a cloth bag tied around their necks. Undoubtedly, bags of garlic. The girl leads me to the bedroom where a young woman a little older than Kit shivers in bed despite the blankets being pulled up to her chin. Her pale skin has a bluish tint, and each breath sounds watery. The smell of musty straw is so strong that I have to breathe through my mouth.

"Is this your aunt? The one who came to nurse your baby brother?" I look down at the little girl.

She looks back up at me, eyes as big as saucers, and nods. She releases my hand so that she can wrap her arms around herself and rock.

"Where is the…oh no." I tie my nursing mask on.

The little girl makes a mewing sound and her eyes overflow with tears. I carefully pull the blanket back. Sure enough, Mrs. Carnes's baby is on the aunt's half-bared chest. He's completely blue. I put my hand on his back. Though heat rolls off his aunt like a furnace, the baby's skin is cold. The truth of the situation punches me in the stomach. I look around the room until I spy a plain shawl. I bite my lip to stop it from quivering as I take the baby from the fever-addled woman. I swaddle the baby and hold it to my chest as if it were still alive.

"I'm sorry. I am so, so sorry." I blink back my tears. "We

need to let your mother know. Can you take me to her?"

The girl shakes her head.

"Please. She needs to know."

The girl shakes her head again.

"How about your father or Sean? Can you take me to them?"

The little girl nods and takes my free hand. I walk beside her wondering how in the world I am going to find the right words to completely break her mother's heart. The Carnes's apartment reeks of musty straw and garlic, too. A dark-haired man sits in the corner, his head bowed and a string of rosary beads looped around his hands. The girl drops my hand and runs to him. She slaps her hand against his arm.

"Marnie, I'm prayin'," the man lightly chastises her. "Please wait."

Marnie vocalizes her insistence and pulls at her father's arm until he stands. She drags him across the room to the door. I take a deep breath.

"Mr. Carnes, I am afraid I have some distressing news. May I see Mrs. Carnes?"

The man looks at me with glassy eyes. "She passed on to be with our dear Lord two days ago. I've sent m' boys away from this place, but nobody would take Marnie."

Hearing her name, the little girl tugs at me and puts out her hands. I hate to burden a child with such a thing, but she is insistent. Finally, I hand her the baby. She grabs him to her chest. Instead of passing the baby to her father, she rushes over to the chair her father was sitting in. She loops the rosary beads around one hand while holding the baby close to her chest with the other. She rocks both of them silently.

"My condolences, Mr. Carnes."

"Virginia?" Daddy pokes his head through the open door. The smell makes him take a step back.

"Do you have any more aspirin?" I say to Daddy. "Mr. Carnes's sister is in a state."

Daddy steps into the apartment to assess the horrific situation. I swoop past him to Marco, who holds a bottle of aspirin out for me. Marco follows me down the hall, back to the sister-in-law's apartment.

"Ma'am, can you sit up?" I say to the groaning woman. "I have some medicine to help with your fever."

Marco puts his hand behind her back to lift the woman to a sitting position. I pull the neck of her nightgown closed. The fabric feels crisp under my fingertips. Suddenly, the woman groans and a flood of blood-tinged froth pours out of her mouth all over my hand and down the sleeve of my coat. Marco and I both step back. I grab a discarded nightgown off a rickety chair and press it up to the woman's mouth.

"Find me a bowl or something," I say to Marco as another wave of froth soaks through the cloth. As I wipe the foam away, I notice mahogany spots near both of her ears. They seep toward the center of her face like an ink blot.

The woman's writhing makes her blankets drop down. Then I see it. The red stain. Down the front of her nightgown, the pillows, fanning out in a circle on the bedclothes underneath her. As I pull the blankets down further, I see a second circle spreading up from under her hips until it meets the first one. You don't have to have a degree from a medical school to know that this woman is not long for this world.

"*Mio Dio*," Marco steps back and crosses himself.

"There's nothing more that we can do for her," Daddy says quietly from the doorway. "She won't make it through the night."

"There's nothing we can do?" I squeeze my eyes shut wishing I could make this whole scene go away.

"We can give her some morphine to ease her suffering until she passes. That is about all we can do." Daddy puts his black bag on the bedside table. He digs out a quarter-full bottle of morphine and draws up a dose into the syringe. He taps the glass window of the syringe to release any air bubbles.

"Who is going to do it?" Daddy holds the syringe across the palm of his hand.

Though Marco reaches for it first, I say, "I am. She is my patient."

"Cleaning the site is a moot point now." Daddy holds out a rubber tube. "Find a vein."

I wrap the tube around the woman's arm tighter and tighter until the slightest outline of a vein shows itself.

Marco stands across from me, his eyes telegraph fear, but he says with confidence, "You can do it."

In theory, I can do it. In practice, I am not so sure. I take the cold, metal-and-glass syringe into my stained hand. The woman gasps, her eyes wide open in fear, as a new stream of fluid adds to both of the circles. She grabs onto Marco's wrist as she tries in vain to pull air into her burbling lungs. Blood trickles out of her nose and tear ducts.

"Do it now, Virginia," Marco says. "Give her some peace."

I plunge the needle into her arm and empty the morphine into it. A moment later, her eyes close and her fingers release their grip on Marco's wrist. I hold the syringe back toward Daddy.

"Leave it. It's too contaminated, and I don't have the time or means to clean it." Daddy methodically packs up his bag. He points to a pitcher and basin in the corner of the room. "Both of you, wash your hands and then go to the Cadillac. Do not stop. No matter what happens. We don't have anything more to give."

When I step out the door a few moments later, I see multiple people crowding the narrow hallway.

"Doctor, please. Some aspirin, please. Nurse, help my child. Where are you going? Where is your Christian charity? You rich people. We deserve help, too. To hell with you." Their voices blend together. People we have failed. People we have to leave behind. People who are going to die. Daddy ducks his head and plows through them to the front door, but I can't keep up with him.

"Miss…Miss…." a skeletal man grabs my arm, pulling me back. I can hear the stitches in my coat's arm hole giving way.

"Get away from her!" Marco doubles back to me.

When the man doesn't let go, Marco shoves him. The man stumbles backward. I hear his head hit the wooden floor.

"Git out 'o here, you bloody Italian." A woman chases after us.

Marco winces as his body absorbs the woman's strikes to his head and back. He tucks the nearly empty crate of medicine under one arm and uses his other one to shield me. The woman continues her assault all the way to the door. Her language alone would send most society women to their fainting couches.

"Madam!" I stop and turn on my heel to face her. "Comport yourself this instant."

The woman, who is Mama's age, silences, her mouth agape. I pull two nearly empty bottles out of Marco's crate. I hold them out to her.

"Take these and attend to your neighbors. If you have the vigor to insult and assault Mr. D'Orio, then you have the vigor to nurse the needy. And now we will be taking our leave to attend others in need. We need every woman to do her part. Please do yours and allow me to do mine."

"Thank you." The woman still doesn't apologize to Marco, but she accepts the medicine from my hands. "God bless you, Miss."

"God have mercy on all of us, Madam."

As we walk down the front steps, Marco lets out an impressed whistle. Daddy gives us a quizzical look, having missed the entire encounter. He notices my coat with the right sleeve ripped halfway off.

"The coat is contaminated." Daddy points at it. "Leave it here."

"On the sidewalk?"

"Yes."

I slide it off. A small amount of bloody secretion has seeped through my coat onto my sleeve. Daddy steps up to me and in one stroke, cuts through the fabric on my forearm with his penknife. He rips the piece downward with such a sharp tug that the buttons at my wrist pop off. He throws the piece of soiled fabric into the gutter. I roll the coat up—Mama will be livid at the loss of such a fine coat—and tuck it next to a fire hydrant. I hope it will become a treasured possession of some young woman after she boils it in lye for a few days.

"Here." Daddy sprinkles the last few drops of carbolic acid onto my hands and arm.

My skin burns. Daddy scrubs my skin dry with the handkerchief I made for him last Christmas, the one with the holly leaf border, before throwing that in the gutter, too. I shiver.

"Take this." Marco wraps his coat around my shoulders.

"I can't take it."

"You saved me from that *una pazza*." Marco rubs the back of his neck where she beat him. "I am forever in your debt."

Daddy opens the back door for me. "Get in. Now. Before the angry horde comes for us."

I slide in, and Marco passes me the box of medicines. Daddy groans and gets in beside me. We ride in silence, each no doubt reliving the horrors we have just witnessed. When we get to the entrance of Devil's Pocket, Daddy snaps out of his trance.

"Go left, Marco. We're taking Virginia home," Daddy says.

"Pardon me?" I say.

"Your mother is right. I don't want you out here. It's too dangerous."

"Daddy, please."

"Sir, Miss Virginia did an admirable job," Marco says. "She even saved me from a mad woman."

"She did, but she is also contaminated. I want you to go home and take a hot bath with a lot of soap. All of your clothes need to be boiled. Or simply burn them. You have a wardrobe full of clothes. Pick another dress."

"No, Daddy. I'll wash my hands thoroughly like Marco when we get to the hospital. You said it yourself. You are desperate for skilled help. I can help. Even if it is only fetching water for feverish patients. Modern women need to do their part, too."

Daddy glares at me with a fire I have never seen before. "For the love of God, I am sick to death of hearing about modern women. We have an epidemic on our hands with people dropping like flies, including doctors and nurses.

If being a modern woman includes disobeying your father and your superiors on a daily—and now it seems hourly—basis, then I don't want any part of it. God made us this way for a reason. We all have roles to fill. Now do yours so I can get on with mine."

The fire spreads to me. "I'm sorry that you were cursed with two girls, Father. Honestly, there are many times I have wished that I were your son. Then I wouldn't have to fight all day every day just to have the door slammed in my face as soon as I get there. I want to be a surgeon. I want to study medicine. I want to go to college. I don't know why this concept is so hard for men to comprehend."

"And this is why we don't want women in the operating room or the battlefield or to have the vote. You are too emotional to make important decisions. This job, in particular, requires a cool head. There is no room for a hysterical woman."

"Then why are you the one raising your voice?"

"Because I am your superior. Do you think I argued with my superiors during the Spanish-American war? That I lectured my colonel about how I took an oath to heal people not kill them? No. I did my goddamn job with shrapnel in my leg and my mouth firmly closed, because *that's what men do*. You want to be in a man's world, then start acting like a man. If you cannot do that, then go back to your woman's world and keep your mouth shut. I don't tell your mother how to do her job. She doesn't tell me how to do mine. That's how a family works."

"But our family *doesn't* work. It's never worked. We are all in our own variations of hell."

Marco looks over his shoulder dumbfounded. I wince expecting Daddy to slap me for my insolence. Instead, he catches whatever words were going to come out of his mouth next and slumps back against his seat.

He rubs his bad leg. "That we are."

I can't stop the tears running down my cheeks. I hate that I am proving him right. That I am too emotional. That I can't follow orders. This is only the beginning of my uphill battle. Men—and some women—are going to be slamming the door in my face every day even after I graduate from medical school. I am already tired of fighting, and I have barely begun.

Marco pulls up in front of our home. Daddy digs into his pocket and pulls out both his pocket watch and his key to the front door.

"Marco, you have exactly three minutes to drop off the contents of this box, refill it with the rest of the medicines on the shelf, and be back behind the wheel ready to go. If you are not, I will start looking for both a new chauffeur and an assistant on Monday. Do I make myself clear?"

Marco leaps out of the car and has the back door open before he says, "Yes, sir."

Marco fairly yanks me out of the Cadillac when he snatches the medicine box from my lap. He is already halfway up the front stairs before my boots even touch the sidewalk. As I climb the stairs, I dig in my pocket looking for a handkerchief to wipe my eyes, forgetting that the coat is not mine. A heavy piece of paper scratches my hand. I pull the folded piece of paper out. It's a license. A marriage license. At the bottom in loopy letters, it says *Marco Francesco D'Orio*. On the other side in less loopy letters it says, *Siobhan Aideen Shannon*. Before I can find the date, Marco rips the paper out of my hand.

"It's not what you think it is," Marco says.

"It looks like a marriage license. Is it?"

"Yes, well no, but yes."

"Which is it?"

"I don't have time to explain." Marco stuffs the paper into his vest pocket and scoops up the box of medicines. "I have to keep my job. My family depends on me."

"Yes, it seems that your family has officially grown."

"We don't have to change anything, Virginia. We can keep on—"

"What? Stealing kisses under apple trees? Dreaming about a future that will never be?"

"No. Yes. I can't do this right now. Please know that I love you. That I can...I will...make things right. Eventually." When Marco leans in to kiss me, I turn my head. "Tell me that you love me, too, Virginia. That we will work things out."

Marco waits for another beat. Waits for me to proclaim my undying love for him, too. But I don't. I can't. My throat tightens.

"Go take care of your family, Marco."

I turn on my heel and dash out of Daddy's office. Marco calls after me as I run up the stairs, but I don't stop. A moment later, the front door slams.

I slam the bathroom door, too, though Marco won't hear it. As hot water fills the bathtub, I alternate between sobbing and cursing while removing my boots and stockings. I heave Marco's coat at the door. Something clinks on the floor and rolls underneath the bathtub. I reach down and pull out a thin, metal disk with letters roughly pressed into it.

DOMENICO D'ORIO
PVT.
M.G. CO.
315th INF.

BREATHE

What's left of a piece of green ribbon pokes through the hole between the letters *S* and *A*. It is Domenico's dog tag. The man who destroyed my chance at happiness with one bad choice in his life. And yet, it's the only thing left of his too short life. That piece of metal and his daughter. I tuck the dog tag back into the pocket of Marco's coat. Daddy can return them both to Marco later.

I slide deep into the tub until the hot water caresses my chin. Ghost-like tendrils of steam rise off the water. I close my eyes and breathe in deeply. The steam picks up the scent of lavender from my soap, the spicy hair tonic on Marco's coat, and the musty straw smell on my clothes.

Bathwater laps into my face and fills my ears as my chest heaves. The pressed silver heart around my neck suddenly feels like an anvil. I take a deep breath and let it weigh me down. Drag me under. Take me to a place of quiet in the middle of this storm. Beams of late afternoon sunlight diffract through the water reminding me of a distant memory. My lungs burn from lack of oxygen, but I don't want to surface. Not yet. I welcome the silence. The reprieve from the horrors outside. Haunting images float through my mind, ebbing and flowing into each other. Kit laughing as she foxtrots with Grayson. Tying off the last stitch in Mr. Grant's arm. Marco in a tuxedo in the moonlight. Sitting in my apple tree. Carving my initials into its bark. My vision darkens.

A hand grabs my arm and jerks me up into the cold air. Water splashes all over the tile floor. I cough and sputter.

"Virginia! Oh, my sweet Virginia." Mama grabs me tightly to her chest and rocks us back and forth. "Why, Virginia, why? Why would you do something like this? I can't bear to lose you, too."

"I'm fine, Mama." I cover myself with my arms.

Mama looks down at the pressed silver heart on my chest, and the groove between her eyebrows deepens. "You are not fine. This is not fine."

Mama shivers, her wet dress clinging to her body. "We're both going to catch the influenza at this rate." She hands me a towel. "Get dressed. Then join me in the kitchen and explain why you were trying to drown yourself."

"I wasn't," I insist. "I just needed the world to go away for a while. Today has been a very trying day."

"For me, too."

"Could you make us hot chocolate like Granny Jackson used to do when I was small? That always brought me comfort on trying days."

"Yes. That would be a comfort. I'll start warming the milk."

Mama turns on her heel and rushes out of the bathroom. Her sobs echo down the hallway.

After I'm dressed again, I flip the pressed silver heart in my hand. Part of me wants to throw it—at Marco's face or at least out the window. Part of me wants to hold onto it, like Mama and the piece of fabric under her desk. I kick out the piece of molding underneath the window and tuck the necklace safely inside.

⊱——⊰

"YOU ARE GOING to catch the influenza with that wet hair," Mama says when I walk through the kitchen door. "Where are you going?"

I place Marco's neatly folded coat on a kitchen chair, but take my wadded up dress with its torn sleeve to the back door and deposit it in the burn bucket.

"A patient contaminated me with her bloody secretions. Daddy said to burn it."

Mama's face pinches in disgust, but she sets two steaming mugs of cocoa down on the table like a good hostess. I don't think I've ever sat in the kitchen with Mama before, even as a small child. We've always had tea—or cocoa when I was small—in the parlor. The throw rug at the base of the settee still hides my clumsy younger self's attempts at being sophisticated.

"Now explain yourself, Virginia." Mama wraps her long fingers around her mug. "And I want complete honesty."

"I was contaminated. Daddy ordered me to come home and take a bath."

Mama tsk-tsks. "A ruined dress is nothing to drown yourself over."

"I wasn't drowning myself."

Mama looks away, hurt clouds her face. "It took me straight back to that horrible day."

"What horrible day? We've had so many, especially recently."

"It was the summer you turned five. We were having a picnic in Fairmount Park, down near the boathouses. It was an oppressively hot day so your father took Katherine to fetch some ice cream for us from the Hokey Pokey man. You wanted to put your feet in the Schuylkill River. One minute you were playing at the water's edge, the next minute you were under the water."

The words trigger a memory from a long time ago. Diffracted light. Mud squishing between my toes. The smell of algae water.

"There was another little girl with me, wasn't there?" The girl's name escapes my memory, but suddenly I can see her clearly in my mind. A little girl in a white dress with a pink sash. Her blond hair done in ringlets. "We were about the same age, but she didn't speak English."

Mama pauses. "She was Russian. Just like her papa."

"Was she my friend?"

"No, just a playmate for the day."

"We were looking at the tadpoles together. She slipped on a rock. She grabbed my hand, or maybe it was my dress. We both fell into the water. I couldn't swim."

Suddenly, I can taste the algae water flooding into my mouth, choking me. I see the afternoon sun diffracting through the water and lighting up the little girl's face. Her eyes open wide in terror. Air from her lungs bubbles up toward the sun-dappled surface as the current pulls at us. My chest burns from lack of air.

Mama puts her hand on mine, bringing me back to our kitchen.

"But you saved us." I remember Mama pulling me out of the water and Daddy carrying me to the picnic blanket. I remember Kit crying over her dropped ice cream cone melting in the grass.

"No, I saved you." Tears well up in Mama's eyes. "But Alexei lost his daughter."

"Alexei?" I remember a blond-haired man beside Mama in the water, shouting words I don't understand, splashing around, and searching.

Mama dabs at her eyes with the handkerchief I made for her last birthday, the one with violets decorating an elaborate E. "Alexei Pavlovich."

"You've never mentioned him—or any Russians— before."

"Actually, I did. Alexei was my checkers friend. The Pavlovich family provided many of the ready-made garments we carried in my father's store. Not the tailored garments my family wore, but the everyday ones most people in our neighborhood could afford." Mama stares deep into her mug reliving some deep memory. "Alexei and I were the same age. We didn't go to school together, for obvious reasons, but I saw him often in the store. He would deliver his family's goods to shops all around Philadelphia."

"And bring you little presents," I say, and Mama nods. I swirl the cocoa around my mug, getting up my courage to ask what I've wanted to ask since I found Alexei's picture. "Did you ever wish that Alexei had courted you?"

Mama gasps at my forwardness, but I don't apologize. I wait for her answer.

"Yes. More than anything. But it was impossible. Especially after the nonsense with Uncle Edward." Mama presses her cocoa mug to her lips, lost in thought. Finally, she puts the mug down and places her hand over mine. "Girls didn't have as many opportunities as you do now. I had to make the best of a bad situation."

Mama has never really talked much about her uncle. Just that they became estranged after her father passed on. Since Grandfather Fisher had no sons, the family business went to her Uncle Edward. A year later, Mama married and, soon after that, the family business closed for good.

"Mama, how did the ink get all over your dress? The cornflower blue one with the lace that Mrs. Maguire couldn't clean." I put my hand on hers so she can't retreat.

"It was a mistake. It started as an innocent flirtation, but things got out of hand. Uncle Edward didn't understand. Oh, Alexei…." Mama closes her eyes, and a pained look passes her face. "They beat him. Within an inch of his life. They accused him of so many things. Vile things. They would have killed him, I'm certain, if Charles hadn't stepped in. For that, I am ever indebted to your father.

"The last time I saw Alexei was the day you almost drowned. I didn't plan it. I didn't even recognize him at first. All I saw was a handsome man wearing a *kippah* on his head like Alexei used to. A doting father talking to his little girl in Russian. A contented man. Until I reminded him of his past. If we hadn't been so distracted, we wouldn't have lost sight of you girls. Alexei would still have his daughter." Tears slip out the corners of Mama's eyes. "Loving me took away his livelihood and then later his daughter. I will have to live with that for the rest of my life."

"Oh, Mama. I'm so sorry."

"I don't want you to repeat my mistake. I saw the necklace Marco gave you and the way he looked at you at Katherine's party. Please, I beg you, don't go down that path. It will bring you nothing but hurt."

I pull my hands away. "It already has. I want to let him go. Why can't I do it?"

"Because the heart is a stupid, stupid organ." Mama dabs at her cheeks with her handkerchief.

"About many things, I'm afraid." I sniff. "Somedays I want to be a surgeon more than anything else in the world. Then I have a trial by fire and people—men—remind me that I am intruding into their world and they don't want me there."

Mama snorts. "Yes, they are quite territorial, aren't they? Uncle Edward was particularly nasty about my talents for facts and figures. 'How unladylike! She'll never marry! Why waste money on further education?' Sometimes I wonder what would have happened if my father's business could have been passed down to me.

Instead, Uncle Edward swooped in and took my father's business—the one Daddy broke his back to build from the ground up—before his brother's body was even cold. And then he ran it into the ground less than a year later."

"He should have kept you on to do the books."

A small smile crosses her face. "Yes, he should have."

Mama collects our mugs and deposits them in the sink. "I used to do your father's ledgers when we were first married. Doctor Porter was the one who put an end to that. He publically shamed Charles for letting me do them."

"I so despise Doctor Porter."

"He is a vile little man, isn't he? Of course, your father said it much more diplomatically. He said that motherhood should be my primary occupation. That I didn't need to worry so much about his business. That he would handle it. And we see how well that went." Mama *hmpfs* and I do too. "If you want to go to medical school, I will support you, but know that it will be a hard road ahead of you. There will be obstacles at every turn. It's exhausting to fight all the time."

"Now you sound like Kit."

"Your sister has her own uphill battle to attend to, I'm afraid. I wanted my daughters' lives to be easier than mine. I have not succeeded." Mama picks up Marco's coat from the chair. "I'll deposit this in Charles's office. You go upstairs and get into bed. I'll bring you up a hot water bottle. I might even attempt to make you soup for dinner."

I stand up and wrap my arms around Mama. She pulls me in tight. Though she is shorter than me now, this is the Mama I remember from my childhood. The soft, patient Mama who smells like roses and cocoa and who would hold me until I was ready to let go.

"Let him go, Virginia," Mama whispers in my ear. "For

both of your sakes."

"I will."

TWENTY-TWO

MARCO'S COAT IS still on Daddy's desk the next morning. They must have spent the night at the hospital. I retrieve the morning newspaper and head to the kitchen. Though my heart is broken, my stomach works quite well. I don't want to wait until Angelina arrives to have breakfast. I'm a modern woman. I'm going to make coffee. And toast. And possibly attempt a fried egg.

⚜

MY FRIED EGG might be a little crunchy thanks to the egg shells that fell into the frying pan while I was cooking, but my toast-making technique has definitely improved. I sit down at the kitchen table with my breakfast and snap the newspaper open.

Millions Pour in for Fourth Liberty Loan Bond
Another Peace Parley is Invited by Austria
President Urges Woman Suffrage as War Measure

Finally, some good news for a change. I want to share the suffrage news with Kit. Maybe now Kit can cancel her Washington plans and work on her wedding plans instead. That would make Mama happy. Maybe Kit can finally have her happily ever after. And if I receive a new silk dress or a fetching hat out of the event, even better.

I sip my coffee and return to the newspaper. A small article hides at the bottom of the first page.

City Orders Schools, Theaters, and "Places of Public Amusement" Closed Until Further Notice Because of Influenza

At least now I don't have to make up an excuse for why I never finished my mathematics homework. The selfish side of me wants to strip my school dress off and crawl back into bed. Instead, I take one last gulp of coffee, rip the newspaper article out of the paper to show Daddy, and brace myself for today's hazardous adventure. I am going to Pennsylvania Hospital to volunteer as a nurse. By myself. By trolley. And no one is going to stop me.

As I pass it, the telephone rings. The grandfather clock hasn't even struck eight yet. That is never good news. The telephone is insistent.

"Daddy?" The voice says before I even have a chance to say my greeting. "Daddy, I need your help."

"Kit? Kit, is that you?"

"Ginny, It's Grayson. He's so sick. I don't know what to do. Where's Daddy?"

"He's at the hospital."

"Can you come then? Quickly. I don't have any more aspirin. I'm at the Bellevue-Stratford Hotel. Room 125. Please hurry."

"I'm on my way. Hold on."

Kit sobs openly before finally hanging up.

❦━━━❧

"WHY AREN'T THEY answering?" Mama slams the telephone receiver down.

"Mama, I can't wait any longer. Kit needs me." I tuck two apples and a heel of bread into my basket. "Keep trying to reach Daddy. I will go to the Bellevue-Stratford Hotel to help Kit."

"It's not safe, Virginia."

"Mama, nothing is safe right now." I pull my mask out and put it on. "And ask Daddy to bring more medicine with him. I'm worried what he gave me won't be enough."

I add medicine to the basket and place my handbag around the bottles to cushion them. We have no medicine to waste. As it is, the aspirin and laudanum are only half full. There is probably enough for one dose of morphine. I use my handkerchief—the one with the viney V stitched in the corner—to hold a disinfected syringe. I pray I won't need it.

❦━━━❧

MAMA USUALLY FORBIDS me to ride the trolley by myself. I soon understand why. A bedraggled young man about Grayson's age sits down next to me though there is plenty of open seating available.

"Whatcha got there, Missy?" The smell of spirits wafts off his clothes and through his mask.

I ignore him and huddle closer into the corner. Instead of realizing his impropriety and apologizing immediately, the man slides even closer to me.

"I said, whatcha got there?"

"Supplies." I pull the basket in front of my chest like a shield. "My friend is very ill."

A dapper middle-aged man comes to my rescue. But instead of chastising the boorish, young man, he asks, "Do you have any medicine? Dover's Powders? What about aspirin? I'll give you five dollars for them. Each."

"It's not for sale." I put a gloved hand on top of my basket.

"Don't need no Dover's powders," the bedraggled man says. "The Missus says camphor will protect you. Each of my boys has a bag of camphor around their necks. That's what's keepin' 'em safe."

"Idiot. Camphor is useless. Onions. Onions will keep you safe." An old woman—who has obviously been eating a large quantity of raw onions recently—butts into the conversation. "And a deer kept beside your bed."

"You don't need no deer. No onions either. Just camphor," the bedraggled man yells back at her.

"Ten dollars," the dapper man yells over the ever-increasing fray. "But I can't go any higher than ten."

"No, sir. I cannot. My friend is desperately ill."

"It's unchristianly of you to hoard medicine, you selfish girl. I have sick loved ones at home, too." The man reaches for my basket, but I put my arms around it like a mother protecting her child.

"She has food, too." The onion woman points at the apples in my basket while the bedraggled man leers at my handbag.

"I deserve half the medicine." The dapper man puts his hand on my arm to pull it away from the basket.

I stand up. "You will unhand me, sir."

"You will give me the basket this instant, girl."

Instead, I slap him. When he takes a step back, the

bedraggled man reaches into my basket to steal my handbag. I elbow him sharply in the nose. In his now addled and bleeding state, the bedraggled man collides with the dapper man who falls into the onion woman. The onion woman screeches obscenities at me as I leap off the trolley even though we aren't at the next stop yet. My boots hit the cobblestones and pain flares up from my ankles. With my hand on top of the basket to keep the bottles from shattering, I run like a doughboy trying to escape enemy fire. I don't stop until I burst into the lobby of the Bellevue-Stratford Hotel.

The sound of my gasping breaths echoes through the lobby. There is no bell hop. No shoeshine boy. No one behind the front desk. The scatter of my footsteps across the lobby's marbled floor is the only sound of life. I take a deep breath before I knock on Room 125. I have seen all kinds of horrors, but nothing prepares me for how broken Kit looks when she opens the door. I take a step back, and my stomach drops. I know her rosy cheeks aren't from rouge. Before I can put my wrist to her forehead to confirm my suspicions, Kit yanks me through the door.

"Ginny," Kit's blood-shot eyes are wide with fear. "Grayson…he's so ill. His fever won't break. I've given him all the aspirin I can find. I don't know what else to do."

"When was the last time you slept or had something to eat?"

"Yesterday? The day before?" Kit pushes a tendril of hair back into her sloppy chignon. "Stop looking at me like that. I know I am in a dreadful state, but I've had more important things to attend to lately than my vanity." Kit grabs my hand and drags me toward the bedroom. "Please, help Grayson."

As soon as I enter the room, a familiar musty straw stench knocks me back a few steps.

"I know." Kit's voice breaks. "I keep washing him, but the smell won't go away."

I no longer recognize the man lying there. The wavy blond hair is the same, but the face beneath it no longer holds any trace of the handsome, virile Grayson Reynolds who foxtrotted so elegantly past me two days ago. Mahogany spots spread from Grayson's ears across his cheeks until they touch his nose.

"Do something, Ginny," Kit pleads. She cups one of Grayson's hands in hers. His nail beds are blue.

I deposit the basket and my gloves on the bedside table and place my wrist against his brow. One could cook an egg on Grayson's forehead. At my touch, Grayson shivers and gurgles. I pull back the sweat-soaked top sheet. A blue tinge washes down Grayson's neck onto his bare torso.

"Kit…he is not getting enough oxygen."

"Do something, Ginny."

Littered on the floor around the bed are fine, monogrammed, hotel towels and what was probably once the satin curtain lining. They are all stained with Grayson's bloody lung secretions.

"How long has he been like this, Kit?"

"Since the middle of the night."

I don't want to tell Kit the truth. I don't want to shatter her heart.

"Damn it all to Hell, Virginia! Do something!" Tears stream down Kit's face as her knees buckle. She sits down on the bed by Grayson's side and strokes his sweat-matted hair. "Anything."

"I can ease his pain." My voice wavers. "I can give him morphine."

"Do it." Kit wraps both of her hands around Grayson's and pulls them up to her cheek. "I'm not ready to let him go."

My shaking hands loosen the knots in the handkerchief and fill the syringe with the last of the morphine. A strip of the white satin curtain lining becomes a tourniquet. It is also my flag of surrender. I hold my breath to steady my hands and empty the morphine into Grayson's dehydrated body. Then we wait.

Daddy, where are you when we need you the most?

Kit continues to whisper sweet nothings to Grayson as the sunlight travels across the room. His breaths become slower and slower, and thinner and thinner. Meanwhile, Kit describes what their wedding would look like. Who would be in attendance. How their home would include a rose garden. What the names of their children would be. All the dreams and domestic aspirations that I didn't know my dear sister even had.

I stumble into the sitting room and collapse onto a plump chair. Why isn't Daddy here yet? It's been hours, surely. Grayson's gold pocket watch and chain sit open on the table beside me waiting for him to march back in the room and pick it up. I would give anything to make that happen. I run my fingertip over the highly-embellished, loopy R engraved on the back. Kit's sudden wail marks Grayson's time of death. 3:47. I cover my ears to dampen the animal-like howls of my sister's grief.

Finally, the sobs—hers and mine—subside. My heart cracks anew when I find Kit curled up asleep next to Grayson, her arm across his blue-tinged chest.

"Kit." I rub her back gently to wake her. "Katherine, he's gone."

Kit releases Grayson's body. She kisses his brow one last

time before pulling the bed sheet over his head.

"Wait here. I'm going to try to find a telephone. I need to call an—someone to assist us with Grayson." I lead Kit out into the sitting room. I grab my handbag and mask. "Then we are going home."

There still isn't a soul in the lobby. So no operator can connect their telephone line for me. Outside, I take several gulps of clean air before putting on my law-required mask. It doesn't stop the stench of musty straw that seems to envelop my whole body. I walk down the sidewalk toward home trying to find an open shop. *Any* open shop. I pass three little girls—in required masks—jumping rope in the street.

I had a little bird,
Its name was Enza.
I opened the window,
And in-flew-enza.

One of the little girls has hair as red as Anna's. Daddy said doctors and nurses are succumbing to the influenza in record numbers. Anna has been on the front lines since Day One. My heart grips. I can't lose her to this horrible disease. We have so many plans together. I can't fathom life without Anna in it.

I spy a masked police officer on the corner standing next to a placard listing the steep fines for spitting in the street or sneezing in public.

"Good day, Officer," I say as I pass, making sure he sees my mask.

The officer nods but doesn't say a word. Beads of sweat dot his brow even though I am shivering in the late afternoon sun. I know he's ill. Probably with the Spanish flu. I look back over my shoulder as I pass. He stands silently at his post kneading the back of his neck. There is nothing I can do for him.

"Another four hundred dead from Spanish flu!" a newsboy waves one of the newspapers he's hawking on the corner in my direction. "Officials say don't panic. Everything's fine. But are they lyin'? Read all about it here!"

"I need an undertaker. Do you know where I might find a telephone around here?" I ask the newsboy.

"Why? They won't be able to help you. The morgues are all filled up, Miss." The man beside me says, flipping a coin at the boy and snatching a newspaper off the stack.

"They are all filled up?" I say as the man walks away.

"Not all of 'em." The boy sells another newspaper before turning his attention back to me. "You can call 'em and find out."

"What's the number?"

"It's in the *Inquirer*, Miss. Only five cents." The boy holds out a copy of the *Philadelphia Inquirer* towards me. "On page three."

I pull a nickel out of my handbag.

"The pharmacy across the street has a telephone." The boy tips his cap at me. "That one's on the house."

After thanking the boy, I hurry across the street.

"Please. Wait!" I wave at the man as he turns over the CLOSED sign on the pharmacy.

"I don't have any Dover's Powders before you ask." Deep grooves etch the man's face though he doesn't look much older than Daddy.

"I need to use your telephone." I put my foot in the door, so he can't close it. "I can pay you. A nickel…a quarter."

The man lets out an exhausted sigh but opens the door

for me. A woman—possibly his wife—pushes a broom around the deserted store. I follow the man into the back office. He pulls out the chair at his desk for me.

"Do you know how to use a telephone?" the man says.

"Of course. We have one at home."

It's obvious that he doesn't believe me. "Holler if you need something, Miss."

I nod and open the newspaper to page three. Sure enough, there is a large advertisement that reads: **Influenza Sufferers, If you need Physicians, Nurses, Ambulances, Motor Vehicles or any other service because of the epidemic, telephone Filbert 100 and when the number answers, say: "Influenza." Filbert 100 answers calls 24 hours a day.**

I remove my mask so I can say "Influenza" when the Filbert 100 operator finally comes on the line.

"I'm sorry. We are experiencing a large number of calls right now, but if you give me the information of the deceased, we will get to you as soon as possible."

"How long might that be?"

"Three, possibly four days," the weary woman's voice says.

"Four days!" I shout into the receiver. "Do you know what a body is going to look like in four days?" Bile rises up in the back of my throat as I remember some of the cadaver pictures Anna showed me one Halloween to frighten me. It still frightens me, even if her stories of cadavers coming back to life is complete bunk. At least, I think it's bunk.

"We are doing our best, Miss."

"Well, it isn't good enough!" I slap my hand down on the man's desk.

"Do you still need our help, Miss?"

It takes all my willpower to comport myself again.

"Yes. I need someone to pick up...my friend. Mr. Grayson Reynolds of the New York City Reynolds. His remains are currently in Room 125 of the Bellevue-Stratford Hotel."

"We'll send someone as soon as we can, Miss. His remains will be taken to the city morgue."

"Thank you," I say, but I don't mean it.

I try telephoning both the Pennsylvania Hospital and my home, but nobody answers. For half a heartbeat, I contemplate calling the D'Orios. Instead, I leave a quarter and the newspaper on the pharmacist's desk, put my mask back on, and decide to be my own knight in shining armor.

TWENTY-THREE

I'VE RIDDEN THE trolley more times today than I have in the last year. This time, the few people left on the trolley give us wide-birth. I'm sure it's due to our shocking appearance. Thankfully, Grayson's coat hides most of the blood stains on the front of Kit's dress.

"Pull up your mask, Kit. We can't afford to be arrested on top of everything else today." When she doesn't comply, I do it for her. The heat coming from her face causes the pit of my stomach to drop.

I prop Kit up under my arm to get her off the trolley once we reach Rittenhouse Square. A few of our neighbors look out their windows as we pass by. No one offers aid. Widow Clark even looks me square in the eye and then pulls her parlor curtain roughly closed. So much for the Golden Rule.

"Wait here." I leave Kit barely standing in the doorway as I run down the hall toward the kitchen. "Mama? Angelina? Nurse Brighton?"

I burst through the kitchen door. My breakfast things still sit on the counter. It doesn't look like Angelina ever came. When I step back into the hallway a moment later, I find Kit melting down the wall like a sandcastle in the evening tide.

I catch Kit's head before it strikes the floor. "We have to get you to bed."

All the muscles in my back scream as I pull Kit off the floor to a stand. I throw her arm around my shoulders and pull Kit step by step up the stairs and into our bedroom.

"Mama!" I yell multiple times toward her boudoir, but she never answers. My stomach clenches as a picture of Grayson slips into my mind. I shake it away. "Let's take this off, Kit."

I throw Grayson's coat toward the old fireplace and then tackle the buttons on the back of Kit's soiled, wrinkled dress. When I pull the first layer of fabric away, a wave of heat rushes off Kit's body. The undergarments beneath cling to her sweaty frame. I ease Kit onto the chair in front of our vanity, so I can unbutton her boots. My heart clenches when I pull off her stockings and find a blackness snaking up from the bottom of her feet. I rub Kit's icy feet, but it doesn't improve her circulation.

In rapid succession, I pull off the corset, chemise, everything, and throw them into the unlit fireplace. A waft of lavender comes out of the top dresser drawer when I dig around inside looking for one of my summer nightgowns. My hand hits the bar of soap that Cecelia had gifted me just a few months ago. Besides the nursing apron she left behind, this little piece of lavender soap is the only thing I have left of Cecelia. Oh, how I wish Cecelia was here. I slide the nightgown over Kit's head as she stares with empty eyes into our vanity mirror.

"I'm going to fetch some water, Kit. I'll only be a moment." I push a sweaty tendril of hair behind Kit's ear.

As I turn to leave, Kit reaches out to take my arm. She grips my arm tighter as a series of racking, wet coughs shake her body. I hold my breath until it passes.

"Let's get you into bed first." I drag Kit across the floor and tuck her into bed.

Kit's eyes flutter closed in exhaustion. My heart clenches when I see mahogany spots dotting the skin in front of her ears.

"Mama?" I take a deep breath before opening the door to Mama's boudoir, expecting the worst. Instead, both Mama's boudoir and her bedroom are cold and empty. I grab the sea sponge off Mama's vanity and fill the china bowl beside it with clean water.

As I sponge Kit's broiling face and neck, the water practically turns to steam. For the next four hours, I force aspirin diluted in water down Kit's throat at regular intervals. Despite my best efforts, Kit continues to burn like Satan's furnace is in the pit of her stomach, and her breathing becomes wetter and wetter.

When the grandfather clock strikes nine, I collapse onto my bed, every ounce of strength sapped from my marrow. As exhaustion pulls me under, I hear the front door open. My heart leaps with hope.

"Daddy?" The person below stomps in with two heavy feet, not Daddy's cane-foot-foot gate or Mama's light, booted gate. My hope turns to fear when I remember that I forgot to lock the front door upon my return.

I'll be damned if I allow some hooligan to break into my family's home and depart with Granny Jackson's silver service or the last of the medication in Daddy's office. Granny Jackson's old-fashioned bed warmer by the fireplace becomes my weapon. I creep downstairs. In the dim moonlight filtering through the window, a hulking figure rifles through Daddy's medicine cabinet.

"Get out of my house, thief!" I turn on the light and

wave the bed warmer in front of me.

"Virginia?" Marco shields his eyes from the sudden bright light.

The light blinds me, too. I step in closer to verify that it truly is Marco because he looks so different. The peacock is nowhere to be seen. In its place is an unshaven, disheveled man with his once pomaded hair now drooping into his bloodshot eyes. Marco takes a bottle of laudanum out of the pocket of his recently reclaimed coat and puts it back on the shelf.

"Sorry if I scared you. The front door was unlocked. I'll only be a moment." Marco turns back to the medicine cabinet and rifles through it. "Where is the aspirin? We had another bottle."

"I'm using it. On my sister."

"There is no aspirin. No Dover's powders. Jesus, Mary, and Joseph! Did you use all the morphine, too?"

"Yes. On Grayson." I push the knot out of my throat. "I couldn't save him."

Marco bangs the medicine cabinet with his fist, making all the now empty or near empty glass bottles rattle.

"Then what am I supposed to use on *my* family?" Marco pounds his fist on his chest. "Angelina, Isabella, Colleen, and now Giorgio all have the Spanish flu. Little Italy's favorite son has called in all of his favors. There is no medicine left in Little Italy tonight."

"So, you came to Rittenhouse Square to steal ours?"

"*Use* not steal. You have no idea what it is like to have to do without, do you? You have never missed a meal. You have never put newspaper in the bottom of your hand-me-down shoes to stop up the holes. You have never had to give up your dreams and aspirations just to make enough money to keep the roof over your mamma's head."

"Aren't I the fortunate one?" I spit out sarcastically though I know he's not wrong. "Well guess what? Money can't buy everything."

"No, money can't buy everything." The fire still rages behind Marco's eyes. "But it can buy medicine on the black market. And, it can buy a good doctor when a Cadillac Phaeton falls off its struts and pins your papà to the ground underneath it while its owner and his well-to-do family are off celebrating Easter in New York City. Then you won't have to rely on the drunk quack filling in for him to drain the bloody lung fluid off your papà's cracked ribs using dirty equipment."

My stomach clenches. Now I know the true reason why Daddy came back to Philadelphia early from our Easter vacation.

"I'm sorry. I am truly sorry." When I reach for Marco's hand, the fire extinguishes in his eyes.

Marco pulls me into an embrace, his chin resting on my head. We cling to each other for several moment until both of our hearts stop racing.

"All the money in the world couldn't have saved Grayson. And now, Kit—" My voice breaks and my eyes sting remembering Kit kissing Grayson goodbye before covering his head with the sheet.

"True, but at least it gave him a fighting chance. My family has no medicine. The odds are stacked against me. They *always* seem stacked against me."

"Me, too." I yawn into Marco's chest. "I am so tired."

"I know. I haven't slept in days. I sure could use a nurse to assist me."

"So could I."

"Yeah." Marco chuckles. "But you have one patient. I have four."

I push Marco away. "Then ask your *wife* to assist you, Mr. D'Orio."

"Siobhan is *not* my wife."

"That's not what that piece of paper said."

"I bought that piece of paper in New York City. There, are you happy now? It's a fake. It's an insurance policy of sorts. It cost me three month's wages."

"And where, pray tell, did you get the money for that expensive piece of paper?"

"It doesn't matter."

"Selling medicine on the black market like Nurse Brighton?" I scoff.

Marco drops his eyes and my heart sinks. Three bottles of aspirin won't bring much, but a full bottle of morphine would fetch a pretty penny.

"I intend on paying Dr. Jackson back for the morphine. Every penny. I am not a thief. I just needed the money quickly. I didn't have a choice."

"Yes, you did." I push Marco back another step. "After everything we have done for you. For your family. You would resort to *stealing* from us?"

"How else could I raise the money to bring Dom's body back to Philadelphia so Mamma could lay her favorite son to rest and buy the fake marriage certificate, too? Unlike some people, I don't have a twenty-first birthday inheritance or expensive jewelry or an automobile or anything I could hock. Angelina and I had to make a choice. Would you have preferred my sister sell her body instead? Is *that* what a modern woman would do?"

I slap Marco's impertinent face.

"You are a child," Marco growls, his hands clenched firmly at his sides. "A selfish, spoiled little girl who knows absolutely nothing about the world outside of her tiny, privileged neighborhood. You can play doctor all you want, but let's face it. You will never make it through medical school if you can't handle how things get done in the real world without collapsing in a fit of self-righteous vapors."

My voice hardens, as well as, my heart. "Get out of my house. And, you can play doctor all *you* want, but let's face it. No one is going to admit a hot-headed chauffeur with grandiose aspirations and an ego to match into their medical school. You don't belong in my world. You never have and you never will."

Marco lets out a string of what are probably wallpaper-peeling curses in Italian with hand gestures to match. I yawn, unimpressed by his theatrics. Marco snatches the last quarter-full bottle of laudanum off the medicine shelf and brushes roughly past me. At the doorway, he stops and turns, his face scarlet and his hair wild.

"Oh, by the way, tell your father…I quit. Angelina, too."

"Fine." I hold out my hand for the laudanum. "And, that belongs to me."

Marco holds it out to me for a brief moment before dropping it into his jacket pocket with a look of gleeful defiance on his lips. "You can deduct that out of this week's pay."

"Bastard," the word slips off my tongue.

Instead of being shocked by my vulgarity, Marco gives me a mocking, overly-dramatic bow.

"GET OUT!"

Marco complies, but slams the front door so hard on his way out that the glass rattles. And with that, the puff of cold autumn air that rolls down the hall snuffs out the last tiny ember in my heart.

"Ginny?" Kit's weak voice floats down the stairs.

I bang my fist on the front door before locking it and then take the stairs two at a time. The smell of musty straw fills my nose before I even step one foot into our room. Kit moans and turns her head to face me. The mahogany spots creep across her high cheekbones like poorly applied rouge.

"Oh no. No. No. No!" The words squeak out of my constricted throat. I take Kit's hand in mine. Her fingernail beds are already blue. "I refuse to let you go. You tell this Spanish flu that it can't have you."

I rub Kit's cold hand trying to get the blood to circulate. "C'mon, Kit. You are the most pig-headed person I know. Don't you dare give in to it. Stand your ground for your sister…your sisters this time."

"Ginny." The word barely escapes before a series of coughs sends bloody foam pouring out of Kit's mouth, soiling the bed clothes.

I envelop Kit's hand in both of mine. My useless hands. Hands that would without hesitation promise to never touch a scalpel if it meant my sister could stay on this earth a while longer.

BY THE TIME the clock strikes five in the morning, bloody rags litter the floor around Kit's bed. The mattress will have to be burned. I can't stop the bloody secretions coming out of her body's every orifice. I sacrificed every towel in the bathroom, all the fabric covering my bed, and the curtain linings, but it's not enough. I will never be able to sleep in this room again. I will never be able to sleep again at all.

As the first rays of dawn bring light to the darkest day of my life, Kit's eyelids crack open slightly. She draws in a watery, ragged breath.

"Ginny?"

"Shhh. Save your strength. Mama and Daddy will be home at any moment. I'm sure of it." I pull Kit's hand to my chest to let her know that she isn't alone.

"Ginny...I'm...sorry."

"Sorry? For what? For ruining my handiwork?" I laugh half-heartedly while running my stained index finger over the equally-stained *K* done in French knots on her pillow case, last year's Christmas present. "You helped nurse me back to health when I had the Spanish flu in July. Now it is my turn to return the favor. Fair is fair."

But this is anything but fair.

"Besides, you promised me. We are going to be the cultured, college-educated, *voting* Jackson sisters. I am going to hold you to that. You simply need a few days of bed rest," I lie, as much for my sake as Kit's. "You will be back in Washington soon enough with your sisters. Marching. Protesting. Being a thorn in the president's backside."

Kit turns her head from side to side.

Tears stream out of my eyes as the words rip out of my chest. "Yes, you will. I am not doing this without you. I refuse to do this without you. I refuse. I refuse. I refuse."

Kit shakes her head. Blood-tinged tears slip out of the corner of her eyes and cut across the mahogany spots soiling her beautiful cheekbones. She doesn't take a breath for almost a minute.

"Please, Kit. Please. Not yet. It's just becoming your time...our time." I try to hold back my tears and smile in encouragement.

Kit mouths through cracked lips: *I love you.*

And as always, Katherine Eleanor Jackson has the last

word.

◆━━━◆

UNFORTUNATELY, OUR PARENTS are too late to hear it.

"Oh dear God." Daddy's hand grasps my shoulder and wrests me away from Kit's body.

As I turn into his chest to sob, I see Mama grab for the doorframe, her face ashen. Daddy pulls me toward the door, but my legs refuse to work anymore. He can't hold me. Daddy's bad leg buckles, and we crumple to the floor.

"Shhhhhhh." Daddy rocks me on the floor like I'm seven, not seventeen.

He looks over his shoulder at Mama, who holds her hand to her chest like her heart has been ripped out of it. With one strong but shaking hand, Daddy reaches back for her. When Mama takes it, he pulls her down to us. Mama loops one arm around Daddy and one around me and pulls us in tight. I so wanted us to be a closer family. But not like this.

TWENTY-FOUR

I DON'T REMEMBER much after Daddy closed the door to my childhood bedroom. Closing off the nightmare inside. Sometime within the next cycle of the sun across the sky, I end up clean, fed, and tucked into Mama's bed.

"Rest now." Mama sits on the end of the bed, stroking my legs through the covers.

Has Mama always had so much gray hair at her temples or is it the product of last night's events?

"Take a sip." Daddy, who is perched on a chair by the bed, holds a glass of pungent liquid out to me. "It will help you sleep. There is nothing more that can be done presently."

I push his hand away. "Then you should take it."

"I can't. Someone might need me."

"Someone *did* need you, Daddy, but you weren't here." I know my words wound him, but I have to know. "Where were you? Kit needed you. *I* needed you."

"And for that, I am truly, *truly* sorry. I made a judgement call." Daddy's breath hitches in his chest. "I had no idea how badly its consequences would play out. If I had known, I would have come to you…to Kit…immediately, well, sooner at least."

"I tried calling the hospital for hours, but I couldn't get through," Mama says. "I finally hired a cab to take me there. I was horrified. There was no one at the front desk. I looked and looked for your father." Mama's voice breaks. "I couldn't find him."

Daddy pats her hand. "There are so few doctors on their feet right now that I was in surgery delivering a baby by Cesarean when your mother arrived at the hospital. First, it was the baby. Then a man with a stroke. Then an automobile accident. And then, and then, and then…and all the Spanish flu patients on top of that. So when Eleanor finally found me and told me that you were taking care of Grayson, I knew he was in good hands. I knew you could handle it until I could get there. I tried to leave. I wanted to leave. Eleanor insisted that we leave. But when we finally did, we were too …." Daddy's voice breaks. "I'm sorry."

I have never seen my father so broken. As Mama wraps her arms around his hunched frame, I fight a swirl of emotions. I want to hate him. I want to blame him. Daddy's racking sobs crack my already fractured heart wide open. After several minutes of healing tears, we finally begin to come out the other side of this nightmarish tunnel.

I take his hand in mine and squeeze. "I forgive you, Daddy."

"Thank you, Virginia." Daddy leans in and kisses my head. "And maybe one day, I will be able to forgive myself."

"Daddy? What do we do about Kit's—" my voice breaks.

"I called Mr. O'Connor's son, the undertaker, but it is going to take some time," Daddy says, back to his your-toe-is-going-to-have-to-be-amputated voice. Mama gasps. "Here. Take a mouthful to calm your nerves, Eleanor." Daddy holds out the glass toward her. "It's for medicinal purposes, of course. Though I am curious, Virginia, why there was rum in your hope chest and why did Katherine…." Daddy pulls out a little note from his pocket. I recognize Kit's looping penmanship immediately. "want you to procure a recipe from Marco for something called *baba*?"

I want to be angry. Instead, a half sob-half laugh erupts out of my chest. Our kitchen dinner party seems a thousand years ago. I would give anything to rewind back time to that night again. That girl didn't have a care in the world. That girl thought she was in love. That girl still had her sister. That girl no longer exists.

I look at Mama, whose lips are pursed. Instead of chastising or questioning me about the rum, she reaches for the glass and takes a gulp.

"Nothing is conventional presently." Mama takes a second gulp before passing it back to Daddy who finishes the glass. "I suggest we all rest for a little while."

I pull the bedclothes back to get out of their bed, but Daddy stops me.

"You two rest here," Daddy says. "The settee and I are well acquainted. One more night won't harm me. Besides, I have a telephone call to make first."

Mama begins unbuttoning her boots. "For a few hours. Then I will trade with you, Charles. You need to rest, too."

"I will." Daddy kisses the top of my head. "Now then, get some rest, my loves."

Daddy and Mama look at each other. When Daddy leans toward her, Mama turns her head so that his lips press into her cheek. It's not much, but I hope it is enough to fan the ember back into at least a small flame.

IT IS MORE than a few hours. Probably twelve. Maybe more. At least Mama's nightmares have finally ceased. Mine have not. I crack my swollen eyelids open. Anything to make the visions of Kit drowning in her own lung secretions cease. My pocket watch sits open on the bedside table. The hands have long stopped, permanently frozen in this nightmare like I am. The sound of Mama's and some other women's voices talking in soothing but earnest tones downstairs makes my heart clench. I can't take any half-hearted condolences right now from the people who looked down their noses at my sister when she was alive. Finally, Mama comes back up the stairs. A moment later, I hear water running in the bathtub.

I take a few moments to tidy myself up, too, but only the most basic of tasks, before descending the stairs to find Daddy. I discover him asleep at his desk, his head resting on his arms, and a blanket draped over his shoulders.

A musical laugh comes from the parlor. I follow it. Two women in dark dresses stand where only a few days ago, Rittenhouse Square's finest members convened around the punchbowl. The women look at me, and the older of the pair's face softens in recognition. She rushes to me, the smell of lavender soap in her wake.

"My Virginia." Nurse Cecelia embraces me before pushing me away. She holds my face in her palms. Her eyes are glassy, and she bites her bottom lip to keep her emotions inside.

I flat out burst into tears, which gives her license to, too.

"I know, sweetheart, I know." Cecelia pulls me tight to her chest and strokes my hair. "This is unbearable for me, too."

Once we compose ourselves—me using my sleeve and Cecelia using the first handkerchief I ever embroidered for her—she introduces her friend.

"Virginia, please meet Nurse Shockey."

"Please call me Florence," the sharp-looking young woman says with a Southern drawl. She offers me a firm, but sympathetic, handshake. "I am so sorry that we are meeting under these circumstances. My condolences for your loss."

Loss? It doesn't seem real. Kit should be coming downstairs any moment now. My heart continues to cycle between numbness and breaking.

"Cecelia has told me so much about you," Florence continues after a beat. A small curl of white-blond hair loops in front of each of her earlobes. "I hope we'll have a chance to get to know each other better while we're here. I'm Cecelia's partner for this post."

"Post?" I say.

"Uncle Sam has dispatched us to Philadelphia for at least the next two weeks to help with the acute nursing shortage. We are reporting for duty, ma'am." Florence does a mock salute.

I give Cecelia a quizzical look and then notice the two cots and matching suitcases that occupy the back corner of the parlor.

"You can thank Dr. Carter. He is the one who pulled the strings to have us posted here instead of Boston as originally ordered." Cecelia looks over her shoulder. "I do feel slightly guilty that our post came with such lavish room and board."

"It's only the parlor," I say. "And Angelina doesn't cook for us anymore."

"Honey, compared to my mama's house up the holler, this house is practically Buckingham Palace." Florence's Southern accent thickens. "And I know my way around a kitchen. Big Granny Shockey taught me how to make biscuits and gravy when I was five."

"Florence," Cecelia chastises in her motherly voice. Surely, Florence can't be more than a year older than me. "Though I appreciate your culinary skills that is not why we were sent to Philadelphia."

My heart hitches. "Cecelia, Kit's body…we have to…."

I can't even say the words.

Cecelia grabs my hands in hers. Her voice is tight, but she says matter-of-factly, "It's already done. I put her in the white dress. Her suffragist uniform. I couldn't find her favorite hat—the blue one with the ostrich feather— but Florence dressed her hair a bit. I even rolled up her suffragist sash and tucked it in her hand. That's how I wanted to remember her. I hope you don't mind."

I shake my head.

"Your father telephoned Mr. O'Connor, Jr. again. Unfortunately, it will still take some time before he can come." Cecelia places a hand on my cheek. "Stay down here."

"Pull up a cot. You are welcome to stay in the Nurses' Dorm," Florence says, pinning a wide-brimmed, black hat into her hair. "I've heard that you are already quite a skilled nurse. Big Granny Shockey always said the best way to heal a grieving heart is to keep your hands busy. You're welcome to join in our post. We start in Rittenhouse Square today and then circle out."

"When you are ready, Virginia." Cecelia squeezes my shoulder. "Maybe tomorrow. Maybe next week. Maybe next month. When you feel called to serve again."

Cecelia fetches her hat from her cot. "Now then, we shall be out all day but will return before dinner to take care of my most important patients. Who knows, maybe Nurse

Shockey will treat us to the aforementioned biscuits and gravy for dinner."

"Thank you," I choke out.

"Now rest, Virginia. Heal." Cecelia kisses my cheek before squaring her shoulders and marching out the front door with Florence.

⚓━━━⚓

THANKS TO CECELIA, I do feel called to serve again. Just for my parents today, but it's a start.

"Shh, try to rest some more," I whisper as I take Mama's luncheon tray from her. "I'll make Daddy something when he wakes again."

With that, Daddy rolls over in their bed with a pained groan. He mumbles some orders before slipping back under into sleep.

After depositing Mama's tray in the kitchen, I tuck myself into the parlor and pull out Mama's Red Cross knitting. I want to be useful. I want to keep my hands busy and dull the pain in my heart. The half-done sock stares back at me for ages before I tuck it back into Mama's basket. It brings me no comfort.

I pull my sewing basket onto the settee next to me and pour out its contents. All the threads and ribbons and pieces of fabric call to me. They invite me to lose myself in them. Heal myself. I pick up the linen handkerchief I started for Anna's birthday. A row of green stems made out of thin green ribbon already decorates the corner, but the blooms are bare. I dig my hand through the pile next to my hip until I find a roll of yellow silk ribbon. Its width isn't even half as wide as my pinky nail, but the ribbon is the perfect color for sunflowers. I dig around in the pile a second time until I find a velvety ribbon of a similar width in a deep chocolate brown color. My heart lightens as I let my hands do the work they know best to create one last gift for my sister.

———

I AM JUST tying off the last knot when there is a rapping on the front door. I take a deep breath and steel myself to face one of my insincere Rittenhouse Square neighbors.

"Everett?"

Everett wavers a bit on my doorstep, his arms weighted down with a large crate. A basket perches precariously on top of it.

"Coward," Everett says and then startles. "Pardon. Not you, Virginia. The man tasked with delivering this box. He saw the white crepe on your door, and the coward turned tail." When Everett jiggles the box, the tell-tale sound of glass bottles tinkles from inside. "I suspect this may be of importance to your father." Everett tips his head at the basket on top. "And this might be of importance to you. And your mother and father, of course."

"Will you bring them to the kitchen? I don't want to disturb my parents," I whisper, and Everett gives me a shocked look like I have suddenly invited him to my boudoir.

Everett clears his throat. "Of course."

"We have given up on formalities for the time being," I say when I introduce Everett to the kitchen. I'm sure he hasn't spent much, if any, time in his.

"I'm sorry that it isn't much, but I wanted to bring you something." Everett places the crate and basket on the kitchen table. "Since your sister...passed. My sincerest condolences. I know you must be crushed."

"Thank you." My voice is tight, but I keep the tears at bay. I don't want to cry in front of Everett. I don't want to cry in front of anyone anymore. I dig in the basket and pull out one of about a dozen perfect red apples. I sniff the ruby skin and my mouth waters. The apples are at the peak of ripeness. "Thank you. Or, your mother, I should say."

Everett pulls at his collar. "About that. If you wouldn't mention it to my mother, I would be obliged. My parents don't know that I am here. In fact, they don't know I borrowed the automobile either."

"Everett," I say, though my tone is more of amusement than chastisement.

"I'm sorry." Everett cowers but then a fire lights behind his slate blue eyes. "No, frankly, I'm not. I don't care what they say. It's not right. We should be helping our neighbors. Our…friends."

I put my hand on Everett's arm. "And your friend is grateful. She would be even more grateful if you would go out to the carriage house and fetch a crowbar so that she could open this crate." I rub the apple on my dress and take a big bite. "Your friend is also eternally grateful for the apples. They bring such a sweetness to this very bitter time."

Everett pulls out an unadorned, white, silk handkerchief from his pocket and wipes a dribble of juice from my chin. He starts to put it away, but I place my hand over his.

"May I keep it for a bit?"

"If you wish," Everett says to my odd request.

"After I launder it, of course, I would like to create something for you. Maybe your initial. Or some ivy. I'm not certain yet. But something for you to remember me by no matter where your travels may take you in the future."

Everett puts his hand over mine. "I would treasure it. Now then, allow me to fetch the crowbar."

I've almost finished the apple by the time Everett returns through the back door with the crowbar in hand and pries the lid of the crate open. I plunge my hand into the sea of wood shavings and fish around. Over a dozen glass bottles of different sizes and shapes clink against each other. I pull each one out and inspect it.

Dover's powders. Digitalis. Laudanum. Castor oil. Vick's VapoRub. But no aspirin.

A letter peeks out the corner of the box. Though it is addressed to Daddy, it isn't Dr. Carter's handwriting. It's Anna's.

September 18, 1918
Boston, Massachusetts

My dear Dr. Jackson,

Thank you for helping my father with his Spanish flu cases earlier this month. Things took a turn for the worse after you departed. I see in the newspapers that Philadelphia has also suffered greatly. You must be working around the clock as we are.

We have been able to narrow down the incubation time of this disease. Most patients present symptoms within 48 to 72 hours. The severe cases are obviously the most contagious, but even the milder cases are easily communicable. Father lost three nurses this week, and three-quarters of the hospital staff are ill or at home attending family members. Now, I'm afraid, Father has fallen to the disease himself while preparing this supply box for you. He has been in bed for the past three days. The good news is that his fever broke this morning. His lungs are very wet, but I believe he will survive, if we can keep the pneumonia at bay. I wish you were here to attend him, but I am doing the best I can with the techniques you taught me earlier. I am including several jars of Vicks VapoRub. A colleague from North Carolina highly recommended it, and it seems to have helped Father immensely.

I pray things are better for you, and that you and your family are well. Please accept this box as a token of my father's friendship and gratitude for your service earlier this month.

Next time, we will have to meet under much more pleasant circumstances. And please bring Virginia with you as promised. I miss her desperately, and we have much planning to do.

Good luck and God bless you.

Warmest regards,

Anna

At the bottom of the letter is a postscript written in Dr. Carter's chicken scratch handwriting.

P.S. CHARLES, APOLOGIES FOR THE LONG DELAY. I FOUND THIS SUPPLY BOX JUST AS MY DEAREST ANNA SUCCUMBED TO THE INFLUENZA. I HAVE NEVER BEEN SO TERRIFIED IN MY LIFE. PLEASE PRAY FOR HER. —JOHN

The letter flutters to the floor as I picture Anna coughing up bloody foam like Kit.

"Oh dear God, no. Please don't take Anna, too. I couldn't bear it."

I put my wrist to my forehead. I'm not any warmer than usual. Has it been more than 72 hours? Am I somehow spared or is the influenza already building in me? How much time do I have left?

"Are you going to faint?" Everett pulls out a kitchen chair and puts a steadying hand on my arm. A panicked look crosses his face. "Are you ill? Should I fetch your father?"

"No, I am…. Honestly, I don't know what I am. Unmoored, perhaps."

"Well then, it's a good thing that I am coxswain of the Chestnut Hill Academy rowing team."

"Pardon?"

"I steer the shell—the boat—for our rowing team. It would be my pleasure to help you navigate through the rough waters—or at least drive you wherever you would like to go—during this tempestuous time. Though that offer may only be good for today, once my father notices his automobile is missing. We could collect some apples off your tree and deliver them to your classmates. Miss Vaughn, perhaps?"

"Who said you were a clodhopper? You, sir, are a knight in shining armor." I go to the pantry and pull out our largest basket. I unhook one of the ropes of onions and throw it in the basket. "Now then, allow me to collect a few more items, and then let's go climb my beloved tree."

TWENTY-FIVE

"ONE LAST STOP for the day," I say when we enter Little Italy. "It's the brick row house at the end of the street on the right. The one with the rosebush underneath the front window."

Little Italy has changed dramatically since my last visit. The once bustling streets are nearly empty. A closed sign hangs in the front window of Mr. Borrelli's shop. The few people out cross each other's paths in wide arcs. Crepe morbidly decorates many doors all down Marco's street. Like all over Philadelphia. Like at my home. A sea of white, black, and gray marks the deaths of the young, the middle-aged, and the elderly, respectively. I say a prayer of thanks when there isn't any crepe on the D'Orios' door.

Forty-eight to 72 hours. My brow is still cool, but my body aches.

"Thank you for today, Everett. I will never forget your kindness."

Everett parks the car. "I will never forget the sight of you climbing that apple tree like you were Tarzan of the Apes."

"And I will never forget the sight of Margaret Vaughn's face when she encountered you on her doorstep, apples in hand." I can't stop the chuckle that sneaks out. Margaret fairly swooned off the front stoop into her mother's prized rose bush when Everett—at my prompting from the automobile—invited her for a future outing.

"Neither will I." A longing smile lights up Everett's face.

I turn away, pull up my mask, and steel myself for the task at hand. "I don't want you to come in. You've been exposed enough today at my home. Allow me to do this alone."

"I can't leave you *here*." Everett gestures at the white crepe fluttering in the wind on both sides of the D'Orios' house. "There is death everywhere here."

"There's death everywhere in Philadelphia. All I can do is try to bring some comfort." I put my gloved hand over Everett's. "Like you did for me."

I give Everett's hand a last squeeze before I gather my basket and exit the automobile. I poke my head back through the door one last time. "Until next time, Mr. Winthrop. God bless you. Stay well."

"You too, Miss Jackson."

I take a deep breath before rapping on the door. Even after a second knock, no one answers. But someone left the door unlocked.

"Mrs. D'Orio?" I call into the empty living room after letting myself in.

Miss Shannon comes down the stairs, looking haggard and holding a whimpering Colleen in her arms. The baby's eyes are sunk deep in her skull.

"Miss Jackson?" Miss Shannon cocks her head to the side.

"Yes. May I help?" I take off my mask and gloves and stuff them into the basket.

"Yes, but Angelina and all the younger children are ill."

"And Colleen is grossly dehydrated." I nod at Colleen,

who doesn't have enough moisture left in her to make tears to go along with her whimpering. "I have some supplies in my basket. Will she nurse?"

Miss Shannon shakes her head no. Without asking permission, I place the basket in the kitchen and begin unpacking it. I slip on my nursing apron and pull out my pocket watch.

"I've brought some vegetables and a little meat. I'll make some soup after I check on the rest of…your family." The words still sting my heart. "Where is Marco?"

"Out looking for medicine," Miss Shannon says.

"I have medicine." I gesture toward the stairs. "May I?"

"Please. Help them. I don't know what more to do."

I take a deep breath to settle my nerves and climb the creaky stairs. Three beds and a crib fill the first room. Angelina and Isabella sleep peacefully in two of them. Sun pours through the window illuminating their lack of mahogany spots. Both sisters sound raspy, but Angelina's breathing is particularly wet. The smaller second bedroom reveals two beds. Giorgio coughs fitfully from beneath a pile of deftly-stitched quilts.

"Giorgio, do you remember me? I'm Virginia. Dr. Jackson's daughter."

Giorgio nods his head, but can't stop coughing long enough to answer. His face is flushed with fever, but thankfully he lacks mahogany spots, too.

"I'm afraid I don't have any aspirin, but I do have some Dover's powders. It should at least help you rest a bit." I pull out my pocket watch from Kit and Grayson. A deep pain twinges in my heart, but I bury it deep. Instead, I flip open the pocket watch and time Giorgio's pulse.

In the middle of my counting, I hear the front door open and feet stomp across the living room floor.

"Why do you have Colleen up?" Marco's voice booms through the house. "You know she's contagious."

Miss Shannon hushes him. "She was crying. I was trying to comfort her."

"Colleen is dehydrated. We've got to find some salt. And some aspirin. And food." I can imagine Marco running his hand through his hair in exasperation. "Let me wash up, and then you must go. Tell Mamma that there has been no change, but *not* to come home. I don't want her to become ill, too. Not with her heart problems."

"Marco, Miss Jackson is —"

"I said I don't want to talk about her."

"But she —"

"Enough, Siobhan. Try to nurse Colleen again. She needs fluids before her kidneys shut down."

I wait until I hear the bathroom door close and water gurgling through the ancient pipes before I return downstairs to the living room. "I'll make the soup after I give Giorgio some medicine for his cough. And don't worry about Marco. He's all bark but no bite."

Miss Shannon melts into Mamma D'Orio's favorite chair and unbuttons her shirtwaist.

"Dom, too. A big softie on the inside, he was. And wouldn't say one cross word to his Mamma. Now, Giorgio, that boy's got a mouth on 'im." Miss Shannon tries unsuccessfully to get Colleen to latch on. "I wish Dom and his father would've gotten to meet Colleen. That's my biggest regret in life. Maybe Colleen could have brought them back together as a family?"

I rummage through my basket in the kitchen and pull out the bottle of Dover's Powders. When I get to the foot of the stairs again, Miss Shannon lets out a sob.

"I don't want Colleen to grow up alone." Miss Shannon

wipes a tear from her cheek with her palm.

I stop. Marco is stubborn and vexing, but I know with the utmost certainty that he wants to keep what is left of his family together.

"Marco doesn't want that either," I say.

Miss Shannon gives up trying to nurse Colleen and buttons up her shirtwaist. "Sometimes I wonder if Marco wishes he was born into your family instead."

The idea is so preposterous that I let out an unladylike snort. "Why? Money can't buy happiness."

"No, but it makes things easier."

Money does make things easier. Going to medical school is hard enough for any woman, but at least I have the funds. I look at Miss Shannon. Her hands are chapped from whatever manual labor she does. I won't throw away my opportunity, no matter how difficult it is.

Giorgio's coughing from upstairs reminds me why I am here. "You rest. I'll be back momentarily."

By the time I return to the living room again, Miss Shannon and Colleen are sound asleep in Mama D'Orio's chair. I set about the task of making soup. Except, I've never made soup before. Surely, it isn't that difficult. I pull the already cooked meat off the chicken bones and throw it into boiling water mixed with a copious amount of salt. I chop up some onions, celery, and carrots and throw them in, too. They aren't the dainty, bite-sized morsels like Angelina makes, but it's good enough. I taste the mixture several minutes later. It's a little salty, but not too bad for my first attempt. What would Angelina put in this soup? Little green specks of something, perhaps?

With Miss Shannon still dozing in the living room, I take the liberty of rifling through Mamma D'Orio's cabinets for spices. I find some minced white pieces that smell like garlic. A stifled sneeze confirms that another jar holds black pepper. I add both to the mixture. There is a jar with some kind of green herb in it. I sniff it. It brings me back to our dinner party in the kitchen. Marco's hearty laughs. Angelina's proud face as she presents spaghetti and meatballs. Kit licking a spot of rum syrup off her fingers. I ache to turn back the clock to that perfect moment.

The door to the bathroom squeaks, breaking me out of my revelry.

"Sorry. I dozed off in the bathtub. What is that smell?" Marco walks into the kitchen. No shoes. No socks. No shirt and wiping leftover shaving foam off his face with a hand towel.

The bottle slips from my hand—thankfully with the lid on—into the soup. I fish around madly with the wooden spoon to get it back out. My face feels like I plunged it into the soup, too.

Marco stands like a statue, a trickle of water running down his chest.

"I brought you something." I pull a perfect red apple out of the basket and hold it out to him like an olive branch. "I also brought Dover's Powders and laudanum for your family. Unfortunately, there isn't any aspirin, but would you like to try Vicks VapoRub on them? Anna sent it to me. She said it helped her father. It's what our colleagues down south are using."

Marco continues to stand dumbfounded and dripping.

"And there's more medicine in the basket." I put the apple down and gesture to the basket at the back of the kitchen. "Please, take it for your patients. I'm sure Little Italy needs fresh supplies as desperately as Rittenhouse Square does. We are happy to share with fellow Philadelphians."

Marco runs a hand through his wet hair and puffs out

his cheeks. "Virginia, I don't know what to say."

"A simple 'thank you' will suffice." I open one cupboard door after another looking for a soup bowl. "We both have a job to do. You can return to yours after you eat."

Marco steps in close, opening the small cupboard above my head. When he reaches up to fetch a bowl, I see all the muscles in his arms and chest straining against his skin. I breathe in the scent coming off his body—a mixture of musky shaving foam and lavender soap.

"Thank you." Marco holds the bowl out in front of him like he is at a soup kitchen. "I didn't know you could cook."

"Neither did I." I put one hand on top of his trembling hand to steady the bowl before I scald the both of us. "I threw a bunch of odds-and-ends from home into a pot of boiling water. It may be good. Or it may be dreadful."

"Aren't you going to join me?" A wisp of steam curls off the top of Marco's bowl.

"Aren't you going to put a shirt on?"

A devilish smile cuts across his face before Marco hands his soup bowl back to me. "Of course. Please avert your eyes, Miss Jackson."

But I don't.

Marco returns a moment later with a clean, but wrinkled shirt and some threadbare socks. He sits down at their roughhewn kitchen table, and I place the bowl of soup and an apple in front of him. Marco reaches for my hand, but I pull it away.

"I want to give thanks for this meal." Marco looks up at me, dark circles under his eyes. "It's the only good thing that's happened to me in days."

I sit down next to Marco and stretch out my hand. Marco's warm fingers curl around mine, his thumb caressing my knuckles as he prays in Italian. I hear my name mentioned. When Marco crosses himself, I add an "Amen." He takes a large bite of the apple before putting it across the table from him.

"Is it bad?" The apple doesn't look rotten from my angle.

"No, it's delicious. That's the problem." Marco looks over at Miss Shannon now sleeping with her mouth wide open in Mamma D'Orio's chair. "Mamma and Siobhan should have it."

"No, *you* should have it. You need to eat. Plus, I brought you a half dozen apples."

Marco grabs the apple back and says through another juicy bite, "Thank you."

"You can thank Everett Winthrop," I say, and, at which, Marco chokes. "The apples were his idea, but I climbed the tree to pick them."

Marco nods and continues to wolf his food down in silence. Meanwhile, I start on the enormous pile of dirty dishes. I plunge my hands deep into the water, pretending not to notice Marco staring at me.

"Mamma would hit me with her wooden spoon if she knew I allowed a guest to do our dishes," Marco says.

"I'm not a guest. I'm a…." I'm not sure what I am to the D'Orios. "I am happy to assist."

Halfway through the dishes, Marco's chair scrapes away from the table. He adds his bowl and spoon to the top of the slowly shrinking pile. I startle when his arms suddenly wrap around my waist. Marco steps in even closer until his chin rests on my shoulder.

"*Grazie, bella.*"

Memories of lemon-flavored kisses at the apple tree flood my mind. My body melts back into Marco's chest. I allow my weary body and soul to rest in the strength of his arms. Marco's lips trail up the side of my neck to the side of my face.

"I apologize for the other night," Marco whispers in my ear.

His words are like a bucket of icy water poured over my head. I jerk away from Marco. Colleen whimpers from the living room. Any remaining domestic fantasy I had bursts like a soap bubble.

"You said you needed a nurse. That is what I am here to do." I brush by Marco to the back of the kitchen and squat down next to the basket on the floor.

"I do, and I am glad." Marco squats down beside me, his lips only inches from mine. "I have also missed you terribly."

Marco's eyes close, and he leans in to kiss me. I dodge his advance and fish out a bottle of laudanum from the basket before standing up.

"Honestly, Marco, you think a little flattery and affection can suddenly make everything better? What kind of vapid woman do you think I am?"

Marco stands up next to me. "I said things the other day that I regret. I apologize. You said some pretty awful things to me, too."

"But there were truths in there. Ugly as they were. Truths you need to face. Truths I need to face."

"This is about the laudanum, isn't it?" Marco strides across the room, grabs something from beside the family *Bible*, and comes back. "Take it." Marco holds the stolen bottle of laudanum out to me. "I didn't use any of it, I swear. I had planned to bring it back the next day, but then Angelina took a turn for the worse."

"Keep it." I push Marco's hand back toward his chest. "Your family needs it more than mine does right now."

"But you still think I'm a thief."

"I...I don't know. Please, Marco. Allow me to attend to your family for a few hours while you rest and then I will go."

"I don't need your help."

"The bags under your eyes are the size of steamer trunks. Please, let me do what I have been trained to do."

"I said I don't need your help," Marco's voice crescendos.

"For God's sake, Marco, stop being such a martyr." Miss Shannon stands at the edge of the kitchen with Colleen in her arms. "Say 'thank you' and accept her help. I know Domenico—God rest his soul—made you promise to take care of us, *all* of us, when he joined the service. And you've made your brother proud, but this is outside of enough. He didn't expect you to carry the entire weight of the family on your shoulders."

Miss Shannon crowds into the kitchen with us. She cups Marco's chin in her hand and makes him look her in the eyes.

"Asking for help is not a sign of weakness," she says.

Marco closes his eyes, trying to hold on to his composure. When he opens his glassy eyes again, they are filled with hurt, anger, and fear.

"Then take the paper, Siobhan," Marco mumbles until Miss Shannon releases his face. "If something happens to me in battle, then you can collect widow's benefits. Like you should have been able to do as Dom's wife, if my parents hadn't been so stubborn and old-fashioned."

"Remember when your mother found Dom's counterfeit American birth certificate after he enlisted? Also purchased from the Camorras, mind you. Don't do that to her heart again." Miss Shannon pokes Marco right square in the sternum. "Or you will regret it."

"But this is different. A marriage certificate—"

Miss Shannon covers Marco's mouth with her poking hand. "Hush. I said no, Marco. And not another word about it. I mean it. Not one bloody word." Miss Shannon removes her hand and her hard exterior begins to melt. "These D'Orio boys. Stubborn. Proud." Miss Shannon gently pats the side of Marco's face. "But loyal and not too hard to look at. Lord help the girls when Giorgio gets older. I hear he's a little heartbreaker at school already."

Upon hearing his name, the little heartbreaker calls from the top of the stairs, "Marco, I'm hungry."

Marco releases his breath and some of the wrinkles in his forehead release, too. *"Grazie a Dio.* I think Giorgio might be on the mend. Coming!"

"I'll go share the good news with your mother," Miss Shannon says.

"Yes, but tell her she *can't* come home. It's not safe yet. For you either. I can't get Angelina's fever to break," Marco says.

"Let me take Colleen and see if I can get some broth into her." I put my arms out for the lethargic baby.

Miss Shannon kisses the top of Colleen's fuzzy head before trusting her most precious possession with me. "Thank you, Nurse Jackson."

"Virginia. Please call her Virginia." Marco places his hand on the small of my back. "We are all *la famiglia* here."

A warmth rises in my chest, and it's not from the feverish baby currently tucked against it.

"And I promise to work on Mamma," he continues to Siobhan. "We are Americans now. It's time to let some of the Old World ideas go."

"Marco!" Giorgio's demanding voice echoes down the stairs.

"I'm hungry, too." Isabella limps halfway down the staircase. Her nightgown is stained from her fevered sweat, but she is standing on her own two feet. The effort causes Isabella to cough, but her face is still thankfully its natural shade.

Marco instructs his siblings in Italian. I hear my name, which with an Italian accent sounds as beautiful as *gelato di limone* on a hot summer's day.

Two hours later, we have the three children fed, bathed, medicated, and tucked back into clean beds. I collapse onto the threadbare settee and tip my head back. It's a wonder the ceiling hasn't caved in considering all the cracks in it. That would put the cherry on top of my Broken Hearts Sundae today. Girl saves patients before being killed by falling plaster. Read all about it in *The Inquirer*. Only five cents.

"What a day today has been." Marco falls onto the settee beside me. "I think it would be easier to bathe the feral cat who sneaks around our garbage can than to ever bathe Giorgio again. I don't know how Angelina slept through all of that."

I chuckle. Bathing Isabella wasn't a picnic in Fairmount Park either. "At least we got some broth into Colleen, and a little water and medicine into Angelina."

"We are good partners, no?" Marco takes my hands and kisses them repeatedly as he says, "Thank you, thank you, and thank you. I am forever in your debt." Marco startles. "I apologize. I have been so concerned with my own family that I forgot to ask about yours."

Big Granny Shockey is right. Keeping your hands busy does help heal a grieving heart. Eventually, at least. Now that my body can rest, my mind reminds me of the horror still waiting for me at home.

"My parents…are grieving. Kit is…." I can't say it, but Marco knows. He can see the truth on my face.

"Oh no." Marco pulls me in tight to his chest. He rocks me gently as I sob openly for a long time. When I finally pull away, I notice that Marco's cheeks are wet, too.

"I'm sorry. I should have stayed to help you." Marco wipes his eyes on the already damp shoulder of his wrinkled shirt.

"There is nothing you could have done." I dig into my apron pocket and pull out my handkerchief. It's the one I made over a year ago. The white thread of the lilies on the white cloth make it look embossed instead of sewn. I dry my face.

"I wish I would have at least comforted you instead of insulting you."

"I'm not proud of my behavior that night either." I wince remembering the vulgar name I called Marco. I straighten my nursing apron. "I really must go. My note said I was out with Everett attending to our neighbors, but that I would be home in time for dinner."

When I stand, Marco's fingers curl gently around my wrist. "Stay. Just a little bit longer. I need your help. For me, this time."

My heart clenches. I sit down and put my inner wrist to Marco's forehead. He's warm, but not feverish.

"Do you have a headache?" I put my fingers to Marco's wrist.

"No," he says, though his pulse hammers at an elevated rate.

"Does your throat ache?"

"No."

"How about your chest?"

"It's been hurting for days."

"Do you feel a tightness or have any wheezing? Oh, how I wish I had a stethoscope with me."

"Can you listen anyway? It's very concerning." Marco pushes one of his suspenders off his shoulders and unbuttons his shirt.

I push the fabric to the side and place my hand over his heart. It pounds a steady, strong beat. When I lean in closer, Marco tucks his chin until his lips rest on the top of my head. Frantic messages telegraph from my fingertips down my spine to the pit of my belly. I take a deep breath to regain my composure.

"I don't hear any wheezing or popping." Though that is mostly because of the sound of my own blood rushing in my ears.

Marco places a hand on my upper back. "Listen closer."

I don't resist when he gently pulls me toward him. Or when he reclines down on the settee bringing me with him. Or even when my cheek rests against the skin of his chest. Instead, I yield, close my eyes, and listen. Air rushes in and out of Marco's lungs.

"What do you think?" Marco's muffled voice says as his fingertips trace the shape of my ear before sliding down the side of my neck.

All of Marco's muscles tense as I leave a trail of kisses from his heart to his throat and on to his ear. "I think— no, I know—that I want to have everything in life that my sister never got to have."

"Katherine wanted the whole heart of an ignorant Italian boy?" The side of Marco's mouth pulls up.

"No, that is what I want for *my* life. And you aren't ignorant. A stubborn, hot-headed peacock on occasion, but not ignorant." I cup Marco's face with my hand. "And definitely not hard to look at."

Marco's lips are warm and full against mine. His hands slide down my sides until they rest on my hips. As our kisses deepen, Marco pulls me up against him even more until our legs intertwine.

"*Ti amo, Marco,*" I whisper. Marco stops and looks at me. "Did I say it wrong?"

"No, *bella*, it was perfect." The late afternoon sun casts a golden glow across Marco's smiling face. "I was just certain that I would never hear you utter those words."

"Then let me say them over and over to you. Even if it is only for today, my Romeo."

"No, I plan on collecting those words long after today, *bella*. And I am very, very stubborn."

I lace my fingers through Marco's and rest our entwined hands between our chests. "We both are, and I plan to hold you to that promise no matter what tomorrow brings."

TWENTY-SIX

WE BURIED KIT, her suffragist sash tucked into one hand and the handkerchief with the sunflowers on it in the other. As the Spanish flu continues to cut through our city, the authorities have prohibited Philadelphians from having elaborate funerals. And Kit's was no exception. At least Mr. O'Connor, Junior didn't make Daddy dig the grave himself as the newspapers have reported other unscrupulous undertakers having done during the shortage. As they lowered the slapdash, rough-hewn pine box into the ground, Mrs. Maguire held Mama's hand and sang *Amazing Grace.*

That day. Only a week ago, yet it feels like a lifetime.

"Would you like some tea before we leave again?" Cecelia's voice pulls me back to the present.

"No, thank you." I return to embroidering my handkerchief—a looping, green J surrounded by roses made from the same yellow ribbon as Kit's sunflowers.

"Virginia?" The concern in Cecelia's voice makes me glance up at her. "We can wait. Surely, your mother will return from her shift at the hospital soon."

"Don't be silly. I'm not five. I can stay home alone."

"The offer still stands." Nurse Shockey picks up the mask

sitting on the third cot—my cot—in the self-designated "Nurses Dorm" in our parlor. "Busy hands heal the heart."

Cecelia shhs her.

"Tomorrow, I promise." I look back up at Cecelia. Tomorrow, I will need busier hands more than ever. "Go, and check on Margaret Vaughn. Everett is going mad with worry."

"Ooh, child, that boy has got it bad." Nurse Shockey hands Cecelia her nursing bag. "Miss Vaughn should be right as rain in a few more days. Now her mama, that's a whole 'nother kettle of fish. Has she always been so… peculiar?"

"Yes," Cecelia and I answer in tandem.

As the pair head out the front door, I make the last stitch. I clip the thread and fold up the finished project. Now, I finally feel ready. The creaking of the stairs echoes around my cold, empty home. I take a deep breath and turn the doorknob. Afternoon sunlight pours through the curtain-less windows, and a light antiseptic smell lingers in the stagnant air.

"Oh, Kit," the words slip out on a sob.

The wooden bedframes are all that is left of both Kit's and my beds. I wanted to redecorate our room. This is not what I meant. The longer I stare at the skeleton of Kit's bed, the deeper the pain in my heart becomes.

Downstairs, the grandfather clock strikes three. I shake my head to remember my task. I open the drawer of the vanity, pull out the tiny cut glass bottle of orange blossom perfume, and dab some on my handkerchief. I tuck the handkerchief inside the top of my shirtwaist next to the unopened letter already there and head to the window. With a quick tug, I pull open the window sash and duck out onto the limb.

A sharp wind cuts through the branches of the apple tree causing me to shiver. I settle into the crook of the tree right below our carving, both for physical and emotional comfort. It's time to finally read the letter.

October 9, 1918
Philadelphia, PA

Dearest Virginia,

On behalf of all our suffragist sisters here in Philadelphia, please accept our sincerest condolences on the loss of our dear sister Katherine. Her absence will be felt deeply throughout our community. Her pen was indeed mightier than a sword. Though your family may not have known about it, Katherine's work was indispensable to our cause. Even as we continue to move forward with our work, know that she will never be replaced and her absence will be felt for a long time. My only consolation is that her beloved Grayson passed with her so she will never be alone. Virginia, please know that I owe your sister a debt that can never be repaid. In that fact, please accept my promise of assistance in any way that you may require in the future. If you need lodging, connections, a hot meal, money for textbooks for medical school or anything, please ask me directly. If I cannot personally fulfill your request, I am confident someone in our vast sisterhood can. It would be my pleasure to do so. All you need do is ask.

Yesterday, I laid my dear cousin, and your teacher, to rest. God have mercy on her soul as well. Please know that she spoke of you often and fondly. I pray this influenza will depart soon.

With warmest regards and deepest respect,
Beatrice Douglas

The sisterhood. A warmth expands in my chest when I tuck the letter back in my shirtwaist. Like all the arms of Kit's suffragist sisters are embracing me. Embracing us.

"No more crying. You promised," I chastise myself while I wipe away a single tear that somehow escaped.

"Virginia?" A voice below me whispers, and I look down.

I blink not recognizing at first the young man in the olive-colored uniform below me.

"I clean up nice, no?" Marco puts his hands out to the sides and turns around. The peacock has returned. "The barber made my hair too short. Ah well, at least I look good in hats."

Marco flicks out his Army-issued cap and puts it back on his head.

"You do cut an impressive figure." The butterflies in my stomach flutter. "This means you are leaving though."

"Yes. Friday. The Army gave me an extra week to report due to...."

I close my eyes and lean into the trunk of the tree for support. So much death. So much sorrow.

"Thank you for coming to Angelina's funeral." Marco's voice is tight. "It meant a lot to me. To my family." Marco clears his throat before continuing. "How is your family?"

"We are still hurting. A lot. But things are changing. Everyday things get a little bit better. Today, however...."

I breathe in deep. The smell of burnt wood, decaying leaves, and musky cologne fills my lungs. When I open my eyes, Marco is on the tree limb below mine. With one arm securely around the trunk, his other arm reaches up for me.

"I went to see your father at the hospital yesterday. I asked him if I could court you *when* I return from war." Marco's warm fingers lace through my cold ones. "He said no. So I told him that I am already in love with you. That I have been for quite a while now. He said, 'Then definitely not.'"

An indignant fire ignites in my stomach. "I'm a modern

woman. I can be courted by whomever I please."

Marco squeezes my hand gently. "It's understandable. I confessed my sin to him before I asked about courting you."

"It wasn't a sin! We didn't do anything to be ashamed of in your living room. I am still very much—"

Marco chuckles. "I was referring to the morphine I stole. I gave him a dollar yesterday. I promised to send him money each month from my Army wages until my debt is paid."

"Then maybe he will rehire you. We could work together again."

Marco shakes his head. "No, Virginia. I burnt that bridge completely to the ground. There's no going back. And I don't want to go back. We have to keep moving forward no matter what comes our way. Together." Marco releases my hand and traces the initials carved in the bark with his index finger. "Can we at least change the incision you made in this tree? I don't know who this A.C. boy is, but I want to punch him in the nose."

I laugh for the first time in what seems like weeks. "A.C. is not my secret paramour, silly. Anna and I carved our initials in this tree when we were thirteen. We sealed our pledge with a blood oath. That we would be truest friends for…life."

"Is she…?"

"I don't know. Dr. Carter's last telegram said she had the worst case of pneumonia that he had ever seen."

Marco climbs up another limb, hitting his head on the branch above. Now that we are closer to the same height, he swings around the back of the tree.

"Come home to me." I place my hand on Marco's cheek and drink in his countenance. "I can't bear to lose you, too."

"I have to. We are *la famiglia*." Marco leans in. His thumb caresses my cheek. "No matter where your studies take you, please come home to me, too."

We seal our promise not with blood, but with a kiss. The distant sound of the telephone ringing echoes through our house and out my open bedroom window. I reach down into the bodice of my shirtwaist and pull out both the pressed silver heart on a chain and the handkerchief.

"You gave me your heart. So I wanted to give you a little piece of mine." I hand the handkerchief to Marco.

"I will treasure it." Marco rubs his thumb over my stitches. "The yellow roses will remind me of the ones outside my home." Marco holds the handkerchief to his face and breathes in deeply. "And the scent will always remind me of you, *bella*, the night of Katherine's party. The most beautiful girl I had ever seen."

"Virginia? Virginia," Mama's voice echoes up the stairs and drifts out the window. "It's Anna!" My heart freezes. "She's alive. She's on the telephone. She wants to talk to you. Virginia, where are you?"

My stomach leaps. I lean in and kiss Marco. "Tonight. Apple tree. Nine o'clock. Will you return?"

"Are you delirious?" A cocky smile pulls across Marco's face. "Of course. Only, meet me *underneath* the tree so I can kiss you back properly."

"Deal." I steal one last kiss from him before pushing up to a stand on the tree limb. Marco still looks convinced that I'm going to fall, but, as always, I slide through my bedroom window with ease.

"Coming, Mama!" I yell. I pause for a moment to watch Marco drop out of the tree. As he walks away, he whistles a joyful tune while doing a little jig with an imaginary tambourine.

Even with Marco thousands of miles away in the thick of battle, I know the ember in my heart for him will never die out. And one day, I will have everything in life that Kit was never able to have: *la famiglia,* meaningful work, and the right to vote.

EPILOGUE

November 2, 1920
Bryn Mawr College
Bryn Mawr, PA

My Dearest Marco,
 I pray that this letter finds you well and adjusting pleasantly to your new assignment in Chicago. I must admit that Anna and I are pea-green with envy over your advancement. While you attend patients, we suffer through endless lectures on Latin conjugation and long-dead poets. Even biology is a chore, as the most interesting thing I have

dissected recently was an onion. I made Daddy promise to take me on morning rounds at the hospital with him when I return home at the end of the term. As per your request, I will accept Isabella's invitation for tea over the Thanksgiving holiday weekend so that I may ascertain the severity of your mother's pleurisy. I will send you a telegraph immediately following. I am sure your mother is not intentionally being deceitful about her medical condition but instead does not want to distract her beloved son from his duties.

Speaking of Isabella, Mama says that Isabella has transitioned smoothly into service at our home. Now if Mama would stop calling her Angelina, God rest her soul, by mistake. I know Isabella still grieves for her sister as much as I do for mine.

I pray daily that you will receive at least a weekend pass for the Christmas holiday. I miss you terribly. Mama keeps insisting that I need an escort for the New Year's ball. At least she finally gave up on Everett. By the way, I hear he and Margaret are expecting their first child this spring. Margaret was positively glowing the last time we went to the cinema together, though if her mother asks, we went to a tea room. Marriage suits her. No, this year I would love for my escort to be a handsome Italian sergeant. Can you make my wish come true?

I will write again later in the week. Presently, I am off to the polling booth to cast my very first vote now afforded to me by the 19th Amendment. Mama even gave me Kit's black-and-gold "Votes for Women" button to wear on my coat.

Anna, of course, finds my sentimentalism silly, but I would give anything to have my sister standing beside me today.

Speaking of Anna, I want to apologize for the pamphlets that were inadvertently tucked in with my last comfort package without my knowledge. I am mortified and didn't talk to my mischievous roommate for three days after the event. Anna oversteps her bounds sometimes. You are training to be a doctor, not one of the sheltered debutants in our dormitory. I'm sure you are already knowledgeable about such things. If the dorm mother finds out about Anna's clandestine activities though, I am afraid that she will be expelled. Anna insists that she is providing a valuable service. I don't think the president of the college would agree.

Please stay healthy and safe. I miss

you dreadfully.

All my love,
Your Virginia

P.S. Daddy is not supportive of my wish to apply to traditional medical schools along with the Woman's Medical College of Pennsylvania. If I cannot bring him around, I may have to call on The Sisterhood once again to help me. Miss Douglas—the new Mrs. Fairbanks—has been my fairy godmother these last few years, but I hate to ask any more of her.

November 15, 1920
United States Public Hospital No. 30
Chicago, IL

My darling Virginia,

I miss you too, bella. Please do not be envious of my new position. Most of my days are spent attending veterans suffering from multiple amputations and mustard gas burns. Young men who wish they would have died on the battlefield rather than live on in these mangled bodies. These men haunt my dreams and often drag a bloodied specter of Domenico with them. Your letters and comfort packages are the only things that keep me going some days. Speaking of...please don't be mortified. I found the pamphlets amusing, and so did my bunkmates who teased me mercilessly about them. I don't care. They are jealous. I have a beautiful girl to come home to and they...need Anna's pamphlets.

I am disappointed to hear about your father. I wish I could help you change his mind. As he has just finally agreed to allow me to step foot in his home again, I don't want to press my luck. Also, I politely remind you that my offer still stands. I could have a ticket to Chicago to you by the end of the week. We have medical schools here, too. Just say the word, bella, and the ticket is yours.

Ti amo,
Marco

P.S. Thank you for the lemon drops. Feel free to include more in your next comfort package, which I hope will be hand-delivered by Miss Jackson, future surgeon and my partner in every sense, herself.

THE END

AUTHOR'S NOTE

Although *Breathe* is a work of fiction, I wanted to weave in as much fact as possible. I have taken creative liberty with some of the facts and details in parts in order to move the story along, but other parts came straight out of historical documents. Yes, some people actually thought keeping a live deer beside your bed would protect you from the flu!

In 1918, the Spanish Flu left its devastating mark in both world and American history. The microscopic killer circled the globe infecting one-third of the world's population and killing over 50 million people. The United States lost more lives to Spanish flu in one year—about 675,000 people—than it did to World War I, World War II, the Korean War, and the Vietnam War combined. What made the Spanish Flu different from the usual seasonal virus strain was the abnormally high mortality rate of people 20-40 years old. Every year the influenza virus mutates (that's why you have to get a new flu shot each year), but researchers still aren't 100 percent sure what made this virus so deadly. At time of publication, the current theory is that the greatly mutated virus caused an over-reaction of the immune system in some people. This "cytokine storm" is what caused the gruesome deaths of some of our characters, who essentially drowned in their own lung secretions. Others survived the influenza virus only to succumb to secondary pneumonia. Unfortunately, penicillin wouldn't be invented for another ten years.

If you want to learn more about the Spanish flu, life in 1918 Philadelphia, women's suffrage, World War I, and more, please go to my website **www.sarafujimura.com** for more facts behind the fiction.

ACKNOWLEDGMENTS

Bringing this project to life required the assistance of many people. First, I want to thank the Arizona Dream Weavers because tapping into their collective creative energy during our 2017 retreat helped me finally unlock this story and hear Virginia's true voice.

Thank you to Molly Phipps for creating stunning covers for both of my books and to Mishka Jaeger for creating the perfect silhouette of Virginia and Marco.

Thank you to historian Evangeline Holland and history teacher extraordinaire Pamela Simon for your expertise.

Thank you to my favorite Italian-American Lana Miersen for helping me bring Marco and the D'Orio family to life.

A huge thanks to the Rowdy Mamas. I know that in 1918, all of you would have been marching beside Kit. A few of you might have even chained yourself to the White House gate, too. The packaging may have changed over the last 100 years, but the sisterhood has not. I am proud to call you my friends.

Finally, to my actual sister, Tara, who helped me hear the echoes of the past and track down the historical details, ate a lot of vintage sweets with me in the name of research, and would not let me quit this project even when I was ready to throw my laptop out the window. I owe you a Broken Hearts Sundae from the Franklin Fountain the next time we are in Philly and a whole lot more.

P.S. Props to the city of Philadelphia. In a case of life imitating art, while I was there doing research for this book, Philly gave me the worst case of influenza that I had ever had. Being a writer, I took copious notes detailing how awful I felt and used them to craft Virginia's bout with the first, less virulent wave of Spanish flu.

ABOUT THE AUTHOR

SARA FUJIMURA is a young adult author, creative writing teacher, and literacy advocate. After earning her degree in Public Health Education from the University of North Carolina, Sara went on to write health-related and other articles for local and national magazines, including a piece on the Spanish Flu for the World Health Organization's *Perspectives in Health*. Her first young adult book, *Tanabata Wish*, is set in Japan. Sara lives in Arizona with her husband and two children.

Find her online at:
WWW.SARAFUJIMURA.COM